THE LEGION
OF
THE LOST

a novel by

Donald Barr Chidsey

WILDSIDE PRESS

To GREGORY CLARK LOESER

THE HOPE OF THE FAMILY

Contents

CHAPTER | | PAGE

1 Mr. Philipse Gives His Orders — 1
2 Guns for a Spy — 7
3 The Best Cook in the Colony — 12
4 Close Quarters — 16
5 The Thing About a Pistol — 21
6 The Windmills of New York — 25
7 A Small Feeling-Out — 29
8 Thirty Stout Lads — 35
9 A Floating Sewer — 41
10 The Menacing Shadows — 46
11 The Treasure of the Ark — 50
12 Bed of Doubloons — 56
13 Life in a Box — 60
14 A Long Way from Home — 66
15 It Was Hot Down There — 71
16 Fumbling in the Dark — 76
17 Murder of a Gunner — 81
18 Frankness in the Dark — 85
19 As the Moon Rose — 91
20 The Great Breakaway — 96
21 Reflections of a Waif — 101
22 Life at Sea — 105
23 Pandemonium — 109
24 A Goddess Out of the Ground — 114
25 The Lap of Luxury — 117
26 We Struggle through Slime — 121
27 The Uncouth One — 126
28 The Dark Escorts — 131
29 Our Verminous Jailers — 136
30 The Fetching of Food — 141

CHAPTER		PAGE
31	The Killing of the Kai-Kai	145
32	Straight through the Throat	149
33	A Path Marked by Skeletons	153
34	Two Gods and a Doormat	157
35	Monkeys and a Crocodile	161
36	Encounter in a Clearing	168
37	The Offenders	173
38	Cutthroat in Satin	178
39	Wicked Lies	183
40	The Man Who Was Lonesome	188
41	Words in Anger	193
42	Hell Ahead of Time	197
43	A Man in the Land of Uz	203
44	Like Toys on a Table	209
45	So Strange a Town	214
46	These Lonesome Men	220
47	No Virgin	225
48	The Crowd Went Wild	230
49	A Dead Man Did It	234
50	Report to the Boss	240
51	He Did It for Drinks	244

THE LEGION OF THE LOST

CHAPTER 1

Mr. Philipse Gives His Orders

THE NIGHT was dark, and I kept clear of the middle of the street, where a ribbon of fog wobbled. In a place so crowded with pirates it was just as well not to show yourself. They were touchy men, those pirates, and, on land anyway, most of the time drunk. They'd burst into blasphemy if you as much as looked at them, and they would yank out a knife at a moment's notice, even if you had never meant them any wrong. Like it says in Proverbs, the wicked flee when no man pursueth.

There had been a great deal of talk among the town fathers about passing a law that would make the owner of every seventh house hang a lantern on a pole in front of his residence, the oil to be paid for by all seven, but so far that was *all* it was, just talk; and so I made my way carefully, staying to the sides of the street, causing no fuss.

The precaution was sensible, but, as it was to prove, wasted. As I neared the corner of Broadway a man lurched out of a doorway, his breath steamy with rum, and grabbed my sleeve.

"I'll have your coins, m'lad, and quick about it!"

There was no doubt that he was drunk, no doubt either

that he knew how to use the knife he held in his right hand, point-out, in the classical knife-fighter's style, as if it was a sword. That knife gave off a great glitter.

There was another precaution I had taken. Behind me as I walked—I never went out at night without it—I carried by a thong around my right wrist a short, whippy cudgel. It was made of hickory, and very light.

I deduced from the ring in his left ear that my accoster was a Brother of the Coast, and these men thought that they owned New York, as indeed they very nearly did. He was desperate for a drink, that much was clear. I had no coins with me, but when he learned this a desperado such as the one I faced might stick me anyway, out of sheer exasperation. So I did not palaver. I stepped back swiftly, and I brought around the cudgel, slamming it down upon the pirate's knuckles.

He gave a horrid screech, and dropped the knife, and, to my amazement, he stumbled away.

I stood there a few moments looking down at the weapon in the mud. It might be argued that this was mine by right of conquest, but it was not a very good one anyway, and I had an idea that the pirate, once the sting was past, would come back looking for it. So I pressed on.

It was the first time that I had ever been to Mr. Philipse's house at night, only maybe the third or fourth I had been there at all. It was in Whitehall Street near Stone, a big square place, in the dark looming even larger than it was, so that you knew right-off that an important man lived there. But this part of the street was not altogether dark, because Mr. Philipse at least *did* have a lantern mounted on a post by the side of his door. Some rich men did this of their own accord when they were expecting guests. But—if Mr. Philipse was expecting guests this night why had he ordered me to call? I plied the knocker.

The door was opened by the biggest servant I had ever seen, a huge broad-shouldered Negro dressed all in black. I was to get to know Moe (that was his name) well, though I never was to find out whether he was a slave or free. It may be

2

that he did not know himself. I had met Negroes like that in New York. What's more, they didn't seem to *care* a great deal. Moe was as pleasant and mild a person as you could ever want to meet, but the first time I saw him, framed in the doorway of Mr. Philipse's house, two steps higher than me, he looked positively Satanic, as if he were just about to hurl a handful of brimstone at me. Instead, he bowed.

"You are expected, sir. Please come in."

Deftly he unlooped the cudgel from my wrist and this he placed in a sort of stand to the left of the door, precisely as though it were a walking-stick and I a gentleman.

Even then, it did not occur to me that the light in the lantern might have been meant for me. I went in, taking my hat off as I did so.

We coursed across the big main hall, me trailing like a gig behind a schooner, and entered a sort of alcove or den, which contained a lot of books on shelves, more than I had ever seen before: There must have been thirty of them. It contained also Mr. Philipse. The servant, to wave me in, executed another deep bow, which made me feel mighty good.

"Come in, Toby," Mr. Philipse called. "Sit down."

He was very grand, not at all the way he was around the counting house, where he wore drab. Tonight he was garbed in a cinnamon-colored cloth coat with skirts to the knees, embroidered four or five inches deep with silver lace and lined with sky-blue silk. His waistcoat was made of red satin woven in with gold, and the breeches, the color of the coat, were trimmed with silver at the pockets and knees. His stockings were dove-colored and they looked to me like real silk. There were scarlet velvet garters just below the knees, and narrow black shoes with red heels and large silver buckles. He wore what they used to call a campaign wig, heaven knows why on a hot night. It was almost as big and full-bottomed as a proper periwig, with heavy curls on top, and the whole thing thickly powdered and scented with ambergris. Quite the smart. He was sipping something that from its tint I took to be French brandy. He didn't offer me any.

3

"It was good of you to come," he said, though he knew perfectly well that I had no other choice. "I have something important to say to you."

He was a very old man, might have been sixty, and he talked like that—slowly, deliberately, as if each syllable were an egg that he wanted to place in a row on the table. There were men in town who told you that Mr. Philipse would never have amounted to anything in what he himself used to speak of as "the world of making money" if it had not been for his wife, Margaret, the Widow De Vries, who had been born a Hardenbrook of Bergen across the river. They said that she brought both property and brains to the union, and that she watched every penny and taught him to do the same. It may be. I never knew her well. When I came into the firm as a junior clerk she was already an old woman, a rickle of sticks and drum-tight skin, who seldom visited the counting house. Anyway, I can avouch personally that, no matter where Mr. Philipse might have learned it, there wasn't a sharper man in town with shillings and pence, or for that matter with moidores, ducats, pistareens, doubloons, and eight-real pieces. He never, as the whist players would say, missed a trick.

Now he set down his drink, and put his elbows on the arms of the chair, and made a church steeple of his fingers.

"Your indenture must be pretty near over, Toby?"

He knew to the day when it was over—would have known to the minute, if there was any written mention of minutes. He never signed anything that he could not remember down to the last crossed "t" and dotted "i."

I said nothing, only bobbed my head.

"You should be a free spirit soon. Except that I'm afraid I am about to postpone that happy time with an assignment. But I'll make it up to you later."

You will, I thought, if I get it down in writing first.

"D'ye know William Kidd, the mariner?" Mr. Philipse asked.

I said that I did. He lived over on Pearl Street at the

4

corner of Hanover, and I did not like him very much—a glum, disagreeable man—but I made no mention of this.

"He's got a pretty wife," I offered.

He swiveled his eyes toward me. They were blue, the way ice is sometimes blue, and for an instant they flickered in amusement. He did not chuckle—I simply could not imagine Mr. Philipse chuckling—but he did give out a small throaty sound, a *gluck*.

"You'd better not let Huysvrouw Van der Donck hear you say that."

It gave me a jolt. I knew of course that my employer had spies everywhere, and anyway New York was a small town in which practically everybody knew practically everything about practically everyone else. But Anneke Van der Donck and I had been very careful. After all, she was a married woman. However, I said nothing; and in a moment Mr. Philipse went on.

"You have heard about his venture?"

"Everybody has heard about that."

"Aye."

For the most part Mr. Philipse had edited out his burr, so that he might have been mistaken for an Englishman, but whenever he said "aye" you saw tartans and claymores, you smelled whisky and wet heather.

"He's got a King's commission to capture pirates out in the Indian seas."

"Why doesn't he start right here, on his own ship? Why go all the way to India?"

Mr. Philipse almost smiled.

"He has got a rough lot," he admitted. "There's an old saying to the effect that it takes a thief to catch a thief. From what I hear, Kidd had a carefully picked crew when he sailed from London in this *Adventure* of his. They were mostly steady family men. But off the Nore he was overhauled by a warship and she took every one of them away—pressed 'em. Kidd went ashore and pounded a table before Admiral Russell, and Russell ordered the men restored. But they weren't the same ones. The captain of the warship, a man named Stewart, he obeyed the letter of his order from the admiral, but not the spirit of it. He sent the same *number* of men back to Kidd, but they were different men, his bad 'uns, the desperate, the trouble makers. And when you've got the dregs of an English naval crew you've really *got* dregs, Toby, you understand?"

"I understand all right, but why did Captain Kidd have to take such sweepings, if he had all that influence at the Admiralty?"

"He had only Admiral Russell, who is one of his backers. This is a private venture, you know?"

"I know."

"Maybe when Kidd went back the second time Russell was out in the country shooting grouse or something. I don't know. Anyway, Kidd had already lost nineteen days in these negotiations, and he was very late sailing for New York here, where he was to outfit the ship and enlist additional crewmen. So he took what he could get and made west."

"And the ones he's picked up here are as wild-eyed a pack of cutthroats as I ever hope to meet."

"It's too bad you feel that way about them, Toby, because you're going to see a great deal of those cutthroats in the near future."

"Eh?"

"You're going to be the supercargo of that ship, Toby. That's why I sent for you."

CHAPTER 2

Guns for a Spy

JUST FOR one crazy moment there I thought that he was funning, though it is hard even for a moment to picture Mr. Philipse making any sort of a joke. But he looked at me again, and I knew he meant it.

I had been brought up in a port, but I had never been to sea. I had never hankered to go. Ever since I finished my schooling—which Mr. Philipse had paid for as a part of the indenture agreement—I had been up to my ears in maritime matters. I had handled invoices, bills of lading, sailing papers, enlistment articles, dockets, and contracts of affreightment, besides any amount of rope, canvas, tar, dead-eves, blocks, sheaves, spars, masts, planking, and so-forth, but the only time I had actually been in any sort of vessel was one day when I crossed on the East River ferry to the little village of Breuckelen, where there was a shipyard. I could not even swim.

I pointed this out to my *bos*, who shrugged airily.

"You'll get used to it," he said. "Oh, you'll be sick for three—four days, maybe a week, but you'll get used to it in time. They all do.

"As for swimming," he added, "very few seamen can. They seldom take the trouble to learn. Curious, isn't it?"

This was a lot for Mr. Philipse to say at one time, and afterward he lapsed into a spell of thoughtfulness in which he might altogether have forgotten me; while I, for my part, tried to find in my mind some plan of escape, for I sure wanted nothing to do with the *Adventure* adventure.

To some it may seem odd that a personage of Mr. Philipse's standing in the community should stoop to putting a spy—for that's what it amounted to—aboard a vessel in which he himself had no financial stake. It was not so if you knew the man.

He liked to know everything that was going on, not only in New York but all around the commercial globe. And though there had been a heap of secrecy about the identity of Captain Kidd's backers, every one of them, I have no doubt, was known to Mr. Philipse. Perhaps he was sore because he had not been allowed into the deal? Or it could be that he was jealous of Robert Livingston, another Scot, another New York merchant, who *had* been. This in itself would be enough to cause Mr. Philipse to act. If Livingston was to make a profit, Mr. Philipse wanted at least to share in it, even if it happened to be on the other side of the world. And pirate-catching might well prove as profitable as piracy itself, while remaining comfortably legal. Stealing on the high seas was of course a crime, but it seemed that stealing stolen goods was not—if you had a commission from the King.

He must have known that I would be loathe to quit an easy life and Anneke Van der Donck for a long and perilous voyage in the midst of a shipload of scoundrels who had reason to be suspicious of me, especially since my term of indenture would be ended in a little over four months. Such a voyage—a privateering voyage, really—might last a year and a half or two years, and what would I do with my freedom when I was tossing on the deep the other side of Africa? I was amazed, for this reason, that he permitted me any time at all in which to cudgel my brains.

8

"They must know that it was you who put me in the post," I started.

"Of course. What of it?"

"What d'ye think my life would be worth among men like that if they knew that I was sent along to spy on them?"

"Tut, tut! No such thing! You will simply be there to study the mercantile situation around and about Madagascar, a neighborhood in which I might soon take an interest. And you'll be making yourself useful while you're at it. You'll be an advance scout for me, yes, but why should they mistreat you? You'll be the only man on board who really knows how to cast up accounts, and the very fact that you are my employee—that you came out of the enemy camp, as a man might say—that fact would give them more confidence in your fairness at estimates and at distributions. They wouldn't trust the Captain himself. Naturally."

Slyly he went on to tell me that as supercargo I would rate two full shares of the total value of any prize or prizes, just like the quartermaster, the chief gunner, and other officers, and he added, what I already knew, that Kidd, in addition to the pirate-taking commission, had also a King's commission to seize any enemy ship he came upon, France and England being at war. In fact, he had already taken one small French prize, on the way to New York from London.

"You might get rich," Mr. Philipse cried.

"And I might also get killed."

"This is a no-purchase-no-pay arrangement. You knew that, didn't you?"

Yes, I had known it, and it meant that the men would receive only their respective shares of the prize money, no regular wages. This was supposed to make them more eager to attack. It might well make them—such men—more eager to turn pirate; but I did not need to tell Mr. Philipse this.

"Right, there's another reason why the supercargo will be so important. And they can't pick and choose. Trained clerks like you don't come a shilling a dozen in this town."

"Yes, I'll bet you are being well paid for my services."

In the end, of course, he won. What could I do? For the next hundred and thirty-three days he owned me, body and soul, just as if I was a black slave. Anything he ordered me to do I had to do, unless it was patently illegal. And this Kidd-*Adventure* business, while there had been a bad smell about it from the beginning, on the surface at least it was legitimate. So I succumbed.

He put a hand that was like a talon on one of my knees. It was like being gripped by a witch. I shivered.

"You won't regret it, my boy."

He got up and hobbled out. You could all but hear him creak.

I waited a while, wondering whether I had been dismissed; but in a few minutes he came back, carrying a handsome mahogany box that might have contained dueling pistols except that it was too short. He opened it, and the pistols that it did contain were so lovely that I caught up my breath.

There were two of them, and they were double-barreled, over-and-under guns, each one not more than four and a half inches long: You could have stuck them into your pockets, one on each side. The barrels were of blued steel. The locks were brass, and brass bands were stipped around the stocks, which were made of Circassian walnut. They sat in red velvet, along with a mold and a flask of powder, and the name of the maker, OSCAR EGG, LONDON, was on a brass plate on the outside of the box.

"Beauties, ain't they?"

"They—are."

"I didn't want you to think that I was sending you forth empty-handed. I'm sure you will never have to fire these, at sea. Just the sight of them would be enough to make any man back off. I'd advise you to get somebody to teach you how to load and fire them, and how to keep them up. But not in public. It'd cause too much talk. Some quiet place like Beekman's Swamp, say. And now, if you'll excuse me—"

The lantern still was burning at the end of its pole when

10

Moe ushered me out, but I sensed that it would soon be extinguished, and sure enough, when I turned around, only a few feet away, Moe was whuffing it. Clinging to my treasures, I tottered on.

The knife no longer lay in the mud near the corner of Broadway, but I scarcely noticed this, for I was not thinking about pirates. I was thinking about how hard it was going to be to tell Anneke.

CHAPTER 3

The Best Cook in the Colony

SHE HAD left a lighted candle in the kitchen for me, and also a pitcher of milk and an *olijkoeck,* which is a sort of doughnut stuffed with apples, citron, and raisins, a Dutch delicacy. Anneke made the best *olijkoeck* in the colony. Whilst I ate and drank I gloated over my new fire-arms. I am no sportsman, and certainly not a duelist, but these guns really were, as my *bos* had said, beauties.

Though it was going to be hard to tell her what I had to tell her, I still could not help hoping that Anneke would be able to come to me that night. It looked so. Their bedroom led right off the kitchen, and the door was a thick one, but even so I could hear Van der Donck snoring. He might have been a stabbed fish. She would be able to get away now. She would be watching the light under the door.

Jan Van der Donck was what New Yorkers called a *zuiplap,* which if you read Dutch tells you all that you need to know. I do not suppose that he had drawn a sober breath since he was married to Anneke, a girl of seventeen then, five years ago, and with no money of his own he was going through hers as fast as he could. Thank God they had no children.

This, to be sure, did not excuse our sinning, as we both acknowledged, but it did make it easier to understand.

After a while, when I had finished eating and drinking, I closed the lid of the pistol box and picked up the candle and started for the attic where I slept, though it was really more of a cockloft—no window.

The Van der Doncks had a low small house that was roofed with old-fashioned thatch instead of tiles. It could be cold up in that attic in winter, but this was August the night I called on Mr. Philipse. There was enough air, even in the warmest weather. When it rained I used to lie and listen to the drops plop into the thatch—round hollow thumps at first, but then, as the drops got smaller and much more numerous, rather a rattling, like the batting together of a lot of thin wooden slats, which, in a way, it was. When it was not raining I would listen to the weathervane. Small though the building was, and low, it had its weathervane, like every second house in New York, where it was always easy to tell which way the wind was blowing. This one scree-ed, a plaintive dry sound. I used to lie there and make bets with myself as to when it would speak again. I suppose because the house was so low the weathervane on top of it, catching all the swoopers, was seldom still for long, no matter how steady the wind. It jerked and complained almost without pause.

This night, though, I listened for a more cheering sound; and pretty soon I heard it. Old Jan the *zuiplap* must have been more than usually sodden, because Anneke took no extra precautions. She was by nature a quiet woman anyway, and sometimes the first I would know of a visit was when she reached out to touch me. This night I did not hear her close the bedroom door, but I did hear her bare feet slish along the kitchen floor toward my ladder. I had blown out the candle and was lying there with no clothes on when she extended her arms. If I did not know better I would have sworn that Anneke had some Indian blood in her, she could move around so quietly.

With no more noise than a snake might make—but she

13

was a great deal more welcome!—she wriggled into bed beside me; and we started kissing, as was our custom.

I was the one who called a halt to that before it got too warm, and held her a little away from me, as much as there was room for. I did not want to wait until afterward, to tell her. It seemed only fair to come out with it right away.

We were adept at whispering. Anneke and I. Anybody who had happened to be down in the kitchen could not have heard us even in the intervals between the scritching of the weathervane, which itself surely would have been audible.

She must have been quivering with excitement to know why it was that Mr. Philipse had sent for me, but she must have wondered at the same time, for just a little while there, why I did not put off telling her until later. She soon learned. I blurted it. I felt her stiffen under my hands, and her skin seemed to grow taut.

"But—why don't you just refuse to go?"

"How can I?"

I did not tell her that Mr. Philipse knew about us, her and me, and what we were doing. It would have shocked her too much. I had no doubt that if I had held out any longer my *bos* would have threatened to reveal our love affair, but I did not tell that to Anneke, who was feeling bad enough as it was.

"Why don't you go before the Council—put yourself at their mercy?"

"Dear heart, Mr. Philipse *is* the Council."

"He's only one member of it!"

"He is the oldest member," I reminded her, "and the richest, and the most powerful. The others might feel sorry for me, but they'd think twice before they went up against Mr. Philipse's personal wishes."

Though our faces were scant inches apart, I could not see the gleam of her eyes, it was so dark in the attic. I could feel her tremble.

"Well, when the new governor comes—what's his name?—"

14

"The new governor will be Lord Bellomont, but he is not due to arrive in America for at least two months yet."

"Two months? But how long—how long—"

I had to tell her what everybody along the waterfront knew. It would have been cruel to keep it back.

"My dear," I said, "Captain Kidd has already got his vessel stocked and manned. All he's been waiting for is a proper clerk, one who is competent to clean up the paper work, the legal work. And now he's got that man—me."

"Then—how long?"

"A week. Maybe ten days, at the very outside."

She began to weep, and I held her close.

It started to rain outside. The vane was still.

Anneke in fact was only about a year older than I was, but she was Dutch, and somewhat squarish, though the lines of her body were dainty, not coarse; and she had had a hard life, and she was a wonderful cook and housekeeper; and for these reasons, and maybe others, I had always thought of her as decidedly older, more of a mother, truly, than a beloved. Now, however, sobbing in my arms, she was pure girl. She wrenched my heart.

The poor thing was denied even the relief that a wail of anguish might have brought. She had to keep her sobs, like her footsteps, unheard. But every one of those sobs went through me, hurting me, just the way they went through her. I patted her with clumsy hands. I was near to bawling myself.

For all of this, I still wanted her body, and she knew it, because when you are so close there can't be any secrets like that. I would not have asked her, her feeling the way she did; but I did not need to. She stopped weeping after a while, and kissed me again: I could feel the wet tears pressing my mouth.

"Then we must make the best of what time we have left," she whispered. "Come on."

So we got out and knelt by the side of the bed and asked forgiveness for what we were about to do; and then we got back into bed and did it.

The next morning I reported to Captain Kidd.

15

CHAPTER 4

Close Quarters

I HAD KNOWN him only by passing him on the street, by having him pointed out. He was of medium height and well set up, a ramrod of a man with dark damn-you eyes and a hawk's beak of a nose. He carried a sword. His linen was expensive, and he wore brave colors, but all the same the impression he gave was one of glumness, sullenness. He looked like a man who would stand for no nonsense. His mouth was incrimped as if he was carrying lemon juice in it instead of spit.

I heard that this man had done well for himself in trade, and certainly his wife, the pretty one I had admired, had brought him from two previous marriages a substantial bit of real estate. I could not help wondering, as I made my way to the *Adventure*, why a prosperous merchant like that would hire himself out as a pirate-chaser and privateer. I suppose the answer is that some men they just never get enough. As St. Paul wrote, the love of money is the root of all evil.

Up close, I learned, I didn't like him any better. For one thing, he had gin on his breath; and that I had noticed this, from several feet away, argued that it was strong gin and that there was plenty of it, for the ship *Adventure*, or *Adven-*

ture Galley, as she was sometimes called, was by no means a fragrant craft.

All ships stink, though this is particularly true at the end of a voyage, whereas the *Adventure* was just about to set forth. When I said that the only vessel I was ever on before this time was the Breuckelen ferry I was not being strictly accurate: What I meant was that the ferry was the only craft I had ever *gone anywhere on.* The course of my work as a Philipse company clerk often took me aboard seagoing or coastwise vessels pulled up alongside one of the New York wharfs or anchored in midstream or even down the bay a little. So I was not unfamiliar with the layout, nor yet was I unfamiliar with the stench—a nauseous compound of tar, oakum, bilge, urine, perspiration, and just plain dirt, besides whatever manner of malodorous cargo the thing might be loaded with—that is to be found on every vessel, certainly below decks. But I had never known this stench to be quite as offensive as it was aboard the *Adventure,* a new vessel after all, and freshly sailing.

The *Adventure* never had been in tropical waters, and it could hardly have collected much bilge on its one London-to-New York run. Nor did it carry any manner of cargo, only its own stores. It was nowhere rotten, yet. I reckoned, when I thought it over, that the exceeding gaminess of the air on board was due rather to the members of the crew.

In the first place, there were too many of them. I estimated, that first morning, that there must have been a hundred and fifty, maybe more, though it was difficult to tell when they and so many of their friends were coming aboard and leaving all the time. Still, she was certainly overmanned. A ship of 284 tons, which is what the *Adventure* was rated at, does not need anywhere near that many men to handle her canvas. The answer was, of course, the guns, of which the *Adventure* mounted no fewer than thirty-four, more than many a warship, and also the making up of boarding parties. Pirates and privateers always carry big crews. If when they are overtaking a victim they can fill the visible deck space with ferociously scowling mariners, all with their heads bandannaed and waving cutlasses and horse pistols, then there is a good chance that the other will be frightened and will strike his colors without further ado. It was always well to get out of fighting, if possible. Then too there was the additional matter of prize crews to be placed aboard captured vessels. All the same, the *Adventure* was hellishly over-crowded.

In the second place, the men themselves were hardly flavorsome. "Dregs," Mr. Philipse had called them, and he selected a good word. There is a saying that he who lies with dogs will rise with fleas, but I never saw a dog as flea-bitten as most of these villains. They were lousy, literally. Even in a less dirty place, even in a *clean* place, they would be foul.

Finally, they had nothing to do—nothing, that is, except loll around and get drunk and be the breeding ground for still more vermin. The deck was a disgrace, but was anyone swabbing it? No. A businesslike skipper, on the ground that the Devil will find work for idle hands to do, especially alongside or at anchor, where it would be so easy to slip away, would have insisted upon swabs and holystones being kept busy all of the time, one right after the other. It was not so with Captain Kidd.

These thoughts passed through my mind as I made for the poop to report. The Captain, at least, was not filthy. He was actually elegant, in a scarlet coat slashed with green, an ostrich plume in his hat, a toothpicker of a sword hanging from a punched leather sling. His countenance showed no such jollity. He was seated on the taffrail, staring forward at nothing in particular, and he did not take the trouble to glance at me when I saluted.

"Yes, I've heard of you," he said, his voice sandpaper. "You're Fred Philipse's prowling penman. Come on." He rose. "I'll show you to your quarters, which will also be your office."

I had feared that he might shove me into the forecastle, which would surely be a pigpen, and I had determined to complain to Mr. Philipse, but instead we went below from right where we were, from the poop. We went *far* below. We must have been under the water line, and we were stooping for the reason that neither of us could have stood upright, when at last he stopped before a hencoopish door with a padlock. He unfastened this door and threw it open.

"There."

I don't know what I had expected. Nothing palatial, certainly. I had mixed among mariners long enough to know that they are required to have, besides leather-lined stomachs, rubber bones. They are required to be double-jointed, if they want to get any sleep at all. This much was common knowledge; but the hole that Captain Kidd showed me surpassed in squeezedness anything I had ever seen or heard of. It was lower, even than the ceiling of the passageway in which we stood. It was nothing, really, but a bunk set into a wall, with a little space underneath for the piling-up of papers. A man could not have sat upright in it. There was a three-legged stool on the bunk, and this I gathered was to be placed in the passageway, so that a man could sit on it whilst he took off his shoes or whilst he was working at a let-down desk that afterward folded back against the bulkhead. A couple of pegs, to hang things on. That was all. There was not even a pottie.

Captain Kidd could not have seen the expression on my face, for my head was not turned in his direction, but I guess he must have *sensed* my dismay. He slammed me in the left shoulder with the heel of his right hand so hard that it spun me half-around until his face was frowning into mine, very close. It was always a dark face, and now it was almost black, and sheened with sweat. A vein throbbed thuddingly in his right temple, blue-purple. His eyes flashed. I am not sure, but I think that there was a fleck of foam at the corners of his mouth.

"*So ye don't like it?*"

His right hand twitched toward the hilt of his sword, and I verily believe that he meant to draw and run me

19

through, though to tug out steel in those close quarters would have been hard. If I did not cringe it was only because I was too badly frightened to think of cringing. I was convinced that I was in the presence of a maniac.

He was screaming like a woman.

"You want something grander, with feather mattresses and all that, eh? Why don't you ask your friend Frederick Philipse for it? Here!"

He threw the key into my face. It was iron, and heavy, and it hit me across the mouth, cutting the lips, so that I could taste the salty blood that came forth. He panted for a moment, licking his lips, and then he wheeled around and strode toward the ladder, his plume brushing the ceiling.

It took me several minutes before I could control my shaking and lock the office-bunk and make my way topside. I went ashore and walked twice around the fort at the lower tip of the island, before I could trust myself to return to the Van der Donck house for dinner and not tremble.

It was the first time I had ever seen one of William Kidd's rages. It was not to be the last.

CHAPTER 5

The Thing About a Pistol

"THE THING about a pistol," Mr. Cripps told me, "is that you can't rely on it going off more than maybe every other time, but the person you're pointing it at—*he* doesn't know that."

"I see," I said.

He was a funny little man, this gunsmith, bald-headed, bespectacled, and as fussy as a hen with only one chick. Somehow, whilst he taught me how to handle my pistols, I associated him with the name of the maker on the box, Oscar Egg. He looked as if he *ought* to be called Oscar Egg. I almost *did* call him that a couple of times. Most assuredly there was nothing dramatic about him, nothing swashbuckling, quite the contrary, but he did know his weapons.

"A pistol's like a sword," he would say. "Just the fact that you are carrying one tends to make other men mind their own business, but when you take it out of its case they run away—that is, if they're not too scared to move. It stiffens the muscles."

We did not seek out the solitude of Beekman's Swamp, as my patron had suggested, but fired into a box of cotton

21

hanging on the wall of a room in back of Mr. Cripps' shop on Rector Street.

"That way, we can retrieve the bullets and melt 'em down again," he said. "And the neighbors are used to the noise."

There was very little shooting anyway, just enough to give me an idea of what Mr. Cripps called the "kick" of the guns, the recoil. I fired with my right hand and then with my left, using first the upper barrels, then the lower ones, and finally both together, which all but knocked me over.

The gunpowder in the flask, he told me, was priming powder, very fine. Ordinarily it would be used only in the flash-pan, while a coarser, less expensive powder would be rammed into the gun barrels.

"That's what a soldier who carries a musket would do. All he could *afford* to do. But you, if you're lucky you'll never have to use these things at all, and maybe you won't have to ever bring them out into the open. And anyway, these're such small barrels they'll only take half a thimbleful apiece. You ought to have enough there to last a lifetime."

There was never any thought of marksmanship. The tiny pistols had no sights, front or back, the way you sometimes see on a sportsman's piece. With the small charge and the big slug of lead—it was almost half an inch across and must have weighed an ounce and a half, a miniature cannonball—the pistols, Mr. Cripps told me, would not carry more than about fifty feet.

"And if they did hit a man at that distance they'd only bruise him a bit. I wouldn't advise you to shoot at anything that's more than ten feet away, if you want to be sure. You don't need sights. Just point one of the things at a man like as if you was pointing your finger. Just make out like you're about to say 'Listen, you—' You'll hit him all right, if he's near enough."

This is not to say that I spent most of the week before sailing at Mr. Cripps' shop. Far from it, I spent only an hour or so there. There was plenty of work to be done aboard the

Adventure Galley, where I spent the greatest part of my time.

The ship's papers—all but thrown at me by Captain Kidd with a contemptuous "Here!" the way you might throw a bone to a dog—were in frightful shape.

The Captain, I soon learned, could write a reasonable hand, and he could read without moving his lips, and surely he was intelligent. But he had no respect for forms. I had encountered the attitude before, though I would never be able to account for it. Such a person thinks that anything legal, anything that has been written down, any record, is petty stuff, fit only for the attention of miserable pen-pushers, never for a man of action. William Kidd, in the absence of a proper clerk, had shamefully neglected to keep up his ship's papers, which of course made it that much harder for me.

I saw very little of the Captain or any members of the crew during that week while we were tied up to the wharf. I was too busy, and all of my time was spent below.

I saw a great deal of Mr. Philipse at his house, usually just after supper, that week. He had all sorts of small orders for me. What it all came to was: Keep your eyes open. I gathered that what he really wanted was a good, firsthand report on the situation in the Indian Ocean by somebody he could trust.

The petty pickings in the Caribbean area—petty, that is, once the English Navy took to escorting the Spanish treasure fleets—had lately been given up by the better-class pirates, who moved, lock, stock, and barrel, to the Indian Ocean, specifically to the entrance of the Red Sea, where they could pick up Moslem pilgrimage ships headed for Jidda, the port of Mecca, that often carried rich cargoes, especially of silk. Being heathen, of course, they didn't count. The navies of Europe would not bother to protect them. But if the pirates took to looting *Christian* ships—well, that would be a different matter.

Mr. Philipse was not thinking of backing pirates openly. He was only interested in keeping them supplied—at a good profit—so that they could stay at sea for months on end. He was thinking too that he might accept his pay in the form of loot, this being much cheaper at Madagascar than it would be off Sandy Hook, where he usually picked it up. But he would never admit this much to me. He wouldn't even use that word "loot." He simply called it "merchandise."

Anneke I yearned for, nights. My days were full enough, and indeed that was a busy week, but at night, when I had finished the conference with Mr. Philipse, there was nothing to do but sit in the kitchen with Anneke and hope that Van der Donck would come home at some reasonable hour. Old Jan, almost as though he suspected something, was changing his habits. It used to be that he would come staggering home, with or without assistance, by midnight at the latest, and then he would fall fast asleep. Now suddenly he began to return much later and not so drunk, so that after he got into bed he tossed a long while, and muttered, and pawed Anneke, who was afraid of him. Only once in that week did we find a chance to get together with no clothes on, and then we were so nervous that it was not very satisfactory. So we suffered.

It could have been just a coincidence, of course, but there were times when I thought—and I believe that Anneke did too—that it might be God's punishment imposed upon us because of how we had sinned.

And so at last it came time to sail.

CHAPTER 6

The Windmills of New York

THE DECK was Babel. "So the Lord scattered them abroad from thence upon the face of all the earth." Strictly speaking, the crew of the *Adventure Galley* were not of many tongues. We had a few Frenchmen, and a few more of Dutchers, a Portagee or two, but English was the accepted language, and from a nationality point of view this gang was no more mixed than any other, rather less than most. But they were confused. They fell over themselves making a lubberly departure. They all wanted to be on deck at once, for the taking-off, and there just was not room for them. No doubt there were efficient experienced mariners among them, and all, excepting me, must have been at sea before. But they were poorly organized, if they could be said to be organized at all. The officers could not make themselves heard; and as for the Captain he stood disdainfully to one side, looking at the crew, when he consented to look at them, as if they were animals in a cage. I noticed that when he did move about a bit the seamen did not fall away before him, as you might have expected. *He* had to go around *them*, on his own vessel! Now and then a man, finding himself suddenly confronted by his skipper, would touch his cap, but this was done not respectfully but absent-mindedly.

There are skippers who have the reputation of being affable on shore but devils incarnate once they are off soundings. I had never heard that William Kidd was such a one. He did not appear to hate his men, only despise them. Which was much the way they felt about him.

It could be that not a little of the confusion was caused by the presence of so large an audience. There were ships leaving New York virtually every day, even on the Sabbath, but they were not ships like the *Adventure*. Piracy might not have been the bread-and-butter of that town, but it was the jam, it was the marmalade. Like every American colony New York was at all times short of money. We were in debt to the English merchants, and getting deeper into debt every year. There was no *legal* way to arrest this sinking. The system being what it was, it would go on and on. Unless England consented to change the laws at least a little bit in our favor, the only ways to make up the difference were smuggling and piracy. I don't suppose a majority of New Yorkers approved of piracy, but they could understand the need for it, conditions being what they were. No doubt this was the reason why Governor Fletcher had been so lenient, not to say co-operative, with the Red Sea men—though I have no doubt that he lined his own pockets in the process. But now it was being said on good authority that Fletcher was to be recalled and that the man who was to be appointed as his replacement, Lord Bellomont, had avowed himself to be an enemy to piracy. It was also whispered that Bellomont was one of the secret backers of the *Adventure* enterprise. There were other outlets for piratical booty in the American colonies—Newport, Boston, Philadelphia—but New York was easily the biggest, and hence New York was the logical place from which to start an anti-piracy campaign. And here was the opening gun, a ship equipped and manned to operate *against* pirates. No wonder its sailing drew a huge crowd, the biggest, I daresay, in the whole history of the port. And this made the crew self-conscious.

Anneke was not a unit in that crowd. She had wished to come, but we talked it over and decided against it. If Mr. Philipse already knew about us, how many others might—or might suspect? To be sure, we did not know at that time—though we might have guessed it—that there would be such a stupendous crowd at the waterfront. As it turned out, one more, in the person of Huysvrouw Van der Donck, would never have been noticed, her presence never remarked upon.

She did not even accompany me to the street door, we both being afraid that we might lose control of ourselves there in the view of passers-by. So we said goodbye in the kitchen, that spotless kitchen where I had fared so well. Old Jan was sleeping one off in the bedroom, and we kissed tenderly.

"Dearest, I'll always, always love you."

"And I'll always love you, no matter what happens."

We shook hands, both of us weeping, and I shouldered my bag and marched away. I did not look back. I didn't dare.

It was September 6, 1696, a bright sunny day.

"Growl ye may but go ye must" is an old maritime expression, and truly there were growls aboard the *Adventure Galley*, and they came soon, even while she was being worked out into the middle of the East River. There were semi-mutinous mutterings as early as that. I paid them no mind, but leaned on the starboard rail and woefully watched the crowd.

The crowd could not have been called apathetic, but neither did it show enthusiasm. Here and there a handkerchief fluttered from a window—no doubt one of them was that of Mrs. William Kidd—but for the most part the folks who had come to see us off just stood there staring stonily. No doubt many of them wondered whether they were witnessing the end of an economic era, the death of a way of life.

A young man setting out for his first trip away from home, under a celebrated skipper, setting out for the other side of the world, for strange exotic sights and unpredictable happenings, should have been exultant, thrilled to the marrow. I was not. I was sad.

I ignored the nastiness behind me, nastiness of which, no doubt, I would get more than enough in the near future, and with doleful eyes I watched Manhattan Island slowly wheel about and float away.

I thought of Anneke and the golden moments we had spent together, even though it was a violation of the Seventh Commandment. I thought of our joy when we learned that we loved one another.

I thought also of what a fine town this disappearing New York was. To be sure, it was the only town I knew, but anyway I was sure that it was kind and comfortable. It was a busy town but a happy one. New Yorkers liked their work and liked their ease as well. They drank their beer, they hoed their gardens, they sat out on their *stoeps* at sunset and smoked long pipes and talked in a desultory, serene fashion. They were a solid, stolid people, and wonderfully clean. They were a *good* people.

We slid down into the lower bay; yet long after I had ceased to hear them I could still see in the distance the windmills of New York. They rose and fell slowly but steadily, their great arms feathered. It came to me that these windmills were a very symbol of the people of New York, reliable, strong, massive, unhurried. They went around and 'round . . . and 'round . . .

It was then that I began to get sick.

CHAPTER 7

A Small Feeling-Out

THE TAR bubbled and seethed in the seams of the deck. It could be that I was mistaken when I thought that I heard it hiss as I walked over it, but certainly it did bubble and burst, so great was the heat. It was a wrench to realize that this was December. Back in New York they might have been skating on the Collect Pond right then, right while I leaned with my forearms on the lardboard rail amidships, sweat drooling all over me, though I did not move, staring out over a sapphire sea.

At least I *was* on deck, and not crammed into my smelly little hole-in-the-wall below. I stayed on the deck as much as I possibly could, day and night. Once we had left New York there was very little supercargo work to do. We had touched at Madeira, which is where that wine comes from, and at the Cape Verde, where we stayed for a few days at anchor. At both of these places we took on wood and water, but at neither were we permitted ashore. Then we sighted St. Helena, but we sailed past it, several miles away. Now we were making for the Cape of Good Hope.

I might have worked and slept in the officers' mess cabin,

such as it was, and sometimes I did do this, but it was customarily crowded and cluttered with card players and with scraps of food, so that the air was hardly better than the air below, which was fetid. Except in the very worst weather I slept on deck. I had a place near the foremast knightheads that I had more or less staked out as my own. I even used to sleep there in the rain sometimes. I had only one change of clothes, but the cook, an immense and very solemn mulatto who liked to cap quotations from the Good Book with me, used to allow me to dry myself beside his fire. He was not a very good cook, but he had a kind heart.

My own bunk was barely bearable, and I avoided it as much as I could. Maybe it was my imagination, but it did seem to me that I had never entirely ridded it of the sour smell of my own vomit, in which, for days on end, when I was at my sickest, I had drenched it. Once more or less well again, after a week of excruciating suffering, I had scrubbed and sanded that bunk and the passageway outside with all my strength; but that same stink, it seemed to me, still hung in the air. I do not like to remember those days and nights when I was too weak to get on my feet. I might have expired there, retching myself to death or choking in my own vomit, for all that anybody cared. Nobody came to me.

How men can make jokes about people being seasick I shall never understand. It isn't funny. It's torture. More than once I had sincerely wished myself dead.

Now, I do not seek here to parade my woes—to weep, as it might be said, on my own shoulder. Plenty of the others must have suffered as much as I did. I mention this only to explain why it was that we had been at sea for almost two weeks before I was strong enough and clear-headed enough to be aware of the whisperings. I had noted the discontentment, it may be recalled, even as we were edging away from the wharf on the East River, but sickness had struck like an evil wind, and for a long while nothing else mattered.

I think that the chief fault lay with the Captain. Something must have been driving him, something that I never was to understand, for certainly he was not happy with what he was doing: He did not, as the saying goes, have his heart in the business. He was unsure of himself, and the crew sensed this. He might well have been physically afraid of them, for indeed, as I have already indicated, they were a graceless pack, the mere sight of which could appall the stoutest soul. Anyway, and whatever the reason, he remained aloof, sometimes staying in his cabin for days on end. After that first outburst he remained fairly civil to me, if distant, sometimes calling me "mister," sometimes just "you," but never addressing me again as "Fred Philipse's prowling penman." I made friends with his two servants, Gabriel Loffe, a Nassau Island boy, and a small Negro, the Barleycorn, who appeared to have no other name; but even they knew little about our Captain and would not venture a guess as to what he might be planning.

Less than halfway across the Atlantic, while I was still lurching from place to place, and the world showed blurry before my eyes, we had met a merchant ship and hailed her. She proved to be Portuguese, so Captain Kidd came back to the *Adventure Galley* and instead of seizing anything he actually gave that merchantman some extra gear and escorted it all the way to Madeira.

To some, as I learned when my head cleared, this was perfectly all right, a natural and sensible way to behave. Since Portugal and England were not at war, to carry away from that ship so much as a single belaying pin would have been an act of piracy punishable by death.

To others it was a discouraging exhibition of the Captain's uncertainty. What if that vessel *was* Portuguese? She was a slow sailer, not armed, and far from any port. She might have contained a heap of treasure—and the Captain did not even look! What sort of a Red Sea man would this make? Or did he maybe really *believe* this tale about setting forth to catch rather than to join pirates?

Few of the hands took the trouble to lower their voices when they discussed this matter, and by the time we had

31

left St. Helena astern I had a clear idea that there was trouble brewing, though exactly the form this trouble might take I did not know. I pretended to hear nothing.

Because I had not mingled much with the men, and because I was after all an officer, I was not asked to join any of the small scowling conferences that so often featured life on the deck. The men probably did not know what I thought, and probably did not care.

This was why I was taken aback, that sunny afternoon in the south Atlantic, when two man ranged up, one on each side of me, and put *their* forearms on the rail in a social manner.

The one on my right I did not know. He was a surly ill-visaged fellow, but as much could be said of most of them. The one on my left was William Moore, a gunner, who was one of the leaders of the incipient mutiny. Moore was an habitual disagree-er—a fault-finder—with him, nothing was ever right or fair. He was a rather babyfaced, tubby, pink man, whose mouth was stubbornly fixed in a pout. It was difficult to take his discontentment seriously, until you heard him speak. His voice did not go with his appearance. It was low, and it sounded like something heavy being dragged over rough gravel.

It was Moore who spoke.

"Lovely day, Mr. Franklin."

Coming from him, this was amazing. Coming from *anybody*, just then, it would have tipped me a mite off-center. Nobody called me by my last name. My first name is Tobiah, but everybody has always called me just Toby.

"Why, yes. Yes, it's lovely," I said after a while.

There was some silence. You could hear the moments march, their fingers to their lips.

"This, uh, this ship has a let-pass, hasn't it, Mr. Franklin?"

"Why, yes. Well, it's more than just a let-pass, really. It's a King's commission."

This flummoxed him, but he elected not to ask what was

the difference. He cleared his throat, his Adam's apple cork-
ing up and down.

"A French one too?"

"Of course not. Why should we? We're at war with
France."

"I know, but I hear that a lot of the ships that operate
where we're headed for—I mean the Indian Ocean—they have
both English *and* French let-passes."

"I've heard that too, and I can only figure that they want
to play it safe if they fall in with a privateer who's sort of
thinking of going on the account."

"I see . . . That's the way you figure it, eh?"

"It's the only way that makes any sense."

"I see."

It should be explained that the expression "going on
the account" is their way of saying "turning pirate." It was
pretty common among seafaring men. Moore and his companion certainly understood it, though it might have jolted
them to learn that I did.

"Could you, uh, could you write one of those French
let-passes, Mr. Franklin? I mean, if you had to?"

"Of course not."

"But why not? You know the form it goes in and all like
that? You know the kind of language?"

"Yes, I do. That's right. What I *don't* happen to know
is one word—not even one word—of French."

"Oh," said Moore. "Oh, it has to be in French, huh?"

This so astonished me that I turned around and gawped
at him. The man was no intellectual wizard, granted, but
still—

He was embarrassed. He stepped away from the rail.

"Well, I'll be moving on," he mumbled.

The other man followed. He had never said a word.

For some little time, standing there, I debated the question of whether I should tell the Captain, and at last I decided not to—yet. If they had got so far down on their list
of possibilities as to approach me it meant that they must

have been conducting tolerably extensive preparations. On the other hand, they would surely not make a move until we had passed the Cape of Good Hope.

I figured that the best thing I could do, meanwhile, was follow Mr. Philipse's advice and keep my eyes open.

CHAPTER 8

Thirty Stout Lads

FOUR DAYS after that we woke up in the morning, a bright blue and silver morning, to find ourselves completely surrounded by warships.

It was like a miracle, as though they were specter ships that had solidified out of the night, the nearest of them not much more than half a mile away. Maybe the miracle was that there had been no collision?

This was a merchantman's nightmare, to have the dawn reveal that he had somehow sailed or drifted during the night, right under the guns of a pirate or privateer. We might have welcomed such an event if the other vessels were unarmed or armed only lightly, but we could not engage a whole fleet of warships: There were four of them.

It would seem that they were quite as flabbergasted by the sight of us as we were by the sight of them. There was a great ado—running back and forth, ringing of bells, piping of whistles, shouted orders.

William Kidd, summoned, came tumbling out of his cabin. He was strapping on a sword right over his nightrail. The first thing he did was order bonnets strung out and an extra spritsail hung. Was· this impulsive? Did the man instinctively run away from authority? Or did he perhaps for a moment believe that these might be *French* warships?

Whatever the reason, it was a foolish move, sure to be counteracted, a giveaway. Those in the other vessels wasted no time. They did not fail to see that spreading of extra canvas. At the nearest vessel, less than a mile abeam of us, there appeared suddenly a great white blob of smoke. Then there was a banshee's shriek just forward of the bowsprit, and immediately after that we heard the explosion itself, which sounded like a distant door-slam in a large empty house.

The next one, if there was to be another, would be right on target.

Captain Kidd's common sense asserted itself, and he ordered all sails furled excepting the regular spritsail, just enough to keep way on.

Scarcely had the smoke streaked off when our neighbor had a boat overside. Even from that distance we could see that it was not an ordinary longboat but a singularly smart, small boat, all white paint and brass. The captain's gig? It could have been. As it came closer we saw that there was an officer in the sternsheets, what we guessed was a bosun's mate in the bow, and three oarsmen on each side. The blades flashed in the early morning light. Perfectly handled, they were a great sight to see.

"There's men who can really row!" I cried.

"They damn' well better not miss a stroke, or they'd get the skin slashed off their backs for it," said a gray-bearded man who stood beside me at the rail. "I know. I've been in the Royal Navy, God help me."

"Bad?"

"Hell."

This same man, I noted, took care to be below decks when the warship's boat did arrive. Doubtless he was a deserter. I have heard it told that the only way to get out of the Royal Navy, while you have still got some strength and spirit left, is by deserting. But if they catch you they hang you. My whiskered acquaintance wasn't taking the chance.

Meanwhile the Barleycorn had sought me out with a message from the Captain, who had retired to his cabin. I was to take to him there all of the pertinent ship's papers, and especially his own commissions.

I found him dressing, very grand, plumed hat and all, the boy Loffe fussing around him. I will say for William Kidd that no matter what the weather, no matter what the circumstances, he was always well turned-out. He was one of the *neatest* men I have ever known. His cabin, too, was spotless.

He told me to leave the papers there, but he gave me a valise—a shiny black thing that I had never seen before—to carry them in in the event that we were summoned to present them before the captain of the neighboring vessel. I gathered that in that case he wished me to trail along after him like a valet: It would make a better impression than just carrying his own papers.

"You think it will come to that, sir?"

"It might," he said. "A Royal Navy captain is arrogant enough ashore. On his own ship on the high seas he can think that he's God Almighty."

This reference to the Deity rather shocked me, but I said nothing.

The Captain strapped on his sword, canted his hat, flicked an infinitesmal speck of dust from his fine muslin steinkirk, and went out to greet his guest.

This was a plump man of middle age, epaulettes on his shoulders, a sword at his side, his eyes poppy, his complexion like raw roast beef.

They bowed.

"Lieutenant Ellison, Royal Navy, at your service."

He pronounced it "lev-tenant," and he did not sound as if he considered himself at anybody's service.

"Captain William Kidd of the *Adventure Galley*, sir, at your service."

They bowed again. It was all very fancy.

"A glass of wine, sir?" asked Captain Kidd.

"Thank you."

They went into the cabin.

When they came out again, two or three hours later, it was obvious that they had had more than just one glass of wine. They did not stagger, but they stepped with elaborate care. Instead of bowing again they shook hands at the ladder; and soon Lieutenant Ellison was no longer with us, and good riddance.

The breeze had been light all night, scarcely perceptible, and now, in the middle of the morning, it fell away completely. We were in a dead calm, five motionless vessels. This troubled the Captain. He paced the deck, a worried frown on his face, and many a time he studied the nearest warship through his glass. He tut-tutted, shaking his head, and he clucked his tongue. He did not take me into his confidence, but it was no magic to read his thoughts. He was uneasy, bearing always in mind what he himself had said—that some R.N. captains on the high seas thought of themselves as little gods. He had satisfied the official curiosity of Lieutenant Ellison, and indeed his papers were in perfect order, as I well knew, but what evidence did he have that one of those four skippers over there would not suddenly make some outrageous demand upon him, such as insisting that he sail in convoy with them when the air picked up, or, worse, impressing half of his crew? It had been know to happen.

The calm stayed with us. There was not a ripple on the sea, which might have been a mirror. It was killingly hot, and the tar seethed in the seams more furiously than before.

Late in the afternoon of the third day of this, the Captain's fear seemed to have materialized. The gig came back, with a midshipman this time. Commodore Warren sent his compliments to Captain Kid and could he see the captain immediately aboard the H.M.S. *Windsor*?

"You come with me," I was commanded.

So I brushed myself off as best I could, and tucked the valise under my arm, and trotted along like a tame dog after him.

I might have spared myself the trouble. Nobody paid any attention to me. Commodore Warren, a large bluff rufous man, seemed entirely satisfied with Lieutenant Ellison's report, and he did not even ask to look at the papers I carried. The midshipman clambered aboard after Captain Kidd, but I simply stayed in the gig, together with the six oarsmen, none of whom said a word to me or even looked at me.

After about an hour and a half Captain Kidd and Commodore Warren came out on deck again, and they had their arms around one another. They were laughing—giggling, really. The midshipman came a-flying, saluted, and scrambled down the ladder to take his place in the sternsheets.

At the top of the ladder Commodore Warren gave Captain Kidd a final affectionate shoulder-squeeze.

"All right, then, that's agreed, eh? Thirty men, first thing in the morning, right?"

"Right, sir! First thing in the morning. I'll see to it personally, sir."

"Stout lads, Captain. Send me good strong ones."

"I sure will, sir. I'll pick them myself."

It left me aghast. Here was my own skipper handing out mariners, men with immortal souls, as casually as though they were cookies. I helped him to his seat—for he was very drunk —but he did not thank me or say anything at all, only stared straight ahead like a man in a trance.

It was dark by the time we got back to the *Adventure*, and as soon as he had reached the deck, and had made sure that the midshipman in the gig was out of earshot, the Captain ordered that all lights be doused and the sweeps be brought up.

The *Adventure Galley* was not truly a galley, despite that name, but it did carry sweeps—immensely long oars—that could be mounted in specially built ports high above the water. These were meant for exactly what we were about to use them for—getting some motion into the vessel when caught in a calm. To be sure, the four warships undoubtedly also carried sweeps, and if they were heavier vessels than ours their manpower was much greater. But how could they chase us if they did not know which way we were going? There would be no moon for the first part of the night—not until well after 1 o'clock.

There were eight sweeps on each side, three men to a sweep, the tallest on the end. The work was done under the main deck, where a space had to be cleared for it. There were no benches. The height of the tholes above the water and the length of the sweeps themselves meant that the power had to be applied from a standing position. Instead of *pulling,* as in ordinary rowing, the men *pushed.* They would walk forward, four long strides at a time, while an unseen overseer—for this was all done in inky darkness—chanted the stroke.

It was backbreaking work. An hour of it at a time was about all that any man could endure, and so we were organized into three working gangs. For I did my share, as did the other officers, and even the Captain took a hand now and then.

The Captain, wisely, had told them the reason for this abrupt departure. That spurred them on.

"He only asked for thirty, but if he catches us sneaking away like this he'll press every last manjack of you! Make no mistake about that! D'ye want to wind up in the Royal Navy?"

There were no murmurs about mutiny that terrible night. There were no feuds or divisions, no squabbles. We all pushed and walked as hard as we could, back and forth, back and forth . . . and when our time was called we would fall to our knees and crawl away to collapse in the darkness, while our relief took over. All too soon we could be called to our feet again, and we would seize those sweeps with freshly blistered hands, and start pushing and walking again, pushing and walking, pushing and walking . . .

Blessedly the dawn revealed an horizon clear on all sides. A small breeze sprang up, the first in four days, and we cracked on everything but the cook's shirt. Then we dropped to the deck in sleep.

CHAPTER 9

A Floating Sewer

ANOTHER thing I should give William Kidd credit for—though the Lord knows that I cannot qualify as a judge here—and that was his navigation. As far as I could make out, none of the officers knew beans about navigation, and the Captain did not pretend to co-operate with them, much less ask their advice. He did it all himself, spending studious hours with his charts, his compass, his opened pocketwatch, and his cross-staff (which they called a "hog-yoke") and astrolabe. Several times I passed a hint that I would not resent learning a little something about this art or science, whichever it was, but he turned a deaf ear. This miffed me. After all, I had plenty of spare time. Aside from reading in my Book, the only educational thing that I could do during those slow hot days was to take a few lessons in the handling of a cutlass.

My teacher was the quartermaster, a brown seamed sinewy man of uncertain age and notable ferocity. He fancied himself in the part, and he was utterly earnest about it.

"This may save your life one day, laddie," he would say. "You never know."

We must have made an outlandish pair standing there in the waist, sweltering in the heaviest leather jackets we could borrow and on our heads a couple of rusty old lobstertail burganets. The cutlasses we used were real, but they were not sharpened for the occasion. A chunk of cork was speared on the point of each, and the cutting edges were stripped with tar. We drew many a catcall, but we stuck to it, he being every whit as dogged as I was.

"Never parry with the flat, lad! *Never!* Not only are you not ready for a return cut, that way, but unless you take it down near the hilt he might slam your own blade back against your face—might put out an eye. No, use the edge—always! That's where your strength is, the strength of your hand and wrist."

How much I benefited was problematical. "You get with a boarding party and you'll be so excited you'll forget anything you ever learned anyway," the other men said. Cutlass fighting, I take it, is largely instinctual. It has not got the elaborate mechanical construction of rapier play, for instance, with its secundas and cartes and tierces and ripostes and all the rest of it.

One thing I do remember, and that was how Adams, the quartermaster, repeatedly stressed that it was well to keep the point forward and a little up, aimed right at the other man's face, when you advanced for an attack.

"Make as if you was just about to cram it right down his throat, the whole length of it. That'll take the fight out of many a man. The edge he don't mind so much, even though your blade's polished bright—as it should be—but the point can faze him. If he gets sliced he may not even feel it at the time, the way you don't feel it at first when you cut your face shaving with a razor. But a stab—that's different."

Another time he said: 'Remember, a man may be affrighted all over, but he is most of all worried about the shielding of four things, and those are his ballocks and his eyes. Remember that."

Since the sun rose almost directly astern of us after that memorable night of toil at the sweeps, I deduced that the Captain had changed from the generally southern course that we had all been taking when we drifted together to a course due west. That is, he was heading straight out into the South Atlantic, away from Africa.

At noon of that same day, after some further fussing with the tools of his mystery, he caused the course to be changed to south again. It looked as though what he meant to do was hook around well to the south of the Cape of Good Hope and Capetown there. No doubt he figured that Commodore Warren and the other English skippers would put in at Capetown for supplies. That is what almost everybody would do. But Captain Kidd, understandably, had no burning desire to encounter Commodore Warren again, in Capetown or anywhere else, so he skipped that supply center, the only one in many hundreds of miles.

This was a logical strategy, and he could not be blamed for following it, but it did serve to make an already long voyage that much longer—by possibly two to three weeks—and it did deprive us of a fresh supply of food and water.

I had been warned many times that the typical ship's diet on the high seas would not be fit for pigs on shore. Indeed, much of it *was* pigs, salt pork, together with hardtack, being the principle item. The men, hardened to such fare, did not seem to be bothered. They even had a little chantey about it:

> "And what d'ye think they got for their dinner?
> 'Twas water soup, but slightly thinner.
> And what d'ye think they got for their suppers?
> Belaying pin soup and a roll in the scuppers."

We did pick up some fresh fruit and vegetables from the bumboats at Madeira and Cape Verde, but these were soon gone. Why we did not stop at St. Helena I will never know. The beer was all gone by that time, and the water was scummy, tasting like tin. The salt pork was rancid—only slightly so, but getting worse. As for the hardtack it was so alive with weevils that you had to close your eyes to bite it off. And we were about to bypass Capetown!

There can be little doubt that it was this added mileage that brought about the outbreak of scurvy.

"Outbreak" may be too strong a word. It *sneaked up on* us. It was insidious, like fumes. It pretended at first to be something else, a touch of sun perhaps, a routine tiredness. At any rate, there was nothing dramatic about its appearance.

I had heard a great deal about scurvy, and had wondered about it. The sufferers I had seen in port after a long voyage would be up and about in a few days, having been fed fresh fruit and as chipper as sparrows after a rainstorm. For this reason I found it difficult to take the malady seriously, though it is significant that few of those who had suffered from it wanted to talk about the experience.

"Scurvy?" one of them had answered me. "Oh, it's nothing much. You just have pains in all your muscles and you can't keep your mind on anything for very long and you can't see well and your hands tremble and your heart thumps. That's just the beginning, of course. It gets worse. You can't hold anything on your stomach. You break out into dark red blotches all over your skin. Your mouth is dry, so that you can't spit. Your eyes water. Your gums bleed, and your teeth start to fall out, and all this while you can't stop shitting. But it isn't bad, really, so long as you don't die of it."

All of those symptoms I have seen, and a few others equally painful. One that my informant did not mention—perhaps because, having it, he was unaware of it—was the fetid breath. A scurvy patient, even in the early stages, stinks like nothing else in this world. Bilge with dead rats floating in it, as is so often the case, exudes no more foul odor.

Given a whole shipload of such patients—and at one time approximately half of the crew were on their backs with this ailment while most of the others had at least the preliminary symptoms—and you get such a massive stench as must have made the very heavens reel in horror.

Truly, I believe that not even all the plagues that the Lord God brought upon the land of Egypt—the rivers-into-blood, the frogs, the lice, the flies, the grievous murrain, the boils, the hail, the locust, the darkness, and the smiting of the firstborns—none of them could exceed this woe of ours, excepting of course in scale.

I? No, I never had a touch of it. The skipper and the surgeon had their own private stocks of liquor, which they made no move to share with us, but otherwise we officers were served the same food and the same liquid as the members of the crew. Several other officers succumbed to the scurvy. But not me.

I can only attribute this to the fact that I had been so violently seasick during the early part of the voyage. I must have sweated all the poisons out of my system at that time, so that I was no longer susceptible.

Our surgeon was a sly, lumbering brute named Robert Bradenham, who was as likely as not to be drunk at any stated time, though like the Captain he always drank alone and was not in the least sociable about it. There was little enough that he could do. He burned tar and vinegar-and-gunpower down below, to try to offset the noxious vapors, and when the patients overcrowded his sick bay—for the men in the forecastle would not tolerate them—he piled them, all groaning, on the deck.

So we sailed, a sewer; and so we were when at long last, January 29, 1697, we made Madagascar.

CHAPTER 10

The Menacing Shadows

THINGS THAT frighten me fascinate me. Madagascar frightened me. Until this time my only glimpse of the tropics had been small, sunbaked, rather drab places, with a few runty dusty palm trees, nothing garish or lush, nothing rich, nothing at all mysterious. Now I was face to face with the real thing, and it filled me with awe.

Madagascar is one of the largest islands in the world, so I had been told, off the east coast of Africa, almost a thousand miles long, north and south, and more than two hundred miles across at the narrowest place. The part we first came to was the southwestern, and we sailed along this almost all day in. a generally northwestern direction only a mile or so offshore, so that I had plenty of time to study it. We were making, the Captain told us, for a place called Telere Bay, where there was supposed to be a good anchorage.

I had pictured the jungle, in my dreams, as a place of teeming life. The place I surveyed from the deck of the *Adventure Galley* brooded as though upon hidden woes. I had thought of it as clamorous, the air filed with the sudden scritches of gay-plumaged birds, the chatter of monkeys, the hiss of slithering, glittering tree snakes. This shore was grimly silent. I had looked to find bright colors everywhere, but what I saw was an overpowering green, a green so dark that it might have been black. It did not suggest death, this shore, not like a tomb, for I *knew* that life was there; but assuredly it suggested desolation.

Since it had a name, Telere Bay must have been visited before we dropped our hook into it. But there was nothing to indicate that. It might have been a remote portion of the world right after the Lord God had created it, still unpeopled by monsters. No smoke stood up against the sky. No fish leapt in the lagoon.

At least you could *smell* this unresponsive place. The smell was dank, damp, depressing. It was the odor of decaying vegetation.

This was late afternoon, and I got the feeling—it was eerie—that the shadows from the shore were reaching out across the lagoon from three sides to gulp us without a sound. The sun did in fact go out abruptly, like a candle that had been snuffed. All of a moment it was dark. Those shadows sneaking out from the shore—it was not at all like a sunset, but rather like dying, like death. I shivered.

In the morning, a brilliant one, there was plenty of work for all of us who could be up and about. The dawn had disclosed what the huddled shadows of yesterday had hidden: There was a narrow beach of white sand, possibly two hundred yards long, stripping the edge of part of the bay. Pegs proved that there was either no tide at all or so little tide that it need not be feared. Immediate preparations were made for ferrying the sick ashore, where they could be laid along the beach. Everybody knew that a sick mariner was better off ashore.

The sailmaker with bits and pieces of canvas and with poles hastily cut for the purpose began to erect a series of tents, to protect the stretched-out patients from the tropical sun and also from any possible rain.

As fast as the patients were carried ashore, clean-up men began mopping the noisome messes that they had left, and later these same men lit and set out a whole battery of fumigation braziers.

A hand was sent up to the crosstrees to scan the sea. Still others were parceled lines and hooks and hardtack and told to fish from all sides of the ship in the hope of bringing in some fresh food.

Three land parties were organized, of one of which I was nominally the leader, though the actual work was done by a durable old bosun's mate named Olsen. We were instructed to spread out three ways, penetrating the jungle at three different points, but being careful to mark our trail as we went, so that we would not get lost. There were no breakers at this point, this Telere Bay, though we had seen many such while we coasted, and hence we would not have such a sound as a direction pointer. The land, as far as we could see, was utterly flat.

We were to search for firewood and fresh water, and of course for wild food of any kind.

Being immersed in the jungle, as you might say, was an even more chilling experience than studying it at a short distance. The shadows blurred your vision, so that you were scarcely sure of your own feet down there. Now and then there would be a blazing shaft of sunlight, which, because of its very glare, would make everything else just that much harder to see.

The ground, if not actually a swamp, was slimy, slippery. Unseen vines, with spikes on them, tore at our clothing and scratched our faces and hands. Whenever we collided with the bole of a tree and reached out to stave it away, the bark would come off, all spongy, in our hands.

When we would stop, panting, you would swear that you could *hear* the process of decay going on all around you. The entire sodden world was falling noiselessly apart.

It might be argued that this was my imagination, and that a twenty-year-old landlubber who had never before visited the tropics was hardly a reliable source of information, but there is no doubt that the others felt the same fear that I did—though for the most part they did not conceal it as well.

We were quiet, speaking, when we had to speak at all, only in whispers. We tended to huddle together; and if one would fall behind a little in order to answer a call of nature, he would come tearing back in panicky haste when he was finished. The thought of being alone in this clammy forest, even for only a little while, was too horrible to bear.

We carried weapons, but we never used them. One of the other parties, on the third day of foraging, did shoot a wild pig; but our own group got nothing like that, only an assortment of rather suspicious-looking berries, which, on being tried, produced a prompt but quick-passing sickness. And water. We did find a spring of sweet fresh water not far from the beach. The stream that it started must have sunk into the earth after a short run, for there was no sign of it down by the sand, but the spring itself was easily accessible—and much used. Wood, no. All the wood we found was rotten, or rotting; it was punky.

The sick, though they must have been somewhat more comfortable on the beach, did not, by and large, get well. A few shook off their ailments, and joined the workers; but most just went on moaning. The scurvy itself they surely had, but as day passed day it began to look as if they had something more, something deadly serious, that maybe our quavering surgeon himself could not identify.

They were not malingerers! Nobody in his right mind, howsoever lazy he might be, would prefer to lie on that open beach day after day to doing a little work around the vessel. What's more, by the articles that they had all signed—or had had somebody sign for them—they would share in any prize that was taken *only* if they were able-bodied and had participated in the seizure. The sick didn't count in an attack. Nor would they be included in a distribution. Yet from where they lay they could see the man who was posted astraddle on the crosstrees, the lookout.

It was on the eighth day that we spent at Telere Bay that the cry came. A bit wearily, I and my scouting group were readying to go ashore for yet another scour, when it rang out loud and clear: *"Sail! Sail in sight!"*

49

CHAPTER 11

The Treasure of the Ark

WILLIAM MOORE the malcontent, and my "fencing master," Harry Adams the quartermaster, were among the few members of the crew I knew well. The one I did not like, the other I did. However, I admired both of them exceedingly when we sallied forth from Telere Bay.

Moore was not the chief gunner, but he was acting as chief now, I suppose because the real chief was one of those men stretched out under canvas on the beach. A big man, given to fat, most of the time he moved lumbrously, but this morning, shouting orders in a seemingly endless stream, he was here, there, and elsewhere, all, it would seem, at once.

We never had been in a position to handle all of our guns—the theory was that we would be fighting only one side of the ship at a time—but now, what with the sickness, we could not have handled more than a quarter of them. Moore actually caused only six to be loaded and shotted, three on each side, in addition to the Long Tom mounted at the bow as a chaser. But he caused *all* of the ports to be raised and *all* of the guns to be run out, so that starboard and larboard alike bristled with muzzles. The reason for this was clear enough. It was a move meant to make us look formidable.

The other fellow could not know, seeing them from the outside, that three quarters of those cannons did not have men behind them. Moore, complainer that he might be, was no fool.

The quartermaster, Adams, had charge of passing out the small arms. All of us who were not actually engaged in handling canvas or manning the guns or holding the helm were supposed to be on the main deck, in plain sight, waving the pistols and cutlasses that Harry Adams passed out to us. He moved fast, but at the same time he was deliberate. He made a note of every weapon, no matter how small, no matter how rusty. He marked them all down, to make sure that he would collect them all afterward.

All this while the bosun was barking orders, topmen were clambering up the ratlines to shake the canvas loose, and half a dozen hands were grunting and singing as they walked the capstern around, hoisting the hook. We creaked, and began to move when the sails whoomed out.

It was an exhilarating experience, and I was as wrought-up as anyone there.

I had not forgoten about my pistols, which were still in their box in my bunk, but I had decided to keep these as surprise weapons, to be produced only if needed in a real emergency. Such an emergency, as I knew from what I saw and heard around me, might be near at hand. The scurvy epidemic did not seem to have diminished the grumbling and might even have caused it to increase. If this prize upon which we were about to pounce proved a prize indeed, a legitimate seizure, it would provide the first money the men had been able to make in almost half a year. If it did not— well, I shuddered to think of what might happen aboard the *Adventure Galley*.

We swept around a wooden spit of land (the man in the crosstrees had been able to look over this) and for the first time came in sight of our quarry.

She was an apple-cheeked ark, high-sided, three-masted, capacious, and certainly slow, though she was spreading a great deal of canvas. She looked to me as though she might have been a John Company hauler, an East Indiaman, and in that event we would of course apologize for having disturbed her. She also looked—and this did not jibe with the East Indiaman supposition—as though she were *confused,* somehow. Maybe her master thought that he was still out in the open Indian Ocean and did not know that he had lately entered the Mozambique Channel between Madagascar and the African mainland. This could be an understandable mistake if the vessel was from out of Capetown, as seemed likely by her generally northern course. As I understand it, the determination of longitude, as distinguished from the more easily fixed latitude, is always more or less a matter of guesswork; and even a John Company skipper could have gone wrong.

The chase was short. For all her billowing canvas, the ark might have been riding at anchor the way we romped up to her. I remember thinking then and there that if we did take her she would be much too slow to help us in our own enterprise. The pirate-catcher, like the pirate, needs, above all else, speed.

When we estimated that we were near enough we let go one gun—and that was the end of it. We might not have been able to reach her with a cannonball, but she did not wait to learn. She dropped everything but her foretopsail, and wallowed there, waiting to be raped.

We had aboard of the *Adventure* three small boats. There were two longboats, upside down on deck, each big enough to transport thirty-odd men, and the Captain's gig, which might have held six in a pinch and which was fitted with a mast. The Captain immediately ordered one of the longboats overside, a skittish operation while we were booming through the water.

Only a few hundred yards away from that ark we put the helm up and swung about, dropping our drawers. It was one of the most expert bits of seamanship I had ever seen, and it spoke well not only for the skill of the *Adventure* mariners but also for their spirits. The longboat, too, had been handled superbly, and now the Captain ordered a group of us, chosen at haphazard as far as I could make out, into her; and he got in himself. Most of the others, the ones who were not rowing, had muskets. I had a cutlass.

It took us scant seconds to get there, so heartily did the oarsmen pull. No resistance was offered: Quite to the contrary, they seemed glad to see us, as though eager to explain something. Captain Kidd, his sword at his side, hastily chose half a dozen men and went up the ladder. The rest of us waited.

There was a swarm of protestations above, now and then shut off by a cabin door, but most of the time audible from the deck. As far as we could make out, below in the boat, it had been proved to the exasperated Captain that the entire cargo was owned by a couple of Dutch merchants, who were aboard the ark right then. Therefore, since England was not at war with Holland, we could not touch that cargo.

There is a popular idea that pirates deal exclusively in coins—doubloons, ducats, pieces of eight, and the like. As a New Yorker working in a maritime agency I knew better. By far the greatest and most important part of all piratically achieved loot, at least from the Red Sea region, was silks and cottons, especially silks. Sagathie, drugget, camlet, doeskin, drap du Barre, muslin, calico, and other such materials would rank second; the ships themselves, as properties, third; and cash, an afterthought, would be far down near the bottom of the list. Not that pirates had any *objection* to coined gold! They took all of it that they could get. But this was a minor matter.

Now, if we could not legally take the cargo, and we did not want the ship itself—whereabouts, out in this part of the world, could we sell it?—we might yet seize the ship's chest.. That would belong not to the owners of the cargo but to the ship itself, the voyage. Was this French or English? Captain Kidd could be heard insisting that it was French and therefore seizable. The others up there—we could not see them from where we sat—avowed that the ship and her owners were English. It could well have been another of those cases where both sets of passes were carried, so that the skipper of the prize could claim that it was French or English, depending upon who asked. Captain Kidd probably suspected this, and wished to look a little harder in the hope of turning up a French let-pass.

He evidently decided meanwhile to take the bull by the horns, for very soon he appeared at the head of the ladder, calling down to us.

"I'm having a chest lowered. Mind you, it's heavy! Take it to the ship, and you, Mister Franklin, take it down to your own quarters. Don't open it."

"Aye, aye, sir," I cried, saluting.

"Then the rest of you come right back here."

The thing *was* heavy. Four men lowered it to us with a rope, and it took up the space of three seats. It was about the size and the general shape of a coffin, only without the wedgelike shoulder protuberances: It was evenly rectangular and was made of walnut and bound with brass bands. The lock was brass. There were leather handles at each end.

Two bosun's mates appointed themselves to be toters, once the thing had been hoisted to the deck of the *Adventure Galley*, where, understandably, it attracted a great deal of attention. I went behind them with a lighted candle when they carried the thing below. Nobody followed us. The situation topside was too tense. The other longboat had been put into the water, and men were filling it, expecting at any moment to be summoned by signal to the stalled ark, where the Captain might be in trouble, a hostage. They were armed, and itching to fight. They hoped, you see, to get the cargo.

For this same reason, the two bosun's mates who had borne it down left the chest in the passageway outside of my hole-in-the-wall, which was just wide enough to take it, and then they hurried off to the main deck.

I stood looking at the thing, wondering how long it would stay there, making it harder than ever for me to climb into my bunk. That was all I thought about just then: the inconvenience of it.

I held the candle in my left hand.

After a little while I happened, just happened, to notice that a brass key still rested in the brass lock of the chest. It was a wonder that it had not been jarred out, so that the chest would have to be smashed open.

Now, large numbers of coins were no novelty to a person in my line of business. All the same, I elected to have a look, see if I could estimate the sum. I was good at that sort of thing.

With my right hand—I still held the candle in my left—I turned the key and lifted the lid of the chest.

There lay, on her back, the loveliest girl I had ever seen. She was dead.

CHAPTER 12

Bed of Doubloons

How LONG I stood rooted there, staring wildly at the vision in the chest—for so she seemed to me then, a vision—I do not know. I was in a daze, stunned, and at the same time frightened. There was a great deal of shouting and running-around up on deck, and once I heard a shot, but to that I paid no attention.

The candle I held wobbled as my hand shook, and the flame wavered. This might have been what did it. Slowly she stirred. She opened her eyes. They were green with yellow flecks in them, and very large. They went right through me. Her mouth too opened a little at the same time, her lips, two rose petals, falling apart.

She was not dead. I had been mistaken, perhaps because of her extreme pallor: She looked as though all the blood had been drained out of her veins, the way they sometimes do with dead people when they want them to keep for a little while; or perhaps it was because of the coffinlike appearance and dimensions of the container in which she lay.

Then too I saw—and saw it just in time to save my sanity —that on each side of this chest, near the middle, high, there

56

was a brass grill. I cannot imagine what these openings were there for. They were not large—maybe one inch by three—but if not obstructed from the inside they would admit air. She *could* be alive, after all. It must have been tarnation uncomfortable in there, but it did not have to be fatal.

She smiled. It was a tremulous uncertain smile, but it dazzled, so that I felt as though the boards beneath me had rocked.

I had a crazy conviction, for a split-second there, that *I* had died and was entering the Life Hereafter. Briefly too, I had the belief—though this was not so crazy—that I was asleep and dreaming a dream. Could it have been that I was having hallucinations as a result of thinking too much about Anneke? I had not glimpsed a woman, even from a distance, in more than three months. Had this affected my reason?

These thoughts, if they could be called thoughts, streamed through my mind as I stood there, not moving, just gawping, my mouth open and my eyes agoggle like those of a fish.

She might have been anywhere from sixteen to twenty-six, though I am a poor judge of age. She was fragile, dainty, reminding me of a piece of Dresden china in the shape of a shepherdess that I had once seen. She was short: Standing, she would probably have come only to my chin. Her feet and the lower part of her arms were bare, and she wore some sort of sleazy brown dress that covered her pretty well. All the same, she had crossed her arms over her breast, tight, as though she sought to protect that part of her body from attack.

Her hair was a *live* brown, as contrasted to the dull brown of her dress. It was very light, fluffy, and maybe it could be called yellow, or the color of cream, I don't know. There was a lot of it, and it was naturally wavy, making a pillow for her head.

Once—still just standing there—it came to me that I ought to waken her with a kiss, like the prince in that fairy story my aunt had told me just before she died and left me alone in the world. But this girl was not sleeping; she was awake and staring at me; and I was no prince.

The smile that had never really clamped itself upon her mouth faded utterly, and she gave a slight, wan pout. She shifted, and I heard the dull clink of coins beneath her. Suddenly, as she looked at me, her eyes filled with tears that gleamed like diamonds in the light of the candle.

"Don't send me back," she whispered. "Those terrible men . . . dirty men . . ."

I heard myself asking: "What did they do to you?" but I could not feel my throat at work. It might have been somebody else.

The eyes shut for a moment, and there came a touch of blood to the cheekbones. "They—they tried to *violate* me," she whispered. "Please don't send me back to them!"

I was filled with fury at "them," whoever "they" were, assumedly some men in the other ship. I would have raged among them, striking right and left. Was I making a fool of myself? I do not think so. Surely it is one of the deepest instincts of any man to protect from molestation his woman; and already, it should be noted, I was thinking of this encoffined belle, this corpse-come-to-life, as "mine." Hadn't I found her?

Before I could perform any knight-errantry, however, there was a scuffle topside and I heard a door open and then steps on the ladder. It sounded like two men.

The girl's eyes epened very wide in fear, but I gave her —and myself—no chance to think. I whisked the padlock key out of my pocket and reached over the open chest and undid the door to my bunk. Then I lifted her out of her bed of doubloons. She was as light as a silken shawl, and warm, tender. Innocent as any baby, she put her arms around my neck for balance.

I heaved her over the open lid of the chest and into my bunk. I closed the bunk door and locked it. As I turned away, two men—the same two bosun's mates who had brought the chest down—loomed out of the darkness above. For one panicky moment I feared that they might have been overcome by avarice and meant to break open and rifle the chest, perhaps killing me in the process; but I soon saw that they were angry, cursing under their breath, and I gathered that they had been ordered to return the chest to the ark across the way. Almost any other pair of *Adventure* hands in the circumstances would have disobeyed such an order, but these two were toughened salts, who followed their skipper instinctively, unthinkingly. No doubt they had been picked for that very reason.

They saw the lid open and saw the scattering of gold coins at the bottom of the chest, and I swear their fingers twitched and sweat stood out on their foreheads. They looked at me, and I knew what they were thinking. They looked at the coins.

"You been counting them, eh?"

"No," I answered, truthfully.

"Huh!"

It was patent that they did not believe me. One of them reached into the chest and pulled out a handful of coins, which he stuffed into a pocket. The other, just as swiftly, did the same. They closed the chest and locked it, and they looked at me, hard. I felt all water. I was like a sponge.

I looked at the ceiling, my eyes rolled up like those of a frog. In a moment or two I heard them lift the thing and start for the ladder.

I listened, standing there, until I heard them get the chest all the way up to the main deck—a bumpy, sweaty business. I had been holding my breath all that while, and now, very slowly, I whooshed it out. I took my key and unlocked the padlock and opened the door of the bunk.

I was looking into the muzzle of a pistol.

CHAPTER 13

Life in a Box

MY HEART until this time had been going thirteen to the dozen, as the saying is, but at the sight of that weapon so close to my face it seemed to stop entirely, as though it was frozen and would never move again. I realized then, and most poignantly, what Mr. Philipse had meant when he warned me of the *ad terrorum* effects of those little guns at close range.

Common sense soon asserted itself, and I was able to reason that the poor girl, locked in a narrow space, fearful that her dreaded pursuers were on their way, in the darkness had fumbled for and found the pistol box, the pistols. Of course she could not have loaded one. Even lifting it was an act of desperation.

My heart started to go again. But I shall never forget the fright I had suffered, for a moment there.

"Better put that down," I said gently. "You wouldn't shoot *me*, would you?"

"Oh . . ."

The pistol dropped into her lap. It had not been cocked.

"I—I'm sorry," she whispered. "I was afraid maybe it was those dirty men again, coming for me. . . ."

I put the candle on the floor, and I sat on the edge of the bunk.

"Don't you think you'd better return? They took the chest back without you, so it looks as if their English papers must be in order. That means we'll be separating soon."

"Oh, no! Please don't send me back!"

She was still whispering, but not with the whisper of one who fears to be overheard: With all the racket up on deck nobody could possibly have heard us. It was rather as though she had not used her vocal cords in a long time and was uncertain whether they would function. How long had she been hiding in that chest?

I tried to talk to her soothingly, the way you would to a frightened child, which is what she was. I pointed out that we had no more right to steal her from the other ship than we had a right to steal the coins in that chest, now that the matter had been straightened out. But she shook her head.

"You wouldn't send me back—to men like that?" she said, looking at me with those enormous green eyes.

We were sitting close together, necessarily. The bunk was not big.

"If somebody was trying to mistreat you, why didn't you appeal to the captain?"

She colored a bit, for the second time.

"He was the worst of the lot," she whispered.

I rattled on, if without any notable spirit; for the truth is, I did not want her to be sent back to that wallowing ark; I wanted her to stay here, somehow.

"You don't understand," I said. "This is not an ordinary ship. The men here are worse than most. I'm sure they are worse than the ones you're trying to run away from. What they'd do if they knew that there was a woman aboard I— well, I hate to think about it. There'd be no place to hide you. There'd be nobody to protect you."

She put a hand on my forearm. She did not press it or wriggle it, just placed it there.

"Couldn't *you* do that?" she asked softly.

61

A tingle went through me, but I pretended not to notice the hand.

"You don't understand," I said again. "I'm the super-cargo, and I am under the Captain's orders just the same as any forecastle hand is. I would have to report that you were here. It'd be my duty."

She did not say anything. But neither did she remove the hand.

Maybe she was a mite hysterical, after that horrible experience. I thought I would urge her to talk. It might make her feel better.

"Tell me about it," I said. "How did you get on that ship in the first place?"

She told me, simply, matter-of-factly. Her name was Eve Shackleton and she came from a small town in Kent, England, and she was an orphan. Her nearest relative, an uncle, lived in Calicut, India, and was employed by the East India Company, as were practically all of the white men in that part of the world. She did not say in what *capacity* he was employed, and maybe she was not clear on this point herself, but she seemed sure that she would not be unwelcome and that her uncle would be able to take care of her at least until the end of his term of service, in three years time. She had taken passage on the *King's Dominion*, the ark, which was not a John Company ship.

"Alone?"

Oh, no. She had been accompanied by what the Spaniards would designate as a duenna, a much older and safely ugly woman whom she called Aunt Stephens, though in fact she was no relation, only an old and poor family friend.

"Nobody would have tried to put a hand on me when Aunt Stephens was there."

Aunt Stephens, however, had died. Last week. Four days out of Capetown. There had been nothing suspicious about her death. She was old, and she had been a long while ailing, and the rigors of the voyage were too much for her, so she quietly passed away; and she was buried at sea.

That was when Miss Shackleton's troubles began. They had scarcely slid Aunt Stephens' remains over the side when the second mate, a man named Aarons, made an indecent suggestion. She fled him, and locked herself in her cabin. Later, after dark, she slipped out and quite properly went to the Captain to report.

"And he was worse than Mr. Aarons."

After that, for six days, she stayed in her cabin most of the time.

"Are you sure that they meant—well, what you thought they meant? Couldn't they have been just acting fatherly?"

"They meant it all right."

"You couldn't have been mistaken?"

"In a matter like that?"

"And there was no other woman on the ship?"

"None."

Nobody brought her meals, and so she took to letting herself out late at night to prowl for food scraps. It was a miserable, humiliating existence, and she did not know whether she could keep it up for the whole voyage, which might last as much as two months longer. But she could not think of anything else.

Oddly enough, one of the best fields for food that she used to exploit was the Captain's own cabin. He must have suffered from what surgeons call insomnia—he couldn't sleep—and he used to walk the poop night after night, by the hour, leaving his cabin door open and a lamp lighted there. Seemingly he did not mess with the men or even with his officers, for there were almost always some bits and pieces of food to be snatched.

On this particular night—two nights ago? three?—she was uncertain about the time—she had found two stale biscuits soaked in molasses, which she wrapped in a kerchief. She was about to pop outside again when she heard a step on the deck—a step she knew to be that of the Captain.

Frantic with fear, she climbed into the only thing in the cabin that would have concealed her—the money chest. It was locked, but the key was in the lock and she turned it and let herself in. She had just lowered the lid, as quietly as she could, when she heard the Captain walk into the cabin.

She lay motionless, for she realized that she was on coins that would click together if she stirred. She heard the Captain for a long while. He moved about, got undressed, harrumphed at nothing, sneezed, shouted for the steward, ordered some more food, took a drink of beer. At long last he whuffed out the light and got into his bunk.

She waited. She waited until he had started to snore, and even then she made herself wait longer, in order to be utterly sure. She decided that she would count to one thousand, slowly, before she let herself out of the chest.

How far she had reached with the count she was never to know. She could remember passing four hundred, making herself go slowly, and without moving her lips. At that point, or soon after, she must either have fainted or, more likely, fallen asleep herself.

When she recovered consciousness, there was no longer any snoring. There was no sound of any sort. She could not know whether it was day or night, and once she was sure that there was nobody else in the cabin she decided to open the lid a little and peeked out in order to determine at least this point. She reached up.

The lid would not budge. She was locked in.

She screamed several times, she believed. There was no answer. She pushed as hard as she could against the lid, but she could not move it. She forced herself to eat one of the molasses-soaked biscuits, which made her exceedingly thirsty. She lost consciousness again.

How long this went on she did not know. She had no way of telling time. It seemed peculiar that she could not hear the ship's bells from the Captain's cabin—surely *he* would have wanted to hear them?—but perhaps the chest itself made all the difference, or maybe she slept or lay in a swoon a lot longer than she supposed. At any rate, at one time she was groggily aware of being jogged around, the chest upended, of being lowered so that she slid noisily. She believed at that time that she was dead. Then there was a light against her eyes, and she opened them and saw me staring down at her. Prince Charming. Yes.

"And I thank you, my friend," she said, and squeezed my arm a little and removed her hand, "from the bottom of my heart."

I rubbered out my lips, as I stroked my chin. I was touched by what I had heard, but we were living in the world and I could not help but think of how she must be suffering. The corridor in which my hole-in-the-wall was located contained nothing else. Seemingly at one time it had been longer and had led elsewhere, but for some reason a partition had been built and now it was no more than a blind alley. At the other end, only a few yards from the bunk, there was a pail I had borrowed from the cook; and I told her about this.

"It's dark," I said, "but I'll turn my back anyway."

"Thank you," she whispered.

I could hear, of course. I could not help that.

Soon she was back, and delicately put the pail by the side of my feet.

"I'll go to the Captain," I said. "He must be back by this time, or on the way. I've got to put it before him. There's no other choice. We'd both get into a peck of trouble if I didn't."

"All right. But—you will plead my case with him?"

"Oh, sure I'll plead your case!"

So, lugging the pail, I made my way up to the deck, where I was greeted by one of the strangest scenes I have ever witnessed.

CHAPTER 14

A Long Way from Home

THE INSTANT my head rose above the level of the main deck I saw that the ark was making off in a northerly direction, all sails spread, eager to get away. She might still be signaled, if I could get the attention of the right persons, but the foreground tableau made this seem unlikely. In fact, I soon forgot about the ark.

William Kidd had just reached the top of the ladder from the longboat, and he was in some danger of being pushed back into the sea, so great was the rush to that spot.

I have mentioned that Captain Kidd did not command the respect of his villainous crew, but until this time I had never noted a display of hatred on their part. Resentments, yes; the customary and almost conventional grievances of seafaring men; but not hatred. It had hitherto been more a matter of indifference or mild contempt. Now, this afternoon, it was a matter of rage.

Men were converging upon that spot in the waist from every quarter of the ship. The canvas hung limp, untended. The wheel swung idly in the absence of any helmsman. The ship drifted.

None of the angry mariners had weapons, as far as I

could make out, but their fists were clenched, their faces worked in fury, and they were loud in their blame of the Captain. One of them, one of the noisiest, was William Moore.

I could sense what had happened. Those who had gone in the longboat were largely loyal to the Captain, and they were all armed. The rest were the trouble-makers, and these had watched with joy when the money chest was brought aboard, but with bewilderment that mounted to rage when unexpectedly it was taken back to the East Indiaman. Even so, at that time they could not believe that a treasure was being returned. Such things, in their world, simply were not done. They must have supposed that there was some trick to it, some technical point that needed clearing up before a final settlement could be made.

Then the longboat had reappeared *without* the chest, and at the same time the ark had spread its wings and flown gratefully off, and a great cry of wrath rose from those crowded into the waist of the *Adventure,* who summoned all their companions to their side.

I said to myself: *This is it!*

My first thought was to hurry back to my berth below, where I could load and cock the pistols and give them to Miss Shackleton, who could use one against the first man to come at her, the other against herself, to save her honor, while I would scramble topside, clutching the cutlass, which I had left on the floor beside the bunk. It was an heroical thought, but a brief one. I did nothing of the sort. I just stood there on that ladder as though transfixed, my head above the level of the deck, a slop-bucket in my left hand.

The men coming up the ladder after the Captain all had guns or swords, and it is likely that they would have made an attempt to protect him, form a bodyguard around him, a movement that would inevitably have resulted in a battle-royal. The Captain did not wait for this. Snarling, he spun himself free. He whipped out his sword.

It was a mere oversized needle, meant for ceremonial

purposes, not for real fighting. It was a symbol of authority and of gentility rather than an instrument of combat. William Kidd probably had never learned to use it. Few men had, even among the aristocracy.

Nevertheless, he kept it canted up, as Quartermaster Adams would have advised, the arcing point directed at a whole semicircle of eyes; and so fierce was his mien, so dark his face, that the men did not advance and some even retreated a little.

"*Back, ye cowhearted bastards!*"

The Captain had been mauled. His hat was tilted, the plume on it broken. His fall was askew, his coat ripped. He had been cut high on the left cheek, a wound in itself not serious but which added to the ferocity of his aspect when the blood from it dribbled down to his chin, to fall off there, drop by drop.

"*Stand back, ye swine!*"

But by this time they had tightened their pluck, and they edged forward instead, the ones in front pushed by the ones behind. It was the Captain who stepped back, carefully, slowly, in a regulated manner, always with the sword sweeping that half-circle of faces, the hand steady, the eyes flashing. I verily believe that if he had lost his nerve and spun around to run for it he would have been ruined: They would have leapt upon him and torn him to pieces.

He came right toward me, where I was standing on a ladder below deck. He did not see me, of course. He did not dare to look that far around.

This was at the break of the poop, and the ladder that led up to that deck and to the Captain's cabin there was only a few feet from my head. Not until he had reached that ladder did he jump. He slapped the sword under his left arm, and whirled around, and went up to the poop with all the speed and agility of a squirrel.

Nobody moved to follow him.

We heard him open his cabin door up there, and then slam it closed, and we heard a heavy balk being thrown.

After that, silence descended upon the ship.

I climbed to the waist and went to the leeward rail and emptied the bucket.

The men stood in small, buzzing groups. Those who had weapons showed some inclination to hold onto them, but Harry Adams would have none of that: followed by two assistants, to whom he passed the pieces, he went in and out among the men, inexorably collecting, checking off each item against his list.

The first mate, a worried man named Carr, climbed to the poop, and we could hear him knocking at the Captain's door. Whether or not he got any answer we could not know, but certainly the door was not unlatched. After a little while Carr came down to the waist and started to issue orders in a voice so hesitant and low that it sounded as though he never expected to be obeyed. Slowly the men drifted toward the halyards, the ratlines, the helm.

The East Indiaman by this time was hull-down. It would have been too late to signal her.

I went below to report all of this to Miss Shackleton. It must be admitted that she took it very calmly. I think that this was due less to her courage—though I would not deny her courage—than to her ignorance. She could not imagine a mutiny. She could not picture the pandemonium that would ensue if one half of the men started to battle the other half. She did not know the nature of these men, already part-outlaws and prepared at any time to cut themselves off from every glimpse of civilization. What is more, she seemed to have a serene confidence in me: She seemed to believe that I could take care of any situation..

The most immediate situation that called for my attention was herself, her physical condition. How long she had been in that money chest we did not know, but her place in my bunk was hardly preferable, there being almost no room in which to move around down there, even in the passageway, which was short, while the air was at all times hot and stale. The thought of taking her out for an elaborately guarded walk on deck in the middle of the night could not be considered; there was always somebody there.

Meanwhile, she must be weak with hunger and thirst. Water was easily obtained now, as a result of the spring our search party had found back of the beach at Telere Bay. She drank it with greed, not even trying to look like a lady. My friendship with the cook stood me in good stead, as it had so many times in the past. I often got food from him on a plate of my own when I did not feel like going to the officers' mess, and he thought nothing of it, knowing me and my ways.

" 'He giveth to the beast his food, and to the young ravens which fly,' " I would say.

"Psalms?"

"Psalms is right, though I can't remember which one."

" 'Put not your faith in princes, nor in the son of man, in whom there is no help,' " he would say. "That's Psalms too."

This day I took the dish to Miss Shackleton, and then excused myself and went up to the officers' mess. It was about the glummest meal that I can remember. The Captain seldom graced our board with his presence, and of course now he was locked in his own cabin, no doubt with a loaded pistol on the table before him. The others were not inclined to chat. Nobody knew what might happen next, and we were a long way from home.

Afterward, though, as I was making my way back to my bunk, I felt the ship shiver, and felt it turn; I heard the canvas crack and snap, and soon even heard a "speaking" at the bows. There rose again the familiar multiplicity of squeals. I grinned to myself. At least we were no longer wallowing like a waterlogged spar. We had hoisted sail, and had turned, and were making back for Telere to pick up the sick. The men were obeying orders.

CHAPTER 15

It Was Hot Down There

THE CAPTAIN stayed in his cabin the greater part of a week, or, if he went forth at all as was reported, it was late at night for a few turns around the deck, and even then with his sword loose in its scabbard, a pistol tucked behind his sash. He would shout orders to his mates when they presented themselves outside of his cabin, but the only ones for whom that door was opened—and then but briefly—were his servants, Babriel Loffe and the Barleycorn. I was on good terms with both of these lads, but they were either too stupid or too loyal to answer the question that we were all asking ourselves: *Was William Kidd afraid of his crew or was he afraid of himself?*

It could be that the man had gone mad. One afternoon I went past his cabin door a couple of times, very close, and I could hear him talking to himself, while he paced up and down. The servants would neither confirm nor deny this; but they were apprehensive.

It is amazing, when I stop to think of it, how readily Miss Shackleton and I fell into our special, furtive way of living, how easily we adopted a sneak's routine.

First of all, it was agreed that in no circumstances was she to go above, with or without me. This was of the utmost importance. She was not even to leave the passage that abutted my bunk, a strip of hall only a few yards long, a few feet wide. Anywhere else, she might get lost, or, worse, encounter some member of the crew; and then the secret would be out.

Nobody ever went down to my cubbyhole—why should anybody?—and it was seldom that anybody came close enough to it to overhear any possible sounds emanating from it— talk, weeping, giggles, whatnot. All the same, I enjoined her to be silent in everything she did, and when we talked together, as we did increasingly, it was by whispers.

We talked about many things, but mostly about ourselves, and I began to notice after a while that *I* was doing most of that talking, though ordinarily I am not what could he called garrulous, having had it drilled into me all of my life that children should be seen and not heard—and sometimes not even seen. This is not to say that I considered myself a child, only that the lesson was a long one, and arduous. In fact, I had passed my twenty-first birthday anniversary some six weeks before this time, which meant that I was no longer an apprentice of Mr. Philipse, for all the good *that* did me—out in the Indian Ocean.

But Miss Shackleton had a way of getting me started about myself by telling me just a little, just a teaser, about her own girlhood in Kent, England, and then asking me suddenly if it had been at all that way with me in New York. Then, while I babbled, she would lean back and listen, her head tipped up, a small affectionate smile at her mouth. She had a genius for listening; and I must admit that it made me feel good.

". . . and then, after supper each night, unless it's nasty weather, everybody goes out on what they call the *stoep,* which is a Dutch word for a sort of wooden platform in front of the door, and they sit there with the woman knitting and the man smoking his big long pipe, and they talk of this and that and the other thing. Sometimes neighbors will drift over, and they'll all join in a slow, easy discussion. That's what they call a *klappernye,* a sort of conference, and it's friendly, it's comfortable. Of course I was never part of one of these, not being Dutch myself, but it was pleasant to know that it was going on all around you—unless it was raining or very cold."

"That's interesting. Tell me more."

And then I would tell her about the windmills, which she said they did not have in Kent, or about how we used to slide and skate on the Collect Pond or sometimes, in a very cold winter, on the river itself. Anyway, it seemed to be me talking nine-tenths of the time, not her.

Getting food for her was easy, because of the way in which I had been living. I could always raise food from Sol the cook and then afterwards eat at the regular officers' mess, without anyone's being the wiser; or I could go back to Sol for seconds, as long as I did not run out of quotations from the Good Book, something that was not likely.

Water too was available at all times, now that our tanks had been filled, and there was nobody to notice—or to care —that I was using somewhat more water than I had used formerly.

You might think at first that emptying the slop-bucket twice as often as before would attract attention; but this was not so. The act was common. At any hour of the day and most hours of the night there could be seen at least a few men along the lee rail heaving their buckets overside at the ends of rope to wash them out in the brine. Another one more or less would cause no comment.

Miss Shackleton could hardly have been cozy in that cramped, hot, all but airless space; but she never did whimper. I, of course, slept on the deck, as I had been doing almost every night since we moved into warm climes, and so my presence there was not remarked upon.

One day Miss Shackleton was cooped up even closer, for a little while. We were sitting on the edge of the bunk, side by side, as we usually sat, and I was asking her again to tell me more about herself as she had been back at home, how she lived, the people she knew, and so forth.

"You wouldn't be amused," she said. "I was just another English country girl."

"I find that hard to believe," I said, meaning it. "What did you used to *eat* in Kent, for instance?"

"Well," she started, "sometimes we would—"

It was at this point that I heard a step on the deck above. It was a heavy step, not that of either of the two servant boys I had asked to call down to me in the event that Captain Kidd elected to come out of his seclusion.

I acted fast. I reached under her legs and whirled her into a lying position on her back in the bunk, and almost with the same motion I closed the bunk door and snapped the padlock. She never said a word, never even squeaked.

I turned—to find myself faced with Harry Adams the quartermaster.

He was a hard case. I think he liked me personally, if only because I had taken cutlass lessons from him, but he was a man who could not have been swerved a hair away from his duty as he saw it.

He took out his list.

"You never returned that cutlass," he said. "The one you were issued when you crossed in the longboat with the Captain."

I snapped impatient fingers.

"You're right. Here it is. Sorry. I'd forgotten about it."

This was true. The weapon had been lying on the floor beside the bunk, unheeded. If the weather had been rough it would have skittered back and forth and I should have had to fasten it down or tuck it away in some manner, but we had been sailing a sea that was like a lake, and now, when Harry Adams came, we were at anchor again in Telere Bay. So there had been nothing to remind me in that dim place of the cutlass. I handed it to him, glad to be rid of it.

Adams swished his nose like a rabbit.

"You only just snuffed out a candle?"

"Yes. In the bunk."

I do not like to lie, unless I have to. But this was no lie. I *had* put out the candle while I lowered Miss Shackleton into the bunk.

"It's damn' hot down here," mumbled Adams.

74

"It always is. I don't spend much time here. Sleep on deck. I just use that," and I nodded to the door of the bunk, "as a sort of storage bin, y'know?"

"Why do you keep it padlocked, then?"

"Leave it open, and it slams back and forth when the ship rolls."

Adams O-ed his eyes.

"But we've got no motion at all on now!" he cried.

I shrugged.

"You know how it is. You never can tell when it's going to start up again."

He put away his list. He nodded, glancing once more at the padlock. And he went topside, without any further remark. I exhaled.

As soon as his footsteps had died I addressed myself to the padlock. With the candle out, only the faintest film of light was filtered down to this remote spot, and the bunk itself, once I got the door open, was utterly dark. I reached in, and my hands fell upon her breast and belly, warm and pulsing beneath that thin gown. I drew those hands back as if they had been burned, as in one sense they had.

"Are you all right?" I hissed, for I had noted that she was trembling.,

"I'm all right. I guess. It scared me. It happened so suddenly."

"Yes."

"Mr. Franklin, stay here a little while longer with me, won't you? Please!"

I shook my head, though it is not likely that she could see it.

"No," I said. "Adams knows that I just put out the candle, and if I stay on down here, in the darkness, he'll wonder about it. He'll get suspicious. He's that kind of man."

"All right," she whispered, and there was a hint of a quaver in her voice.

As I started up the ladder I thought that I heard the faintest of sobs from the bunk below. I paused, but the sound was not repeated, and I went on up.

CHAPTER 16

Fumbling in the Dark

OUR WATER and firewood gangs having completed their work at Telere Bay, it only remained to bring in the sick from the beach. Making sure that Quartermaster Adams had seen me, I paused on the poop to survey this work.

That beach would not be deep enough to careen the *Adventure Galley,* and there was talk that as soon as we got all the sick on board we would seek out a more favorable place for this operation.

"Careening" means tipping the vessel over in such a way as to expose her bottom, or most of it, which is then scraped. I had never seen this done, but I had heard that it was a long and painful process. First the vessel must be emptied of all her guns and supplies, which are taken ashore. Then the lightened craft is hauled up on the beach as far as possible, and tilted to her side with lines attached high on her masts and worked by means of jury-built capsterns—that is, *walked around,* precisely as is done when the hook is hoisted. Then comes the scraping, in itself a major undertaking. And finally the ship must be worked out into deep water again, and restocked and regunned by means of the longboats. Laborious as all this is, it is better than having a vessel that has been slowed by the barnacles on its bottom, not to mention the sea worms, growths that greatly increase in warm waters. Once again, we had to remember that speed might prove to be our best friend.

There is a way to careen a vessel right out at sea, if no suitable beach presents itself. This is called "boot-topping," and it is done only in an extremity, an emergency, and then only in a calm sea. All canvas is struck, and all guns and supplies are shifted to one side of the ship, so that she keels far over, the side that is weighted being virtually dead-eyes-under. Then the exposed bottom can be scraped, at least partway. After that everything is shifted to the other side, and the process is reversed. A boot-topping operation often takes two weeks or more, and all that while the vessel is in a perilous position, for a squall could capsize her, while a suddenly appearing pirate or enemy privateer or warship would have her at its mercy, flight being impossible, fight equally so.

It was not likely, I reckoned, that we would employ boot-topping.

Except for the unpalatable berries my own party had found when we first entered Telere Bay, the additions to our larder consisted only of a wild pig, a few rather tough sea fowl, and many fishes fished right out of the bay itself. This was all flesh, not the vegetables and fruits that the scurvy sufferers needed.

They were not doing well. The stretch on the beach had improved few of them, and some, as I noted from the poop when they were brought back aboard, were worse than they had been when we left them. Besides their other symptoms, the scurvy symptoms, some of them had red eyes and thick dry furry tongues, and under their armpits and in their crotches clumps of what looked like tiny warts. And all of them still, without exception, stank.

They probably were wishing that we would leave them alone. They would have to be taken ashore and back on board once again, if and when we careened. It was an unpleasant prospect.

At last we got under way, into the Mozambique Channel, and made for the north. Once out of the bay, to where there was some motion of air, it seemed to me that poor Miss Shackleton down below might at last get some relief from the heat. I hoped that she did not think it mean of me to go up on deck every now and then, but I really believed that I should let myself be seen lest stories start. It would be easy for any inquisitive party to follow me below.

I walked around the deck several times and made sure that my staked-out sleeping place by the fore knightheads had not been usurped, and then very casually I drifted below.

I made no attempt to tread softly, but neither did I, as I approached the last ladder, yoohoo on a quiet note ahead to announce my coming. I don't know why I failed in that. Just forgot it, maybe.

The candle was not lit. That was an understanding: The candle was not to be lighted unless I was there. This made it hard on her, but we were obliged to play safe. If somebody who a moment before had seen me on deck just happened to pass the head of that last ladder and glimpsed a light from below, he might investigate.

After the rowdydowdy sunshine of topside I found the passageway so dark that I could proceed only by groping like a blind man. My hands found the open bunk all right, but Miss Shackleton was not there. The bunk was warm, but she was not there.

Cold sweat leapt out all over me. I reeled.

A thought came. I dashed for the end of the passageway, a very short distance. It did not occur to me, in my agitation, that if she was using the pail it would result in an embarrassment for both of us, despite the darkness.

My hands encountered only wall. The pail was there; I found it with a kick, and it clanked, empty.

This was what I had most feared! She had become panicky, or perhaps just more bored than she thought that she could endure, and had ventured up the ladder—meaning, no doubt, to go only a little distance. Or—had somebody *dragged* her out?

It must have happened only a little while ago, either way, a matter of minutes, for the bunk was warm from her body. Yet in that case, why had I not met her on my way down?

Were rough tarry hands on her even now, feeling her flesh? Were they ripping off her gown?

Then, and for all of my state of distraction, I heard a scuffling, gurgling sound that could only have come from *under* the bunk. There was a sort of small doorless wall locker there, not much more than an inset shelf really, where I kept some of my gear. I had not thought of looking there, or rather feeling there, because it had not occurred to me that anybody, no matter how small, no matter how lithe-limbed and pliable, could have worked his way into that skimpy space.

I got down on my knees and raised the door of the bunk, exposing the space beyond, and there she was. How she had succeeded in getting into that tiny compartment I will never know. Fear must have lent her strength and suppleness. She had heard my step but no yoohoo, so that she thought some stranger was coming, and she had scrambled out of bed and onto the inset shelf. Once there, she could not move; and even when she recognized me from the way I patted the mattress and the way I kicked the pail, she could not draw attention to herself. The dangling door of the bunk held her there, and in that cramped position she could not summon the strength to push it away.

It was a ludicrous situation, I suppose, but it had badly shaken both of us, and when I got her to her feet we were laughing and sobbing at the same time, like a couple of idiots, and we were holding onto one another like ship-wrecked men holding onto a raft.

"I—I'll light the candle."

"No, no," she cried. "Let's just stay this way for a little while."

We were very close together, squeezing one another,

our hands flat, our hearts thumping. What might have happened next I can only surmise, because at just this time there came Gabriel Loffe's voice from above.

"Mr. Franklin?"

"Yes?" I called.

I must have sounded strange, half strangled maybe, for he was worried about me.

"Are you all right, Mr. Franklin? Should I come down there?"

"No, I'm all right. What is it?"

"You asked me to let you know whenever the Captain came out of his cabin. You wanted to talk to him about something, I believe?"

"That's right."

"Well, he's out now. He's walking the deck. But—I don't think that you'd better talk to him about anything, Mr. Franklin."

"Why not?"

"Because I think he has gone out of his mind. I wish you'd come and look at him, Mr. Franklin."

"I'll be right there," I said.

And I was.

CHAPTER 17

Murder of a Gunner

SEEN FROM behind, as I first saw him on this day, Captain Kidd did not look either insane or drunk. A tallish man, he walked with a long swinging confident stride. His back was straight. He was not wearing his sword, nor did I see a pistol or any other weapon on him. His attire, as always, was clean and neat and even brave.

When he turned around, however, I changed my mind. His face, naturally dark, was almost black. His lips were working, as though he chewed something. His eyes blazed. Cheekbones and forehead glistered with sweat. That protuberant vein in his right temple that I had noticed when I first met him, throbbed more violently than ever before.

In short, he was a man to stay away from.

There might have been sixty-five or seventy of the members of the crew strewn along both rails, on their feet, watching him. They were troubled: I could see that. They were puzzled and afraid.

The only person who seemed to pay the Captain no mind, at first, was William Moore the gunner, who sat on a bollard amidships, where he placidly sharpened a chisel. In fact, though, it soon developed that Moore was the one who was provoking our commander, taunting him in a low voice, perhaps cursing him. Every time the Captain passed that pig-faced man his back stiffened, his pace quickened. Moore never looked up, but he was acutely aware of the Captain's presence.

It was a curious scene, and somehow it gave me the creeps.

From where I stood, in the companionway, I could catch only an occasional word of what Moore said: "We'd be rich by now . . . a man who's afraid to fight . . ." But the jeering note was unmistakable, and he was playing up to the crew, their passions, their disappointments.

Captain Kidd was like a man who deliberately tortures himself, though why he should have done so it was impossible to say. He might have left. He might have returned to the cabin where he had been skulking for so long. But he paced back and forth, fuming, his face working, his hands, clasped behind him, all atwitch.

Abruptly he seemed to realize that he was making a spectacle of himself before almost half of the crew. He heeled to a halt, only a few feet from the gunner Moore, who kept up his steady patter of recrimination.

Kidd wheeled upon him.

"Shut your mouth, you lousy dog!"

Moore did not even look up. He was sure of himself. He knew that he had an audience, and he believed that he was about to win.

"If I am a lousy dog," he said loudly, "it is you who have made me so."

I thought then that Captain Kidd would, literally, explode; I thought that he would burst, blow up.

He snatched a bucket that chanced to be near his feet. It was a heavy oaken thing bound with iron, and with an iron handle. He raised it high.

Somebody screamed. I heard that. But it was not Moore, who didn't even raise his head.

Moore had no hat or cap on, either.

The sound was a sort of "thunk!" It was as though two

heavy logs had banged against one another. It was loud, solid, authoritative.

Captain Kidd dropped the bucket. Afterward he shook his fingers in strong distaste, as though he had cast aside a snake.

William Moore slipped forward so that his face slapped against the deck, the nose first. His arms were spread, the honing stone slithering out of one hand, the chisel out of the other. Thereafter he did not move.

Neither did anybody else move, for a moment. Then, stiffly, Captain Kidd straightened his waistcoat, straightened his fall, and walked, marionette-like, away. He seemed to *jerk* as he walked. He went to his cabin, and let himself in. He did not slam the door, but he did shut it firmly, and so quiet was everything on the deck that we could all hear the ponderous wooden balk being pushed into place.

I was the first to go into action, I don't know why. The others appeared to be spellbound, gawping, gaping, their mouths open.

I ran to William Moore. The top of his head—and he had been hit right smacketty-dab on top—did not show a bruise or as much as a droplet of blood. The hair was not even mussed. It was dry thin hair, the color of moldy hay.

I turned him over, and slipped a hand beneath his shirt and tried to feel his heart, if it still beat. I *thought* that I could feel it, but I wasn't sure.

Moore's eyes were closed. He did not tremble or move in any way. I spit on my right forefinger and held this before his mouth, which was open, but I could not be sure whether I detected breath.

"Somebody throw water on him," I yelled, and then I ran below to summon Dr. Bradenham.

He was drunk, as I suppose I might have expected. It took considerable shaking to bring him to a blurred awareness of how serious my message was. Then he blinked wildly, and started topside; but his step was unsteady, his breath was foul.

They had wetted William Moore with seawater. They

must have almost drowned him, right there on the deck, for I suppose that everybody felt ashamed about how they had stood there doing nothing for so long, and tried to make up for it with frantic activity once I was gone.

Bradenham, in a wavering, squeaking voice, ordered him to be carried below, to the passageway outside of his, Bradenham's cabin. There would be no room in the cabin itself, he mumbled by way of apology. I guess it was too crowded with bottles of rum.

William Moore lived for three days, during which time nothing whatever happened. He never did recover consciousness. We sewed him up in an old jib and slid him over the side.

The Captain did not come out of his cabin for that ceremony.

CHAPTER 18

Frankness in the Dark

IT WAS THEN that I decided to jump ship.

Many a mariner could afford to make this decision lightly. He does not like the skipper, or the food, or the sleeping arrangements, or perhaps he finds his shipmates unsociable, so one night in port, any port, he simply slips over the side. He might lose whatever pay is due to him, but what of that? It would be little enough at best, and as he knows from bitter experience every effort would be made at the end of his enlistment period to cheat him of even that little.

Seafaring men live in a sort of international society that is distinctively their own, and they look askance at anybody outside of it. They converse in an argot that is unintelligible to anyone else, and it has been said that if a true salt ventured more than half a mile from the waterfront and went into a barber's shop he would have to take an interpreter with him in order to explain that he wanted a haircut. They have their own rooming houses, their own taverns. It is never difficult to get another berth. Seasoned sailors in any port are so hard to come by—who, after all, would resign himself, knowingly, to such an existence?—that skippers in general adopt a policy of no-questions-asked. The worst our deserter can expect, if he does not ship on another vessel promptly, is to be nabbed by a couple of bosun's mates from his own, or by a press gang. Either way, except for a broken nose and a few bumps on the head, he is no worse off than he was in the first place.

My own case was different. I was a clerk, and had signed the articles in person, not merely made an "x" by the side of my name after somebody had read them to me. It is true that I'd had no other course to pursue, being at the time an indentured servant; but this is no excuse, legally. I did not belong to the maritime fraternity and could not take advantage of their hideaways, their protective blocs, their favored taverns. On the contrary, as an outsider I would be regarded with suspicion and might well be turned in. Most telling of all, I was in a savage land on the far side of the earth.

My obligation to Mr. Philipse had run out, but not my obligation to Captain Kidd and his backers, by repute a powerful pack. Even still considering Mr. Philipse, as I was no longer obliged to do, couldn't I get more of the information he wanted by playing my part alone than I could by traipsing across the seas with a shipload of discontented scoundrels? I thought so. It was my plan, in a general way, to get, somehow, to the northeast coast of Madagascar, or rather St. Mary's Island, just off that coast, where it was said there was a large pirate colony. Without stooping to become a real pirate, I could make myself useful in many ways. I could do accounts. I could keep books. I knew the difference between the coins of various nationalities, and that without stopping to think. Among ignorant men these are skills worth cultivating.

What could I learn, where would I get, by staying aboard the *Adventure Galley?* It was not, truly, my assigned post.

I have heard it said by cynical persons that every man has at least a little larceny in his heart; but *this* collection of cutthroats among which I found myself were truly pirates in their souls, no matter how long William Kidd could succeed in restraining them from going on the account. The killing of William Moore had impressed them, but only momentarily. Another leader would rise, and he would be careful to keep away from the Captain when there were any buckets close at hand.

One of two things was going to happen on this doomed vessel. Either the crew would kill the Captain and go on a cruise of their own, raiding everything they met, or else they would force the Captain to go on the account with them. The latter was the more likely, since Captain Kidd was the only one who knew about navigation, and they would be babes afloat without him. But where would I end, no matter *which* happened? I would be regarded as a spy, as indeed I was, and one day I would wake up, as the seamen put it, with sand in my ears—at the bottom of the sea. It is very easy to get rid of a body in the middle of the Mozambique Channel.

There were drawbacks, yes. I was in good health, indubitably, but how was I to know that on land I would not come down with some hitherto unknown virulent tropical fever? It was a part of my plan—if I could be said to have a plan—to steal the Captain's gig for my getaway; yet I knew nothing about navigation, nothing about the handling of a boat, *and* I could not swim.

The highest hurdle of them all would be Miss Shackleton. It was unthinkable that I should sneak away and leave her to starve in the darkness or to give herself up, perforce, to profanation. That I simply could not do. But would she consent to go with me in what might well seem a hare-brained excursion, a plunge into the jungle of an unknown, dark land? It seemed unlikely.

The only way to find out, of course, was to ask her; and this I did.

It was a night when I sat with her on the bunk and watched her eat the supper I had brought. If I wanted any supper for myself I would need to get to the mess cabin in a little while; but I did not care to ask her such a delicate question—would she consent to run away with me?—while she was still munching. So I waited.

Would I mislead her? After she had heard me out, would

she feel that she should not refuse to agree to my perilous proposal because she was under obligations to me, who had saved her? I hoped not. I desired her honest opinion.

At times like this, when I was mixed in my thoughts and verging on a momentous decision, I used often to wonder what Anneke Van der Donck would have advised, she who was so good to me in many ways besides being such a good cook. Anneke had a fine level firm Dutch understanding, and she never did anything hastily. But it was just as well not to think of her at a time like this, when I was cramped into that small space with Miss Shackleton. It made me think of sinning, which was not comfortable.

"Ma'am," I said at last, when she had finished her food, "there is something that I want to ask you."

"Yes?" she said, wiping her mouth and leaning toward me, those fine big green eyes shining in the candlelight.

"Something important."

"Oh?"

I swallowed. This would be hard. But I plunged in, and I told her about my plans, as well as my reason for making them. I did not hide from her that it would be a very dangerous and difficult thing to do.

She reflected, leaning back a little, very graceful. She put a finger to her lips, as though to stem words that might have come forth too fast.

It occurred to me then that I had never really seen this girl in the light of day, and that even now, after several weeks of dim undertoned acquaintance, I could think of her only as a pair of large lustrous green eyes, a somewhat pear-shaped face, a rose-petal mouth, a preternaturally pale skin, and, considering her slight size, luscious large breasts. It was well not to think of these things. I shook my head pettishly, as if I had just walked into a spider's web.

"Are you sure that it would not be safe for me on this ship, here?" she asked after a while.

"Certain of it. All hell will break out at any time now, if you'll forgive the expression. These men are *jumping* for a chance to hurt somebody, anybody. They are almost beyond control. And the sight of you would set them mad. I mean it."

She paused, finger yet upheld.

"I don't know whether I like to hear that or not."

"You wouldn't like to experience it—*that* many men!"

"Of course not!" She considered further. "Well then, are you so sure that we would be better off at St. Mary's? They're practically *all* pirates there, from what I hear."

"That's right. But they have at least got some kind of organization. They even have a city, they call it Libertatia."

"I've heard of that place. Every man has a vote. It must be unusual."

"Well, I expect there's nothing else like it on earth. But at least they've got some form of government there."

Her response was a whit sharp.

"Do you think that a form of government would make me less desirable?"

I covered, promptly.

"I did not mean that. I meant that they wouldn't even pretend to have an outpost of civilization there, as you might say, without having *some* women. They might be heathens, they might even be blacks, but at least they'd be women."

"I see."

It made my face feel hot, to be talking about such intimate matters with a young female, but she took it all calmly and very well.

"And then too, in a place like that, with ships coming and going all the time, we'd have a much better chance of getting you a passage to Calicut."

"Calicut?"

"So that you could join your uncle, the way you started out to do."

"Oh yes, of course."

She was silent for a moment, and then suddenly she leaned forward again and put both her hands over both of mine.

"Anywhere you go I want to go," she cried. "So that settles that."

"Good."

I got up, and whuffed out the candle.

"Last mess bell ringing up there," I explained. "I'll have to hurry, if I'm going to get anything at all to eat."

I thought I heard her sigh a little, as I turned toward the ladder, but I suppose that was just from nervousness. It must have been a worrisome decision to make.

Halfway up the ladder I heard a topman call: "*Land ho!*" and I wondered whether this would prove to be the place where we would careen. It was in the course of the careening, when everything would be topsyturvy, that I planned to escape.

CHAPTER 19

As the Moon Rose

UNDERSTANDABLY, and in spite of the Captain's reluctance to attend, the funeral of William Moore the gunner had been well attended. This was not so of the death services that followed. They became too common to attract attention. For the plague—it could only be called that, not a simple epidemic of scurvy—was suddenly intensified. There were no new victims, but those who were already suffering began to die like flies. It was as though the Devil himself was in our midst, laying about him blindly. By the time we had raised the little island of Mehila there were no fewer than five corpses sewn in canvas and laid out on the forward deck.

The reason we did not slip these over the side, as had been done with the remains of Moore, was because there was a serious shortage of malleable lead, and a succession of unweighted bodies, we feared, would cause sharks to follow the ship right into whatever anchorage we might find.

Mehila, a hilly, thickly wooded island, offered us an ideal beach immediately: It was almost as if it had been waiting there for us, expecting our arrival. It was a beach of light yellow sand, deep, gently sloping, void of serious rocks, and it lay at the bottom of a small but well protected bay near the southwest corner of the island. Unless we got a blow from that very direction—that is, from the southwest—we would be perfectly snug in that small space. And such a flow was highly unlikely at that season of the year, March, when the prevailing trade wind, or "monsoon" as they call it out that way, was just the opposite, blowing from the northeast. It was a good wind that we had, steady, sturdy, not often straked with rain.

This would be a busy time for everybody, even for me, who, as the ship's clerk, had to keep a record of each death and of the personal effects of the dead men entrusted to my care. Both of the longboats and the Captain's gig as well were put into the water, and thereafter in all daylight hours they plied back and forth between beach and ship.

Though there was no reason to believe that the island ever had been inhabited, there *was* ample reason to believe that it had been visited from time to time by mariners in the same straits as ourselves. The hinterland—what little we saw of it—was without evidence of human life; but the beach itself was strewn with leftovers from other callers—a rusty capstern bar, part of a ship's lantern, a marlinspike, snippets of rope, even an occasional plank. The sand was smooth—the wind would have seen to that—but many of the trees behind it were scarred where cables had been wrapped around them preparatory to the process of dragging ships ashore. And when Apperson, our new chief gunner, who had succeeded Moore, went up a hill that clearly commanded the entrance of the bay, he found to his delight that the previous visitors had left there a firmly constructed gun platform, saving him a heap of work. The first guns to be rowed ashore were hauled up there and mounted on that platform, where too a magazine was built. For a man's ship was not safe in these waters, which teemed with pirates, and we had no intention of getting caught with our breeches down.

In one of the first boats to go ashore there were the five corpses of which we had cheated the sharks. We buried them far up on the beach, where the high tide would not reach them; and even while we were performing this lugubrious task, two more men died on the ship.

This made me all the more eager to get away. The hand of God, it seemed certain, was against this venture. The escape should be made, I reasoned, when the *Adventure Galley* was riding the lightest, just before she would be hauled ashore, but I was not seaman enough to be sure when this would be—after the last of the guns had been taken ashore, assumedly—and I would rather make my exit too early than too late. If the *Adventure* was dragged up on the beach with Eve Shackleton still aboard, it might prove awkward to feed her. Then there was the matter of the gig. It must be stolen early on the chosen night, so that we could put a great deal of water between ourselves and the *Adventure* before the theft was discovered. The gig was in the water all the time these days; and at night, ordinarily, it was tied astern, just under the counter, the painter indeed being made fast to one of the uprights of the taffrail that half-rimmed the poop. This would make it difficult to stock, a task that must be put off until the last moment, for the Captain used the gig a great deal during the daylight hours, or at least always had it manned and on call.

And with *what* would I stock it? Food and water mostly. The water was easy to get: There was a good spring ashore, and our tanks were full. The food would be something different. Here again my friendship with Sol the cook stood me in good stead. For some time I had been drawing what virtually amounted to double rations twice a day, and now could I ask for even *more?* I believed that Sol suspected something but just didn't care, but if I should ask for *more* he would surely begin to question me. I decided to steal the extra stuff. This was easy, since I had the run of the galley, and what I took from there I supplemented with scraps of food—"orts" the mariners called them—from the officers' mess. These, together with several leather jacks containing water, I stored in the inset shelf below my bunk, the same space into which Miss Shackleton had squeezed herself when she heard me coming. It was not much. It consisted mostly of rancid pork and broken hardtack.

As for weapons, I had a sheath knife I'd picked up somewhere, my pistols, and a cutlass. The cutlass I had found in plain sight on the deck one afternoon. I suppose it must have been dropped in the confusion of moving. Most of the guns and stores and more than half of the men already had been moved to the beach, where a widespread tent colony had sprung up, and it was only to be expected that something would get mislaid. Also, there was a boathook in the gig, and it was left there nights. They did *not* leave the two pairs of oars, but I knew where these were stored and I had no doubt that I could get them at the last moment. The thole pins were kept in the boat: I had checked that. I had in fact been studying the gig very carefully for the past week, without, I hope, having seemed to do so.

At last our night came. March 30, 1697. To wait any longer would have been to risk being hauled ashore, where, incidentally, our burial ground grew larger every day.

We could not know about the weather. That was a chance we took—one of many.

We were almost alone on the *Adventure Galley*, which we shared with the Captain and his two servants, and a handful of salts in the forecastle. All of the officers, excepting me, were ashore. Both longboats were ashore. Even the cook was there. It was the perfect time.

As soon as it got dark I made my way below and alerted my companion and took the provisions and oars topside and placed them in a companionway near the opening to the poop. While I did this I scanned the poop itself. It was utterly empty. In ordinary times there would have been an officer and two helmsmen stationed there all night, but now there was nobody and the wheel swung free.

Crossing that poop deck to the taffrail, from where we could slide down the painter to the gig, would be the most risky part of the whole performance. A gibbous moon was inching itself over the horizon: In a little while the whole space would be flooded with light.

I had not been able to plan any other way of getting to the gig. There was no port near it, and neither Miss Shackleton nor I could swim. So it had to be the painter.

I went down to my bunk again, where I gathered up my pistols, my sword, and my passenger.

It was necessary to guide the girl carefully up the various ladders and around the various corners, for it was as dark as pitch down there, and she had never made the trip before—except when she was carried in the chest. I held her close.

I stopped her in the corridor just a little short of the door to the poop, standing her right beside the provisions I had piled there. I tiptoed ahead, to have another peek at the poop.

It was well that I did. There was a man there. William Kidd.

CHAPTER 20

The Great Breakaway

HE WAS TALL and very straight in profile to me from where I lurked in the shadows. He did not stir. He was gazing toward the land, the beach, where a score of campfires winked like lightning bugs.

He stood near the taffrail, his left knee scant inches from the rope that was my goal.

There was pain at his mouth. It was not a spasm, a passing emotion; it was etched there. Did he too realize that the hand of God was turned against this voyage? There had been three more burials that very afternoon.

Was he, like me, wildly wishing that he could escape, and did he concede that because of the responsibilities of his high position and because of his advanced age—he must have been near fifty—this was unthinkable?

I felt sorry for the man, as I watched him standing there. I had no reason to love him, except in the broad sense that he was a man and we are taught that all men are brothers and that we should love our brothers, but at least I could feel sorry for him. His was a bitter pill to swallow.

I don't know how long I watched him. The moon was fully up and his figure and features were clear. At last he gave a sigh that sounded as if it really came up from the heart, and his shoulders sagged a little, the first time I had ever seen them do that, and he turned and walked back to his cabin, leaving the poop clear. I heard the door close. I heard the balk.

We wasted no time then, but hurried all the food and the weapons and the oars out to the upright of the taffrail to which the painter was tied.

Up close like that, I was more than ever impressed by the squeakiness of our escape, by the flimsiness of the line on which it depended. The painter in truth was little more than a cord of the sort a housewife might hang her washing on. There were no knots in it, and it was chafed in many places. It was almost taut, only slightly arched. A good twenty-five feet below, the gig, a slim white craft of perhaps eighteen feet overall, bobbed. She was scarcely beamier than a fisherman's dory, and looked as if she might be hard to hit down there.

I went first, as was only fair. If it would hold me, it would hold her.

I took with me one of the oars, some personal effects slung over my shoulders, most of the water bottles in various pockets, the box of pistols, and, clenched between my teeth, the cutlass. The descent was uneventful, and I managed to drop into the boat without any noise. Nevertheless, I felt curiously exposed. The *Adventure's* stern was wrapped in shadow, for the moon, still low, lay forward; yet I found it hard to believe that the men on shore, in that sprawling camp, could not see me. They were only a few hundred feet away, and I could see them moving about among the fires, and could hear their voices coming clear across the water. But there was no outcry.

I signaled for Miss Shackleton to slide down, which she did with a notable agility. She carried the other oar, the remaining water bottles, and as much of the food as she could hold.

That left the bulk of the food still up on the poop, and it was my duty to go and fetch it.

Climbing was a much more exhausting job than sliding

down had been. The painter cut my hands and refused to stay firm between my legs, it was so thin. All the while too, and contrary to the promptings of common sense, I had the conviction that men were watching me from the beach. They had the two longboats over there, twelve-oared craft. They could have caught us up before we got out of the bay.

Seated on the taffrail, I moved fast. Here I *was* in full sight of anybody who cared to look.

By means of a sort of basket that Miss Shackleton had woven of palm fronds I'd brought aboard from the edge of the beach, I was able to pack all of the remaining food containers on my shoulders and back, but I was woefully overloaded and had all I could do to keep from slipping.

I was about halfway down to the gig when I thought I heard something that might have been a footstep on the deck, and I looked up quickly.

That might have been what did it, that movement. Anyway the rope pipped apart a few feet above my head, and after a sickening split-second I found myself lying in the bottom of the boat.

I was not badly hurt, though the breath had been knocked out of me and no doubt I would find bruises later. The food, fortunately, all had descended into the boat with me, and indeed some of it had helped to break my fall and conceivably spared me broken bones.

But the noise was stupendous, deafening. There was one great splash, and then the gig bobbed eratically, sending out waves on either side. The oars rattled, the cutlass jumped, and I think that Miss Shackleton screamed for an instant, cutting it short when she clapped both of her hands over her mouth.

It was unbelievable that this would not be heard by the men ashore as well as those still aboard. I got full-length on the bottom of the boat and pulled Eve Shackleton down with me. As much as possible we worked ourselves under the thwarts, where we lay perfectly still, putting a somewhat vaporous trust in the shadows.

Nothing whatever happened. At last we crawled out, incredulous, and rose. The shadows no longer swathed us. The gig, unhitched, had drifted out of them, and now we were in a blaze of moonlight. Yet nobody hailed us.

It had been a part of my plan to row us clear out of the bay, and not to try to spread the sail until we were well beyond sight and hearing, inasmuch as I was so lubberly in that respect and would probably make a lot of noise. Now, when I saw that we were miraculously unperceived, I jumped to a rowing seat and got going.

Miss Shackleton sat in the sternsheets, leaning forward earnestly toward me, as though to urge me on.

It was a pity that we had not been able to bring all four oars, for these were not equipped with leather welts to prevent them from slipping into the sea if they were for an instant neglected, and it occurred to me right away that if we lost one—we who could not swim—we would be all but helpless. I spoke of this to Miss Shackleton and showed her where the boathook was kept and begged her to stay awake and watch carefully in case I nodded or slipped. She promised that she would.

It was a long pull, much longer than it had looked from the *Adventure Galley,* but we got there at last, to the entrance of the bay, the edge of the open sea. There, after several clumsy tries, once almost capsizing us, I did manage to spread the sail, and we started to slish through the water at a gratifying speed.

I fitted the tiller into place, reflecting as I did so that in an emergency it could be used as a cudgel.

We rounded the farther tip of entrance to the bay and made in a direction that I knew to be due east, heading for Madagascar. How long we would hold that course was another matter. I lined us up with a star, and did the best I could to keep us going in a straight line, but I was not bubbling over with confidence. The wind might shift during the night and I not be mariner enough to notice it. We might go around in a circle, the way they say that men lost in the woods sometimes go in circles, though they think that they are going straight. That was a risk that we must take. At any rate, and wherever we were going, we were on our way.

I waved my arm.

"Eastward ho!" I cried.

Miss Shackleton giggled.

CHAPTER 21

Reflections of a Waif

THAT MUST have been the longest night in history. Because of all my exertions I had reason to believe that sleep would come soon; but this proved to be a mistake. Weary though I was—muscle weary, bone weary—I could not nod. Eve Shackleton, with a fortitude I was to come to admire, cast off her cares and curled up like a cat on the bottom of the boat, where she slept the sleep of innocence. Blessedly, she did not snore. But I, thought my eyes throbbed and felt dry, stayed twitchy, groggy of mind but in body all jerks, like a quockerwodger on a stick.

It was a dreary time, that long, long night. I did not even have the satisfaction of gloating upon the beauty of my companion, for I had not yet seen her in a full light, and now, the moon being still low, she lay in the shadows of the thwarts, a mottled mass, a blur. Would she prove, in reality, as lovely as I had pictured her in my mind all this while? Or would the dawn reveal her as a blotched creature after all?

And that dawn—would it never come? And if it did come, and when it came, would it be straight ahead? If we missed the northern tip of Madagascar, a possibility, there would be many thousands of miles of open ocean before us. In that event we would assuredly die of hunger or thirst.

I had started to steer by a star, but the stars in that part of the world were in a different pattern from the stars at home, the ones with which I was tolerably familiar, and it came about that soon I was no longer certain which one was the one I had picked. Besides, I had heard somewhere that stars are not reliable direction-pointers because they move around in the sky; or maybe it is the earth that moves; I was never clear about this. The wind seemed safer, more dependable. There was no gust, just a steady, firm breeze. Once I had got the sail into a position where it seemed to be pulling best, I never touched it. Even so, there was always that pesky possibility that we might be sailing in circles. I had nothing to go by. For a while I could look back and see the island of Mehila bathed in moonlight, but soon it faded, a mere thickening of the horizon, and then there was nothing but sea and sky, a magnificent blank.

The bows of the boat "spoke" with a soft sibilant whisper. Now and then, too, I heard or thought I heard a small splash, a sound that could have been made by flying fishes, of which there were many in these waters, or perhaps by a shark or a porpoise. For the rest, the world was wrapped in a terrifying silence, and there were times when I almost wished that Miss Shackleton *would* snore. I had never before been so horribly alone.

The minutes crawled past like wounded animals looking for a place to die.

To get my mind away from the two self-pitying subjects that occupied it so much of the time—my hunger for Anneke Van der Donck and my bitterness about being dispatched to a faraway sea just before my term of indenture was about to run out—I deliberately made myself think back on my boyhood, a happy one.

I remembered our old schoolmaster, Mr. de Groot, the man who probably had more effect on my life and character than anybody else, excepting always Mr. Philipse. I thought of him that way, as "old," though in truth he might have been less than thirty when he pounded the three "r"s into me, among others. Still, he always *looked* old, with his thinning hair, his spectacles, his earnestness of manner. Or rather, he looked as if he had never been young, as if he had been born the way I knew him, without a boyhood, without any youth.

He was an excitable man, was Mr. de Groot, and he used to switch unwittingly into Dutch when he lost his temper, spluttering. Thin-chested, thin-faced, stiff in his movements, and perhaps defensive because of this, he was partial to the rod, and was often criticized for harshness. My own small backside was not unacquainted with that instrument of correction, but on the whole, I will admit, Mr. de Groot was kinder to me than, probably, I deserved. I think that this was because he felt sorry for me, an orphan.

When I stopped to think of it, as I not infrequently did, I simply could not feel compassion for myself because I lacked living parents, but apparently I was alone in this. I had never really known either my mother or my father anyway, so that there was no lingering sense of loss. From what I heard, they had been highly likable persons, and there were a great many friends who went out of their way to be pleasant to me, their only survivor, for I had no brothers or sisters. Even when Aunt Fanny Sanders died, after having done her ineffectual best to be a mother to me, there were those who persisted in watching to make sure that I was not missing anything because of my condition of orphanage. I was asked to all the parties and outings. When the Collect froze I was given a pair of skates and carefully taught how to use them. At May pole time I was always allotted one of the ribbons. Whenever, at a share-out, there was one cookie left over, or one apple, it was given to me, the orphan. I joined in all the songs, whether Dutch or English. The English and the Dutch in New York, though they get along together all right, and are good neighbors, *socially* don't mix much. They go to different churches and have different bees. They seldom visit one another, except maybe on business, and never bowl or hunt together. But

I was welcome in either camp, as much at home in a Dutch kitchen like the Van der Doncks' as in an English one. There are advantages in not having parents.

Nor did my aloneness make any difference in my fate as a clerk. We were poor, so I understood, and had no land, so that almost certainly if my mother and father had lived I would have been apprenticed to Mr. Philipse or somebody like him anyway. It was the only way to learn a trade.

All things considered, I thought to myself as I sat in that boat and stared hard at the horizon, I had been pretty lucky.

Did I perhaps doze a little, after all? Despite my staring, the dawn took me unawares. At one moment there was no sign of it, but at the next it was smearing itself all over the sky, pinks and purples and blue-grays, the clouds glowing as though from lights inside of them.

And—it was straight ahead!

I saw nothing *else* ahead, no land, nor was there any in sight to the north or the south, nor yet behind us. But the dawn was in the right place, that was all that counted just then. We were on course. I take no credit for this minor miracle of navigation. It was the wind that did it.

Something stirred at my feet, and life began all over again for one who had so lately been a miserable wretch. Eve Shackleton rose, blinking, stretching, patting down her dress. Except for a complexion admittedly a bit on the pasty side, she was the epitome of loveliness. The rays of the rising sun shone on her hair, and her eyes were as large and as lustrous as I had remembered them.

The dawn, that is, did nothing to damage her. She gave me a dazzling smile. She pointed astern. "Now, turn your head for a little while," she directed.

CHAPTER 22

Life at Sea

I HAD BEEN at sea for six months, but not until now had I been acutely conscious of the water. This was different, being right down there with it at its own level. From almost every part of this small boat you could reach out and dip your hand into the Indian Ocean, the immensity of which was only just coming home to me.

We had the whole world to ourselves, and it was more than a little frightening. In that first silver-gray glimmering of the dawn I was not so carried away with delight to see it ahead of us that I forgot to look behind as well, and throughout that morning, from time to time, I tossed a backward glance, fearful, in spite of myself, that I might see a speeding longboat. This was probably stupid. None of them knew of the existence of my companion, and as for me they probably would not even miss me for a while and might well think that the Captain's gig had simply snapped its painter and drifted off into the night. I had always been a loner on that ship anyway, keeping to myself most of the time. Not until somebody else died and they looked around for the clerk to record this fact and to give a receipt for the personal effects, would they be likely to note that I was no longer present. Even then they would probably only say "Good riddance." My books were in order; I knew that.

Aboard the *Adventure Galley* there was always a multitude of sounds, even on the stillest night. There were the squeal of strained lines, the snap and crack of canvas and the rattle of reef points, the snores or shouts of seamen, the shush of the bows, the gurgle of the wake, and at all times, even when I was in my hole-in-the-wall, there was the insistent scree of timbers being rubbed together. Now, in the gig, everything was silent. We had only ourselves, Miss Shackleton and I, and we did not speak much to one another. Could this have been because we were afraid to? I know *I* was.

As she had been in the dimness of my bunk, she was for the most part rather grave than merry in her manner, her voice low and serious, her speech slow. Now and then she would flash that sensational smile, causing my heart to miss a beat, and on occasion she could even be playful. For instance, the painter had broken near its upper end when it spilled me into the boat the previous night, and that left us seventeen or eighteen feet of rope. It was not very good rope, but I racked my brains to find an immediate use for it. At last I decreed that it should be used at all times to lash the helmsman to the tiller. Though the sea had been smooth and the wind steady it was only natural that one or the other of us should always be at the tiller. Now, a sudden squall or a shift of the wind could cause that stick to give a great sideways shove that might possibly knock the helmsman into the sea if he or she was not fastened. I explained this to Miss Shackleton, and I waggled a forefinger at her as I did so.

"There must be no exceptions, understand?"

She saluted, chanting "Aye, aye, Cap'n," which sent us both off into gales of laughter.

Water—drinking water, that is—was our prime consideration, as we both appreciated from the start. We had six jacks of it, leather bottles, each containing about a quart, but we should have had four or five times that much. A gallon and a half seems like a lot of drinking water, but for two persons in an open boat in the tropics it decidedly is not. The sun was merciless, the breeze unpausing, and both the hardtack and the salt pork made us ravenously thirsty. We did not dole out the water, so many shares at such-and-such intervals, but we did agree, early on that first morning, not to wash except in sea water and not to take a drink until we thought that we couldn't stand it any longer.

"Hold it in your mouth a long while before you swallow it," she suggested. "They say that makes it go farther."

A thought that I suppose could be called whimsical struck me. I spread my arms, turning around.

"Water everywhere! Every place you look! As far as you can see, everywhere! And yet we have to take it a drop at a time when we want it to drink. Don't you think that that's ironic? Don't you think that maybe some poet ought to make a poem out of it?"

She looked at me and smiled, though the smile was a mite tremulous. I suppose she thought that I was a bit touched by the sun. We were each of us expecting the other one to start talking foolishness.

I slept, off and on, a good part of that first day, but it was not a restful, refreshing sleep. Miss Shackleton held the tiller, to which she had obediently fastened herself. At sunset we reversed these positions, and she dropped off easily, her face, in slumber, free of strain or worry.

In all that time we had not seen or heard a thing. No fishes jumped. No gulls flew overhead.

Next morning, soon after first light, we got an unexpected treat. I was slumped over the tiller, I am afraid half-asleep, when there was a whirring sound in the air at my left, and a school of flying fishes started to skim right over the gig. They are small things and they move mighty fast. Groggy, I let most of them plop back into the water on the starboard side, but I did get awake soon enough to bat down three of them with my open hands, slamming them upon the recumbent Miss Shackleton, who thereupon awoke.

With my sheath knife I scaled them and cut off their

107

heads and tails, and with my fingers I boned them: They fairly bristled with bones. There was not much left after that, but such as there was we divided it evenly, and we ate it on the spot.

I had never eaten flying fish before, but I had heard—and so, it turned out, had Miss Shackleton—that they were delicious. That must have meant cooked. We had not the means of cooking or even heating them, and raw they were not pleasant. But we were in no position to be squeamish. At least it was a change.

However, like the hardtack and the salt pork, it left us more thirsty than ever.

Here was a long day and a hot one, and I verily believe that we *would* have been jabbering slobbery-slup before it was over, had not Miss Shackleton got the idea of making us hats against the sun. She did this by taking apart the baskets she had woven from palm fronds, and reweaving them. The result was wide-brimmed and pointed on top, and we must have looked ridiculous in them, but by that time we were in no mood for laughing at one another or at anything else.

We were down to a bottle and a half—three pints—of water, and there still had been no driftwood or floating coconuts or flying birds to indicate land. I for one was badly scared, though I strove to prevent my fear from showing. Miss Shackleton, as she had done each of the previous nights, calmly curled up on the bottom of the boat and went to sleep.

I went to sleep myself, lashed to the helm as I was, and despite my fears. I did not do this intentionally, of course. I just dozed off, not being a good skipper on my first command.

When I awoke the sky was dark, no moon, no stars, and the air smelled of rain. What had awakened me was a sound ahead of us and very near at hand. It was a sound I had never heard before, yet I knew it instantly.

It was the sound of breakers.

CHAPTER 23

Pandemonium

THE NOISE was immense, and very near. The wonder was that it had not wakened me sooner. A sudden shift in the wind, perhaps? I noticed now, for the first time, that the sail was wambling violently.

We had only a single sail, a triangular one made of Dutch linen and sewn with round needles. It was a good sail, a strong one, nearly new, but it had never been meant for such heavy work. A Captain's gig, after all, seldom goes to sea. I had had thunderation's own time hoisting it and fastening it into place, but since then there had been no need to touch it. But now the previously placid thing had gone wild, flapping and slopping like a bird caught in lime. It's urgency was shrill compared with the heavier urgency of the unseen breakers just ahead, and between them they filled the air.

I knew that I must do something fast.

I reached out with a foot and jogged Eve Shackleton, who got to her hands and knees, looking up in inquiry. She must have seen that there was something wrong with the sail, and she must have heard the ominous thudding of the sea along the shore or on a reef, but seemingly neither of these circumstances alarmed her. She continued to believe that I was capable of handling any situation.

I signaled to her to take the tiller, and she did so without hesitation. There was no time for her to lash herself to it.

I sprang for the preventer, but at this moment it elected to snap in half, and before I could drop to the deck the boom had whammed against my right shoulder and the upper part of my right arm, pinning me against the larboard bulkhead. An instant later, in answer to another crazy lurch of the boat, that boom swung away: Otherwise I would have been forced over the side.

I made the preventer fast somehow, but clearly the sail was rigged wrong and it would not stay in that position. I signaled to Miss Shackleton to put the tiller far over to starboard, because I thought that I had caught a diminution or at least a dull spot in the sound of the breakers to larboard.

Just then, as though to confirm my ears, the moon peeped briefly through a rift in the clouds, illuminating the water around us. It was only for a moment, but it gave us a chance to glimpse the fury of the sea at the reef and the dark solemnity of the land beyond. Would we ever reach that land?

Both were awesomely close. The reef—surely it *was* a reef?—was a smother of foam and high, angry, hissing, spitting, white water. There must have been an off-land wind, for already we felt the sting of spray like a million needles pricking our faces.

Then everything was black again, the moon having gone. But I had seen the break in the reef, if it could be called a break. It was only a little to larboard of us.

There was no question, now, of fighting clear of the reef itself. We were virtually upon it. The sail was flapping furiously.

When the full impact of our plight struck Miss Shackleton, in that moment of moonglare, she screamed. At least, she opened her mouth very wide, popping her eyes. The roar of the water was such that any sound from her could not be heard.

110

I signaled to her to keep the tiller far over, and I grabbed the oars from the bottom of the boat, and sat on a seat and set them between the tholes on either side.

Then I thought, or sensed, that something was wrong on my right, and I supposed that the boom had come undone again, and I ducked my head lest it be smashed like a pumpkin.

The boom did not come. It was still secure. But my movement in ducking brought about the very thing that I had most feared—it caused one of the oars to slip out of my wet grasp and to slither down between the tholes and into the sea.

There could be no thought of fishing for and recovering it. The thing was gone for good, snatched out of sight as soon as it struck the water.

I seized the other oar in both hands and used it like a canoe paddle on the starboard side of the boat. In this way I hoped, with the aid of the rudder, to steer us into the pass to larboard. What the tactic did was swing us sideways, the worst possible position, but by dint of desperate paddling I got us around completely, so that we entered the pass stern-first, or, as the mariners would have said, arse-backwards.

It was not truly a pass, only a low place in the reef. We were slammed with water—solid water, no longer just spray. The oar was wrenched out of my hands, and I fumbled my way back to the sternsheets, where Miss Shackleton sat. The tiller yawed with a lunatic uncertainty, and I worked it off and dropped it to the bottom of the boat. I threw my arms around Miss Shackelton, as she had thrown her arms me.

Then suddenly, all sound ceased.

We could see nothing at all.

Was I dead? This was the first thought that came. Yet I had an arm around Eve Shackleton, and she was trembling, so *she* wasn't dead anyway.

The next thought to come came on the heels of the first, and it seemed more logical. We were underwater. We had somehow been pitched into the sea, no doubt in a stunned condition—the boom? the mast?—and we were drowning or about to drown.

It seemed to me that we were whirling around and around rather than sinking; but then, what did I know about being underwater, I who had never gone swimming with the other boys, not in the dirty East River with all its ships and other vessels but in the nice, clear, sweet-smelling North River or Hudson's River, as they called it upstate? Maybe this was the way the experience did affect people.

I had heard, though, that if you were sure to drown, if you were doomed, the best thing to do was not struggle but just open your mouth and get the business over with.

So I opened my mouth.

No water rushed in, but I was swept by something wet and sticky, and then the truth came to me.

The sail! It had tumbled over both of us, as we sat there in the sternsheets. It had enveloped us, shutting out every other thing.

I worked it away. Miss Shackleton was still clinging to me.

The breakers on the reef were loud, but not as loud as they had been a little while before, and they seemed to be receding. We were going around and around, yes, but sluggishly, not dizzyingly; and the water in which we found ourselves was not turbulent but rather suggested a millpond.

We were not immersed in this water, only up to our ankles. The mast had been snapped off a few feet above the bottom of the boat and was now no more than a jagged mass of splinters. There was a large hole in the floor, but though water swirled around our feet we were still afloat.

Close together, pitifully wet, we began to giggle. It seemed funny, somehow.

And that is the way we drifted ashore, sliding gently up on a gentle sandy beach, giggling like a couple of silly schoolgirls, giggling and sniggering irrepressibly—and hysterically.

We stumbled out. We found a fallen coconut tree, and sat on it, still convulsed with laughter.

After a while I rose. I knew that I should go walking

along the edge of the lagoon in search, even on such a dark night, of whatever odds and ends might have been washed ashore, aside from the remains of the battered boat itself.

"You know," I said to her, once I had got control of myself, "if we ever get out of this alive, I'm going to take swimming lessons."

She grinned at me, and even in that moonlessness I could see the gleam of her eyes.

"You know," she said, "so am I."

CHAPTER 24

A Goddess out of the Ground

THERE WAS plenty. Five of the six leather jacks, the empty ones, bobbed in the shallows in five different places. All the food, though soaked, was still in the boat, as were my cutlass and my box of pistols. I did not at first find the tiller, but I did find the second oar, which had been scraped but not smashed. The boat itself, as I could tell even in the dark, was wrecked beyond my poor ability to mend. Our sleazy hats had been blown off, and the salt water as it dried stiffened our clothes and itched our skins. We were still thirsty, too. One of the first things I must look for when daytime came, I told myself, is fresh water. The only thing that Miss Shackleton had complained of, during our two days and two and a half nights at sea, was the absence of water for washing.

My most notable find was the sail, which, though ripped in a few places, was essentially intact. Attached to it still were the boom that had given me so much trouble and the snapped-off mast. I did not see, immediately, how we could use these two spars, but something might suggest itself later, in the daytime, so I detached them carefully and placed them in the high part of the beach, out of the reach of the tide.

The sail itself I triumphantly carried back toward the spot where I had left Miss Shackleton.

You might have thought that, what with all the exertions of the last few hours, I would have been more than ready for sleep. The very opposite was true. In the whole half year since I left New York there had never been a time when I felt so tortured by carnal thoughts, thoughts of Anneke Van der Donck so far away, even hotter thoughts of Eve Shackleton right here. I did my best to shake these off, but they returned with the persistence of flies to a dung heap. I was ashamed of myself, but shame did not help either.

In the all-but-airless bunk aboard the *Adventure Galley* I had scarcely glimpsed her, never in full, and though I suffered when occasionally our bodies brushed briefly, I survived. In the gig, because of the sun, the wind, and the fact that each of us at any given time was lashed to the tiller, it had not been as bad, though bad enough. She might have had a few unclean thoughts of her own, in the course of that voyage. I had caught her, several times, looking at me with a very strange look. But now, out in the open, on a sandy beach, I would, assumedly, lie down by the very side of Eve Shackleton. I would need every ounce of will power I could muster, and it might even be well, I told myself, as I started back with the sail, if I prayed for more.

Since I did feel that way, it was a wonder that I heard the stream, a very small one, trickling in a thin channel through the sand. I knelt and tested it, and the water was sweet. Glad to have such good news for Miss Shackleton, I hurried ahead, following this tiny stream with the thought of tracing it to its spring unless that was hidden in the jungle.

A goddess rose out of the ground before me, and I stopped short.

She had found this same stream, farther up, doubtless hearing it while I was down by the edge of the lagoon. She was bathing in it, such as it was. She had been bending far over to scoop up water, and now she straightened, rising full-length, ever going up on her toes.

She was stark naked.

Her head was tilted back, her eyes were closed in sheer ecstacy. Her forearms were crossed over her breasts, not in modesty—for I was sure that she had not heard me coming—but in order to empty two palmsful of precious fresh water over her two shoulders, right hand to left shoulder and the other way 'round, so that it could run all down her body, a delicious thrill.

I dropped the sail.

She heard that, and opened her eyes. Her arms tightened, squeezing the breasts flat. She swayed, as though she might fall in a faint. Then her head went back again, and her eyes closed, and her forearms loosened, releasing the crushed breasts, which swung free. She reached out toward me, where I stood.

I jumped over the sail.

We kissed for a long time, holding one another tight, and when at last I did release her her knees buckled and she fell to the sand.

I spread the sail, and literally dragged her onto it. She was conscious, for she moaned. I stripped off my clothes . . .

It was worth having waited for. At one time toward the end I could not even hear the crash of the waves upon the reef, though this was near at hand, and the sound came again as soon as I had finished and fallen off.

We lay for a long while, panting, on our backs. She reached out with her right arm, and I reached out with my left, and we clasped hands, pressing very hard.

There was no need to say anything aloud, but I did tell myself, without words, that I must be fair to this beautiful woman. She had given herself to me, and I must prove worthy of the gift.

It was while thinking this or something similar, and still clutching her hand and no doubt smiling like a fatuous fool, that I fell asleep.

CHAPTER 25

The Lap of Luxury

For a week we indulged ourselves. After the hot stench of the *Adventure*—and this was even more true of Eve than of me—it was Heaven to have shade when we wanted it, sun when we wanted that, and fresh air at all times. The sand was soft. The weather was mild, the wind caressive.

We were about to embark upon a journey that would be fraught with hardships and perils, and it seemed common sense to rest for a little while and regain our strength in this minor but orthodox Eden.

We no longer trembled at the thought of pursuit. Land-lubber though I might have been, I did know something about supplies and storage, about spars and the stepping of masts, and I could assure Eve that it would take at least five or six days of furious work to reassemble the *Adventure Galley*, even supposing that the careening project was abandoned; and as she herself put it, "Nobody but a pair of lunatics like us would make that trip in an open boat." We did scan the sea from time to time, but it was for fear of pirates, not because of any apprehension that my late associates would reappear.

There were thousands of coconuts, more than we could have consumed in a lifetime. We would pick and choose among them, pushing aside the green ones, the rat-eaten ones, and the too-old, over ripe ones. The coconut world is very wasteful.

I mentioned rats. I suppose that they are everywhere in this earth. We seldom saw one, though there is no doubt that they were there, interested only in the coconut trees, of which there was a plentitude. The rats ruined many coconuts, true; but there was more than enough to go around, for them as well as for us. We never heard them scurry or scamper. Maybe they stayed up in the trees? At any rate, they were by no means as noisy and *obtrusive* as the rats on the ship had been. They did not constitute a menace, or even a nuisance, as elsewhere they would have done.

I seldom went into the jungle, and never very far, for it was a dank place and packed with gloom, but when I did I had much better luck foraging than I'd enjoyed at Telere Bay, coming back each time with wild grapes, berries, gourds, melons, and several kinds of fruit that we could not identify. Not all of these were good to eat, but most of them were, and not being famished we could taste each gingerly, putting it aside if it did not immediately tickle our palates.

The lagoon teemed with fish. The wreck of the gig, reinforced by the lashed-on mast and boom, was sufficiently waterworthy to serve as a raft, with the one remaining oar as a paddle, and from this I fished, using a net woven by Eve out of palm leaves. This net was not very durable, but it served our simple purposes, and it could be thrown away before it fell apart. It was the same as with our hats. If they blew off we did not chase them. Eve simply wove more. There were always plenty of palm fronds.

If the menu sounds monotonous, I can assure you that to persons like us, who had been at sea for months on end, it was a paragon of variety and delicacy. We threw away what remained of the salt pork and the weevil-ridden hardtack, for our new food, praise the Lord, was *fresh*. We esteemed ourselves lucky, as indeed we were. Once I did hear Eve express a half-playful wish that she could have some bubble-and-squeak, and as near as I could make out this was a kind of suet pudding; but I myself, I never even in my innermost mind yearned for a tasty Dutch *olijkoeck,* for which failure I should have been ashamed of myself, though I wasn't, being too happy.

Fire was no problem. My flint and steel had been in my wallet all the while, and tinder was easy to obtain, so that most of our meals were cooked.

Eve spent a great deal of time blissfully bathing—her nudity did not embarrass her in the least—while I walked the beach in search of interesting and perhaps useful shells. She had produced from somewhere a comb and a needle and thread, and she would comb her hair by the hour, until it sparkled in the sun, and she would mend rents in her dress and in my breeches, though the sail, of course, was too tough for her.

That sail! We spent long periods of time recumbent upon it, either sinning or preparing for sin or recovering from it. We would not wait for the coming of night, but would do it any time we felt like it, the way I suppose wild animals act. Just at first I found it a mite disconcerting to sin in broad daylight on an open beach, where you could be seen from miles away if there had been anybody to look. The rats did not seem to mind. Still, it *was* unsettling to feel the wind on your back and on your buttocks while you were engaged like that. I got used to it after a while, but I was always to prefer the dark, which seems more natural.

Make no mistake about it: My darling of the beach had not been a virgin. She was much too expert. Anneke Van der Donck was the only other woman I had ever possessed, so I cannot be said to be a man of the world, but certain basic facts about virginity are known to every boy over the age of twelve; and I repeat that Eve Shackleton was not, nor had she recently been, a virgin.

This did not lower her in my eyes. Just because some

other man, some unprincipled scoundrel, had taken advantage of her innocence and then had left her, that did not mean that I too should brush her off at the first chance I got. I fully intended to do the right thing, as soon as that was possible.

It occurred to me one afternoon, while we were lolling on the sail in the shade of a casuarina tree and watching the sunlit wavelets of the lagoon, that she might be a married woman, which could account for the experience.

"Are you married, Eve?" I asked idly.

(I called her Eve now, and she called me Toby, which was pleasant.)

She laughed, but it was not really a light laugh.

"Who would want to marry *me?*" she countered.

No, the laugh had not been lighthearted, nor was her voice as flirtatious as she had meant it to be: There was an edge of bitterness in it.

I sat up. I took her hands in mine.

"I would," I answered. "And as soon as we get to a parson we'll have it done."

She actually blushed. She turned her head away, but I had seen it. And there was a glint of tears at the corners of her eyes. I had seen that too.

"Toby," she whispered, "you're sweet."

We did not pursue this particular conversation any further.

It was not until the eighth day after the washing-ashore that at last we shook off our languor and packed our pitifully slight things and prepared to set forth on a long trek to, we hoped, Libertatia. We were not jubilant, not confident. We both feared that this would prove to be anything but a dance around a Maypole, and we were right.

CHAPTER 26

We Struggle through Slime

It was like walking through a door into another world, the change was that dramatic, that abrupt. The air on the beach had been dry and light; in the jungle it was heavy and wet. On the beach a man felt like frisking about, like a young goat, leaping, dancing; in the jungle he instinctively cringed, his head flipping back and forth as he steeled himself against an expected assault from behind.

We always felt in that place as if somebody was about to leap on our backs.

It was not an abode of sodden silence, as I had found the jungle at Telere Bay. There were noises, but they were small, furtive, *sneaky* noises, all from nearby, all swiftly hushed muffled, gulped whole by the dank air. It was impossible to think of any echo being formed there.

That Eve Shackleton felt the same about the jungle was instantly apparent in the way she kept near to me. The tiller at last had floated ashore, and though I still thought that it would have made a good cudgel we had left it behind as being too heavy. I had my cutlass, which I used in a manner that Quartermaster Adams never taught me, hacking the vines and creepers away where they were thickest, so that we could get through. This kept me in front, but Eve was always close behind, and I was glad of this. We did not talk much—the atmosphere hardly encouraged chitchat—but I knew from the beginning that she was frightened. I at least had been given an advance warning, the foraging party at Telere Bay; but it came as a shock to Eve.

Aside from the sinning, there had been about life on the beach an idyllic quality. It had been different from anything we ever knew before. But in the jungle, life was sheer slog. You *forced* your way ahead. I am sure that Eve and I were as fond of one another as at any time we had been, but it is awkward to wax romantic when you happen to be up to your ankles in mud.

"I wonder if we'll ever be dry again," was the way she put it.

Half an hour after she so spoke it began to rain.

We had known, in a general way, though only by hearing it, that the rainy season, the season of the southwest monsoon, was about to begin. Nevertheless the first squalls surprised us. Instead of a steady drenching downpour, to which we might have accustomed ourselves, against which we might have hardened our bodies, there was an erratic series of *outbursts* of rain: That is the only way I can describe it. There was no regularity about it, but rather a frenzied vindictiveness, as though a madman in the skies were lashing the top of the jungle with a million studded whips. Much of the moisture must have been caught in the vegetation above our heads, to ooze a gradual way downward and eventually to be lost in the already soggy earth. What reached us directly was fine, almost a film, almost a fog, and with all of a fog's pesky persistence. It was not a bit like a familiar, friendly shower at home, though it got you just as wet, or wetter, in the long run.

These storms, squalls, call them what you will, seldom lasted for a long time, but they were hellishly frequent, one slamming earthwards on the very heels of the other, with scarcely a chance to gasp in between.

This made it hard for us to keep our tinder dry, so that

122

fires became rare, breathless occasions. Not that we had much to cook. We gathered grapes and melons as we went along, but for flesh we lacked. The multitude of slim sly sounds around us—and all of them sounding very close—had convinced us that the jungle was inhabited by many small animals, such as squirrels, coneys, woodchucks, or the tropical equivalant of such creatures, but though I kept my cutlass cocked like my ears I never even caught sight of a critter, much less got a swipe at one. This worried me, and I think that it worried Eve as well. We would have given a great deal for a fried chicken.

Of water there was, understandably, too much; but it was not easy to find *sweet-tasting* water, most of it being scummy, stale, bitter.

Another thing that had me troubled was direction. Which way were we going? We had been, I was sure, on the west coast of Madagascar, probably near the northern end of the Mozambique Channel. From there, in order to get to Libertatia on the east coast—or *near* the east coast—we could have followed the shore north and east and then south, but I had decided to strike through the interior, which might be much more rugged and even perilous, but would certainly be shorter. Our course was to be due east, unless mountains intervened. Walk into the sunrise, with the sunset at your back: There was our intention. It is a sketchy way at best of telling direction, but it was the only one I knew. At home men who pretended to understand the woods used to say that you could always tell the direction of north because more moss grew on the trees on that side. But would this apply to Madagascar, below the Equator? And in fact when I did encircle with my arms some of the half-seen trees that hedged us in, it was only to find that there were creepers or vines or a fungus growth of some sort on *all* sides of them, not just one side.

The trouble was, floundering through that matted morass, sliding and sludging through that sea of mire, the sun seemed to have gone out. We traveled in a state of nighttime abated only now and then, here and there, skimpily, by a shaft of sunlight so motled and twisted, so shattered and shorn, that we could only *guess* which direction it had come from. There was no question of sunrise or sunset, nor would there be until we got out into the clear.

I have called this place a jungle, but I could just as well call it a swamp, at least at first. We had to skirt many small, stagnant, stinking pools of water, pools we could scarcely see. Eve was especially leery of these pools, as she believed they were alive with snakes, and she was deathly afraid of snakes, though we never did see one. However, as we proceeded, these pools became fewer; and this fact, added to the fact that our leg muscles were tired unexpectedly early each day, led us to the belief that we were gently going *up*. If this was true—and we fervently wished that it was—we could hope to find ourselves at some time soon struggling out of that dank, drear place. After all, swamps don't climb slopes.

Sure enough, on the afternoon of the fifth day (though Eve insisted that it was the *sixth* day, which gives you some idea of how furry had become our sense of time) we emerged upon an upsloping plain or plateau, almost treeless, and without any pools or streams that we could see. Miraculously, it was not raining. The sky was clear. The earliest of the stars were prinking out up there, low near the horizon.

"The Lord has delivered us from the Amalekites," I cried.

"What are those?" she asked.

I told her.

What is more, it was here, mere minutes after we had emerged from the slime, that I killed our first animal. Without warning of any sort, it scurried before us, so that Eve, thinking it a large rat, retreated, squealing, but I, with my still-upheld cutlass, slashed down, cutting the thing in half.

If it was a rat it was the biggest I had ever seen, and singularly blunt-nosed. At home I would have called it a ground hog, which I guess is a sort of rat after all. Anyway, we had plently of dry wood now, and we built a fire much larger than we really needed, and we cooked that beastie and and ate it.

We felt good. It seemed as if we had the world all to ourselves: There was not a sign of any human habitation. We spread the sail on the ground, and sinned with gusto. Afterwards we fell asleep.

When we woke, the next morning, it was to find ourselves face to face with a tall, broad-shouldered man who had long yellow hair. He was smoking a pipe.

CHAPTER 27

The Uncouth One

HE HAD A beard like a doormat, and small snake's eyes. He was not attractive; but he did seem to be perfectly at home. His clothing could only be described as heterogenous, for it was made up of scraps and pieces of all sorts, some of them furs or pelts; yet he did not show *ragged,* somehow. He was thick-thewed but nowhere fat, and though he was by no means young he rested easily on the balls of his feet, giving the impression of a man who in a pinch could move almighty fast.

He carried no weapon that I could see, but he did grip, in his right hand, a walking stick that was not at all the tall, slim, stylish, silver-handled thing that might be flourished by a smart at home, but rather a short, thick, knobby one that would serve very well as a club.

I did not think that I liked the looks of this man.

We both sat up, flummoxed.

"Who are you?" I asked. "Where did you come from?"

He looked puzzled. Frowning, he shook his head. He leaned forward. He began to talk haltingly in a language I had never heard before. When he paused, having perceived from our faces that we were not getting one word of what he said, I tried him again in English, speaking very slowly and loudly, so that it seemed almost unbelievable that he could not understand it if he really tried. He shook his head in helplessness.

He did not have rubbery lips or a flat nose, though the skin of his face was as dark as any Negro's, and copiously creased. His hair alone would stamp him as a white man. It was a Viking's head of hair, pale yellow, straight, shiny, and it fell to his shoulders.

Then the pipe, a long curved-stem thing, gave me an idea. The man did not *look* like a Dutchman, but there would be no harm in trying.

"*Spreekt U Hollands?*"

That did it. Delighted, the visitor burst into a torrent of Dutch that buffeted me, leaving me agasp. I had to beg him to stop and start all over again, taking it much slower. He grinned apologetically, and complied.

His name was Jan Calkoen, and he had lived on this island many years, so many that he no longer made any attempt to count them. How had he come here in the first place? This was a subject he clearly did not wish to discuss; and I formed the belief that he had been marooned from a pirate vessel because of some shipboard offense. Pirates, I had always heard, were exceedingly strict in moral matters while aboard their ships, which are customarily overcrowded, and the punishment for theft, attempted murder, and so forth is likely to be swift—and likely, too, to take the form of marooning. So our new acquaintance had been thrown out by the lowest of the low? It did not auger well for his usefulness as a companion.

After that first outburst his speech slowed, and indeed he seemed at times to have trouble finding the right words. He explained this by saying that it was so long that he had spoken his native Dutch that he was, to his own vexation, unsure of it. However, this was all the better for me.

Eve thought that it was a marvel that I could interpret almost everything the man said.

"I learn something new about you every day," she cried. "You're wonderful!"

I was gratified, but she might have saved her admiration. Anybody who was brought up in New York, as I was, and did not learn to speak and understand at least a little Dutch, would have been a halfwit or less. It is as common as English there, in the shops, in the gristmills and taverns, along the waterfront. A lot of New Yorkers who don't have a drop of Dutch blood in their veins still speak a mixture of Dutch and English when they are among their own kind, when they are not on their finest manners. It comes natural to them, as it did to me. My Dutch was fluent, though grammatically it might have leaked, and I could not read or write the language very well, only speak and understand it.

What did Mijnheer Calkoen, then, do in Madagascar? How did he make a living?

Well, it seems that he traded with the natives among the various tribes, of which there were a great many, he said, in all this the northern part of the island. He had picked up their language, which had many dialects, but was essentially the same all though his chosen territory, and in addition to his own native Dutch he had some command of French and could even manage a little Portagee. Thus he could be valuable as a go-between when slavers scoured the coasts. He could talk to the slavers on the one hand, to the local *dean,* or lord, on the other.

"When any of these beggars is called *dean* so-and-so or so-and-so *dean,* be respectful to him. You're really supposed to kneel down and kiss one of his heels, but you don't have to go that far. But be respectful."

And what did the slavers pay for their slaves? Liquor?

Oh, no. The blacks had their own liquor, a stuff called *toaka,* which they made out of a nut something like a coconut, only smaller. And when you took a drink of this you first hoisted it and said *"salama,"* which meant health, happiness, well-being.

"No, they either want help in some feud against some

other tribe, or else muskets, which amounts to the same thing. They'll do anything for a musket."

I asked him if when he made contact with other white men like that, didn't he ever think of getting a post on a ship and sailing back to civilization?

He answered no, he was perfectly happy here, but he dropped the topic with alacrity and I gathered that the reason he did not go back to Holland was that he might get his neck stretched if he did.

We invited him to sit down and join us at breakfast, which would be the remains of the ground hog, and he did so gladly and with a good appetite.

I noticed that he was eyeing my box of pistols, and soon he asked me what it was. I showed him the weapons, for I was proud of them, though admittedly they had never been of any service to me. Our Dutchman was delighted. They would be as magic in his hands the next time he dealt with a *dean*, he said. Would I sell them?

Now, in fact the pistol box had come to be something of a dead-weight, and I was favorable to an offer to rid myself of it, but I could not think what to ask.

"For what?"

"For money, of course. I've got money!"

He seemed indignant that I had ever doubted it.

"I'll give you two eight-pieces for them," he offered.

A Spanish eight-real piece, or piece of eight, a silver coin, was worth only a little over six English shillings at that time.

I laughed at him.

He seemed to expect that, and we fell to haggling hammer-and-tongs, poor Eve being left out of this because of her ignorance of Dutch. Not until about an hour later, when he had positively refused to go higher than four eight-pieces, did we drop the subject—to Eve's great relief.

This scarecrow stayed with us for three days. They were lazy days, filled with sunshine, and we were comfortable in our little camp in a hollow not far from the edge of the swamp. There was a stream of sweet water near at hand, and we took things easy. Eve did not agree, but I had decided that she was entitled to a good rest after that struggle through the swamp; she should regain the strength she would need for the trek to St. Mary's.

Calkoen was a sly old rogue, but a born diplomat. He saw right away that Eve and I were in love—and not only in love but *actively* in love, as you might say—and without any eye-rolling or simpering he contrived to sleep well apart from us. He never showed any wish to share our sail, which would not have been large enough for the three of us anyway, but with the coming of darkness would walk to a nearby tree and sit on the ground behind it and go to sleep, or at any rate pretend to go to sleep. He was a man who seemingly could sleep at any time and in any position. All the same, we didn't like it, Eve Shackleton and I. It made us nervous.

The morning of the fourth day when we rose he was not there, no longer behind his tree or anywhere else in sight. But others were there, thirty-odd of them, standing all around and staring at us.

They were black men, completely naked, and they carried spears.

CHAPTER 28

The Dark Escorts

Eve and i had more than once commented upon the fact that we seemed to fall off to sleep at the same time and almost invariably woke up at the same time, as though we were both activated by one lever. We said that this was proof that God had meant us for one another.

It was so this morning, when the blacks encircled us. Up on one elbow, I knew without looking around that she too had just opened her eyes.

"Shall I go for the sword?" I whispered.

"No," she sensibly said.

The cutlass lay on the ground about four feet off my left elbow. It was not a striking blade. There was no sort of sheath or scabbard for it, and what with all the wet traveling it had begun to rust, a dusty flaky red-brown. Also, it badly needed honing, for I had wielded it against all manner of vines and tree branches. Nevertheless, swung with spirit it might still be formidable. Undoubtedly I could have got two or three of these savages before they downed me; but then—what would happen to Eve?

She was right. I did nothing. I did not even stir.

Neither did the blacks. They just stood there staring at us, as if they had never seen anything like that before, which was very likely the case. They did not show anger, but neither did they smile. And they all had those javelins, which looked sharp. Some had three or four.

I never saw so many sets of private parts in my life. It was embarrassing. I did not dare to look at Eve.

I call these men blacks, and that's what they were. I am aware that the word is used loosely to describe Negroes who can be a dark or even a light brown. But these men really were *black*. They were of slightly less than what to us would be medium height, and they were somewhat slenderly built, with smallish bones; yet they looked healthy enough. Not only did they wear not a stitch of clothing but they were not even decorated in any way—no beads, no tattooing, no bracelets, nothing.

After a long while, very slowly, I rose to my feet. I was scrupulously careful not to lean—or even *sway*—toward the cutlass. Solicitous, a cavalier, I helped Eve to her feet. My courtesy on this occasion was exaggerated, for I had some thought that it might help us if the men saw that I valued my companion; and she, sensing this, gravely accepted my attentions.

"I wish they'd *do* something," she whispered. "I wish they wouldn't just *stand* there."

There were about thirty of them, and when she spoke they edged a little closer, for all the world as if they were straining their ears to hear what she had to say.

Then something, some movement, caught a corner of my eye.

"Look out!"

Instinctively I ducked, pressing Eve down a little.

It was a false alarm. The man I had seen move had himself noted a movement out of the corner of *his* eye, and had turned to see an animal running across the plain. It was the same sort of animal that I had killed the previous night, the one that resembled a ground hog. The man threw his javelin at it.

I say "threw" but in fact the movement was so swift that it almost seemed as if he had *willed* the weapon toward that small, speeding animal. The distance was seventy-five to eighty feet, and the javelin struck right smacketty-dab in the middle, pinning the beast to the ground.

"My God!" whispered Eve; and I knew how she felt. It was the fastest thing I ever had seen.

The man who had thrown the javelin trotted over to his prey, yanked the thing out, picked up the ground hog, and hurried back to his previous position. He was not interested in the animal; he was interested in *us*. None of the others paid him any particular attention.

"We'd better do as they say," I whispered.

"If they only *would* say something!"

It was then that I had my inspiration. Keeping a grave face, as indeed we both did, and speaking in a low serious voice, I proposed that we simply pack our belongings and continue our journey as though nothing had happened, always moving, of course, slowly.

"You mean on the theory that if you don't look at them they might go away?"

"Not exactly. But it could be that they won't do anything to stop us. They don't look angry. In fact, they don't really look like men at all—more like apes."

"No ape could throw a spear like that."

However, she consented to try it, and so we did. We ignored the blacks—or at least we pretended that we were ignoring them—and went ahead to assemble our kit just as though nothing had happened. Neither of us cared to answer a call of nature with *that* audience gaping at us, but otherwise our routine, such as it was, was unchanged. We scanned the skyline for smoke, and saw none. We breakfasted on the few grapes we still had left. We folded our sail, which was getting mighty spotty, and we picked up our things. When I lifted the cutlass and tucked it under my belt I'll admit that I held my breath, but I tried not to let this show. Nothing happened. It could be that these men did not even know what a cutlass was. None of them appeared to have knives. I could not help wondering, as we started for the east, how they could skin the animals they killed.

We started off side by side. The ground was grassy only in patches, which gave it a somewhat *chewed* appearance, but it was not rocky. It sloped up, in a general way. In the distance we could see gray cloud-wrapped mountains. But it was definitely east that we were going: That we knew, now.

The blacks fell into a semicircle behind us, just a few yards away. It made us edgy, knowing that they were back there.

Only once, and then fleetingly, did I think of Calkoen and wonder why he had disappeared as quietly as he had appeared in the first place. I attributed it to a sort of jungle instinct developed over many years by a hunted man. Actually, I was glad to get rid of him.

We did not have far to go. After only a little over a mile what seemed like a miracle happened: A village sprang into view.

In fact it had been hidden, whether by accident or design, behind a fold in the ground that was not evident until you were almost upon it; but at the time it sure seemed miraculous to us.

It was not a difficult village *to* hide. It consisted of thirty-five to forty circular thatched huts, rather low and mean, each smelling like a jakes. It was dusty. There were no streets, nor was there any sort of central square or common. There were mangy dogs, which barked at us. There were fat women, all eyes. There were children. And a few old men.

If we had not expected them, they most assuredly had expected us, for they were all lined up, agog. No doubt a runner had been sent back with the news.

It was almost incredible. The whole place was only a little over a mile and a half from where we had camped, yet never until now had we so much as suspected its existence. There were no fires, so that no spirals of smoke stood up against the sky. Even so, you would have thought that we could hear the barking of the dogs.

Eve and I, without preliminary conference, started to slant our steps to the right, in order to bypass this unattractive settlement, but our escorts acted firmly for the first time, those on our right flank, as it were, hurrying forward to head us off. They made no threatening gesture, but it was clear that unless we were willing to jostle our way through their ranks we would be obliged to straighten our course and continue right into the village; and this, to be sure, we did.

I have said that there was no sort of central plaza, and this is true; but the crowd seemed to know where they were going, and almost imperceptibly, without ever touching us, or even coming very close, they steered us to a large man who was seated on a stump before one of the houses. He had a small skirt, a sort of kilt, around his waist, similar to the ones the women wore, but he was every inch a man, a large, strapping, solemn fellow. He reminded me, indeed, of Mr. Philipse's Moe back at Whitehall and Stone, though he was much darker of complexion. He had that same stateliness, the same impressive proportions.

Each of the members of the squad that had brought us in bowed low before this potentate and kissed one of his bare heels—whether the right or the left, it didn't seem to matter: They were equally dirty. I was glad that we were not expected to perform this obeisance.

This man immediately started to deliver an address to us, as if we two alone were a public meeting. He went on and on, while Eve and I, uneasy enough at best, shifted from one foot to the other. He did not seem to be aware that we couldn't understand a word he said. Moreover, he made no sort of manual gesture and never raised his voice. He did not even work his way to a peroration, but simply stopped talking after a long while, and stood up and walked away.

Thereafter we were shown—unsmilingly but without any sullenness—to a small hut, which, it was indicated, was to be ours. Eager to get out of the crowd, we stepped inside. There were a few grass mats on the ground, but no furniture.

"Well," I said, "it seems like we've been taken into the tribe."

"God bless our home," muttered Eve Shackleton.

CHAPTER 29

Our Verminous Jailers

WE SPENT three months in that wretched place, one day crawling snail-like after another until they merged into a seemingly interminable gray smear. Actually, after the first week or so it was not bad, only uncomfortable and degrading. They say that you can get used to anything. It was the way a man in prison must feel—lost to every glimmer of hope, cut off from all that is human, with no change in those drab surroundings from day to day, yet all the while filled with the intensest feeling of *frustration*, a rage at the *senselessness* of the whole system.

Our durance, if undeniably vile, was not rigorous. The savages for the most part did not watch us, or didn't seem to. It was only when, together, Eve and I drifted to the outskirts of town, that we became aware of a casual gathering of the hunters, each with his javelin. There was never any scowling. These men simply got between us and liberty, as though they had done so by the merest chance; and we would turn back. What else could we do?

Stupid as they were—inhuman, it sometimes seemed, certainly *sub*human—these aborigines had learned one important thing. They knew that Eve Shackleton and I were in love. It was a marvel that people who seemed only brutish could sense so tender a passion; but they did. Only when we were together did they watch us. Apart, they knew that we were safe, for they knew that neither would run away without the other.

In every other respect they were almost unbelievably obtuse. Virtually every day throughout that long time we asked them, separately or in a group, what was their name, their tribe? They never hesitated to answer, but the answer was different every time. Of course, it was possible that they thought we were asking something different each time, but the name of the tribe or clan was the first thing that we *would* ask, naturally, and we had reason to believe that in this respect at least they understood us. Yet invariably a different answer emerged. We could only conclude that they had a different tribal name for every day of the month, or that the tribe was named in accordance with the day-names of the heathen gods, which they might have counted by the score, the hundred. *Something* like that must have been the truth.

Consider this: Not once did they make any attempt to master the meaning of any words of English or to learn what our own names were, nor yet did they try to teach us their language, which indeed they persisted in supposing that we already knew. That tall man who reminded me of Mr. Philipse's butler—he was evidently a chief, and we seldom saw him—was not the only savage to regale us at length in words we knew nothing of, himself meanwhile catching from the blankness of our expressions no hint that we were without comprehension.

There was no such thing as a chair or stool or bench in all the colony, if we except the mat-covered tree stump before the chief's house, and that appeared to have some symbolic significance, like a king's throne in a civilized land. The natives did not hunker down on their heels, as we might have expected, but sat flat on their bare behinds, whether indoors or out. Then they brought their knees up to their chins and wrapped their arms around their legs, and in this position they could and frequently would sit talking for hours on end. They would come into our house at any hour of the day, though never at night, and take up this position, lecturing us at length about we knew not what. They never seemed to tire. If the rain ceased for a little while, and I got up and went out of the hut, they would fall silent and follow me, looking puzzled, wondering, no doubt, how they had offended.

When a man sat down, in those circumstances, he first took care to put a hand under his dangling testicles, which he would rather gracefully lift to one side, so that he would not sit on them. It was a deed that never failed to remind me of a fop at home fastidiously spreading the tails of his coat as he prepared to sit; and it never failed, too, to make Eve Shackleton giggle.

They did not take offense at that giggle, and may only have thought that she was belching in a slightly different, ladylike way. They themselves never smiled, guffawed, snickered, or grinned. The children of the village romped boisterously and bawled when they were spanked, as elsewhere; and the women, with whom Eve sometimes tentatively mingled, used to chatter like birds, and now and then even utter a laugh of sorts, as they plaited their palm fronds into kilts; but the men were the glummest lot conceivable.

The rain was not unremitting, but it might as well have been. It had ceased to be the maniacal fury we knew in the jungle, and had settled down to a series of long gray slanting curtains, without shimmer of any sort, penetrating, yet thin. It would chuff into the thatch of our roof as we lay on mats and tried not to think about sinning in the daytime for fear of unasked visitors. It reminded me of the rain in New York, on the Van der Donck roof, only there was more of it, much more.

Possibly it was the rain, at least in part, that so dulled my sense of obligation to Heaven? I had never lost sight of the fact that every man is born with an immortal soul, which he keeps unless he is depraved enough to make a deal with the Devil, and that God loves one and all regardless. There were

138

times when I reflected that I ought to make a greater effort to learn the nature of our hosts' gibberish and to bring to them the message of God the Father and of Jesus Christ. Had they never been exposed to that message? Had they never had a chance to be saved?

But then would come the thought: *Are* they men, after all? Do they have immortal souls? I could see nothing to support such a supposition, and in the absence of a competent adviser I decided to do nothing. Besides, I had Eve to think of.

I had the means of conversion with me, if I had been called upon, for my Book, wrapped in oiled silk against the moisture, was tucked behind my shirt and went with me everywhere. I used to read from it to Eve every morning in the hut, starting with Genesis and skipping nothing. It was a mite hard when I floundered through the begats, what with all those jawbreaking Jewish names, but I stuck to it, and Eve appreciated my persistence. Indeed, I don't know what we would have done—we could well have gone mad—without the Word.

It might have been the eleventh or twelfth morning, in that miserable village of no name, that I saw Jan Calkoen.

Eve was not with me at the time, which was odd, for in those first days, when we were still afraid of our verminous jailers, we seldom were out of touch with one another, literally. But I was alone for a little while that morning, when, rounding a hut near the king's throne-stump, I came almost face to face with the Wandering Dutchman.

He looked right past me.

He was talking lickettysplit to three or four impassive blacks, and he must have seen me, at a distance of no more than twelve or fifteen feet, but he gave not the slightest sign of recognition; he did not so much as turn his head.

I reasoned: He must have a reason. The man's a meddler, was the way I put it to myself, but he's no fool.

So I walked right past, paying no mind to *him*.

If Eve had been with me, surely she would have greeted him, for I truly think that she was fond of the old fraud, whereas I had said all along good riddance. Indeed, we had come close to tiffing about this, which would have been a shame. When I told her afterward that I had seen Calkoen she was flushed for a little while with hope that he might somehow romantically rescue us from our plight; but the fact is, we never saw him in that village again.

This was the state of affairs when we ceased to entertain vague, amorphous ideas of a supernatural deliverance, and began instead to lay plans for escape.

CHAPTER 30

The Fetching of Food

THERE WAS nothing haphazard about
the way we attacked the problem of escape. We went at it in a
scientific spirit.

"What's the most remarkable thing about these people
we find ourselves among?" I asked one night.

Eve was lying on her back on a raffia mat, and she smiled
up at me. She had been patching yet again her poor shapeless
dress, and she wore only a pair of drawers. Eve Shackleton was
a modest woman, and she would not have so shamelessly
exposed her breasts if it had been daytime, for though every
remaining woman in the village went around bare to the
waist Eve preferred to cling to her genteel ideals.

"I don't see anything at all remarkable about them,"
she answered, "except that they're so dirty."

"You *don't?*" I stopped in my striding and stared down
at her, but the sight of those breasts was so disconcerting that
I started to pace again. "You don't see anything remarkable
about a people that hasn't got any religion?"

"How d'ye know they haven't any religion, just because
it isn't like ours?"

"You see a church anywhere? Or an altar? Or even any-

141

thing like a totem pole or a prayer wheel? Are there any shamans in this town? Or soothsayers, or medicine men? For that matter, do you see any soldiers?"

"What have soldiers got to do with it?"

"Here's a tribe that doesn't make war and it doesn't worship God. So—what *does* it do?"

"It hunts for food," she said.

"Exactly! It hunts for food! And that's *all* it does! It is entirely absorbed in a search for food. That's both its strong point and its weak point."

"I don't see the connection, but never mind."

I had paused again, and was looking down at her. She gave me one of those smiles. She extended her arms toward me, wriggling her fingers.

"Let's not talk about it now," she said.

Nevertheless, when a little later I resumed my thinking, I decided, there in the dark, that I was on the right track, and next morning I made a few more pertinent observations.

I had noted that while the village was strewn with dry fish bones it did not stink of fish, nor had we ever been served fish or any other water animal in our daily meal. This argued that the fishing was done, perhaps in the nearby jungle-swamp, during certain seasons assumedly dictated by super-sitition. Perhaps the women did the fishing? The women tended the grubby little pease patches scattered around the outside of the village, producing large quantities of small round gray vegetables that did indeed resemble a pea in shape and size, though not in color and certainly not in taste: They were pasty, with almost no flavor. For the rest, the food was brought to the village by the party of hunters that went forth each morning—the very party that had found us and brought us in. They seemed to have no Holy Day.

"Behold, as wild asses in the desert, go they forth to their work; rising betimes for a prey: The wilderness yieldeth food for them and for their children," as it says in Job.

Though they were gone all day, these unclad Nimrods brought little back.

They brought coconuts. There were scattered coco palms on the plain, though they were never in the profusion in which he had found them along the beach. The natives cracked these by smashing them on rocks. I noted that none of them had been chawed by rats, from which I inferred that there were no rats in this particular part of Madagascar. The hunters would surely have brought them in for food, if there had been.

They brought, sometimes, a beast they called a "kai-kai," as nearly as I could make out. This was like an enormous black lobster, heavily armored. I wondered how they caught these things, which made excellent eating. Their lances would hardly have been enough; and the kai-kai looked like an animal it would be well to keep away from.

They brought hedgehogs. These were slightly larger than our American hedgehogs, but much the same. They were not good eating, being acrid and greasy; but we ate them all the same.

They brought in many of those ground-hog-like animals I had first seen on the edge of the plain. They called these "tandrakas." They were about the size of a cat, only with shorter legs, and they had bristles on their face and along the top of their back, and no tail. This sounds silly, and to tell the truth they *looked* silly, but they were delicious when fried, resembling roast pork.

They brought yams, much bigger ones than any I had ever before seen, which obviously had just been dug out of the earth.

They did not dress the tandrakas or the ground hogs, but roasted and ate them whole, skins, entrails, and everything. This was unpleasant, but so were our hosts.

Eve and I had our own fire—a brand was always available —so I skinned out the animals we were given with my sheath knife. I always did this privately, not wishing to let them know that the knife was, in a way, a weapon. They were still living in the Stone Age, and as far as we could see had no metal.

Then one evening they brought in many substantial chunks of beef, which had been freshly cut. It was stringy and tough, but it was indubitably beef. It must have represented at least two cows. There was no sign of hide. They could not have done *that* with javelins, I told myself.

I suggested, by sign language, that they invite me to go along with them the next morning. They were delighted, some of them almost going so far as to smile.

And so I left my cutlass and a kiss with Eve, and we hunters sallied forth.

CHAPTER 31

The Killing of the Kai-Kai

THEY HAD never learned to laugh, those poor people. Their stubborn stoicism permitted no show of feeling whatever. Eve was to mix more with the women, once I was away for the day, and she even picked up a little of the language. She reported to me that they often talked among themselves in a lilting, gay sort of way, though they did not actually smile, but in the presence of their menfolk they were solemn. The men themselves remained immovably glum.

Once we saw them execute a man—for what offense we were never to learn, for to our knowledge there had been no crime committed and no manner of trial held. The poor wretch—he was a comparatively young man too—made no struggle. He knelt on a flat piece of ground just outside of the village, and the hunters passed him one by one, each hitting him full-force with a club, which club he thereafter passed to the next in line. The victim—it seemed to be a point of honor —did not raise his arms, though these were not bound, and he stayed erect as long as he possibly could. He must have been dead before the last man reached him, for both of his shoulders were broken and his head had been laid open in several places, blood and brain being splattered for many feet on all sides.

You might think that in the performance of such a messy, cold-blooded killing the blacks would show some manner of rage, if only for the sake of their own nerves. They did not. They showed no expression at all, and neither did the women who had gathered to watch.

If they had a laugh in them it would surely have come out when they saw me practice with a javelin. They themselves were all experts in the handling of this weapon. The javelins were about four feet long and very thin. I don't know what kind of wood was used; it was none that I had ever seen before. Though light in weight, the weapons were unexpectedly sturdy, resilient, whippy. They were plain, not barbed or feathered in any way, and not provided with throwing loops. How the hunters kept them sharp I do not know, but they always *were* sharp.

Whether because the wood was hard to come by, or the process of peeling was arduous, or whether it was just because men, all men, naturally love weapons with which they can kill, these blacks treasured their spears. For this reason, when the first day out I asked, by means of sign language, if I could borrow one. I expected a refusal. But as soon as they grasped my meaning four or five of the hunters offered me their javelins.

It looked easy, as I had watched them. I first took a shot at a thick palmetto about fifty feet away, and I missed it by at least two yards. Anybody else in the world would have roared with laughter, but not these blacks.

After that, after many more tries, I got to be a little less maladroit; but I was never really good with the things.

As it turned out, there were very few thrown lances in the hunts I attended. The men used the javelins rather for stabbing and for digging.

These men did not "walk" up sloping coconut trees, as I have been told the natives in the South Pacifice islands do. Instead they picked up fallen nuts.

It was necessary to dig for the yams, which they called

something like "oovie." This is the root of a vine that climbs trees, and the blacks were swift to spot such vines. I guess that when they tore up the root they killed the vine, but this did not worry them. These oovies were very big: I have seen them as large around as a man and weighing close to a hundred pounds. They are bright red on the outside, though the skin is thin and can be stripped off with the fingers. Inside, the meat is white shading into a very pale pink. It is eaten raw, and it tastes somewhat like watermelon, only there are no seeds.

The hedgehogs and the tandrakas were in hibernation at that season, and they had to be sought out, and then, in their stupor, slain. The hedgehogs were holed up in the larger trees, and I never did find out how the hunters spotted them. Perhaps they smelled them? At any rate, though they did not get many, neither did they waste much time in searching.

The tandraka dug himself into the ground like a mole, only deeper. He was clever about covering his tracks behind him, but the blacks were cleverer still in finding him, though sometimes they were obliged to dig long trenches.

The javelins in these cases were used both for the digging and for the kill. In the case of the kai-kai they were not used at all.

The killing of the kai-kai shows the blacks at their best. I have watched it many times, and I never ceased to marvel at the ingenuity displayed by these otherwise stupid men.

I have described the kai-kai as resembling a black oversized lobster, but it is strictly a land animal, and is not only larger than a lobster but fiercer. It looks slow, awkward, but it has a truculent disposition, and its snap is like lightning, its two foreclaws incalculably strong. I suppose that it could bite the hand off a man. At the very least it would give him a nasty wound. Moreover, its armor is such that only by a fluke could any lance find a chink in it.

The kai-kai can crush coconuts in those claws, and the coco indeed is its favorite food. It does not wait for the nuts to fall. It climbs the tree and gets them.

This sight—and it has to be seen to be believed—is

astounding. All coconut palms, of course, are curved, and the kai-kai, moving briskly at first, uses the flatter side. It goes *up* the tree headfirst. It comes *down* the tree tailfirst, now moving slowly, feeling its way behind it.

It does not eat the coconuts up in the tree but drops them to the ground for a more leisurely consumption.

When the black hunters know that a kai-kai is up in a coconut tree—whether because they have seen it climb or because coconuts are being tossed out—they reach up the bole of that tree as high as they can—say seven feet—and fasten around it a basket of fronds, into which they place pebbles and earth, together with torn-up tufts of grass. Then they collect rocks, and wait.

Mr. Kai-kai takes the descent a bit carelessly, being eager for the treat below. When his tail touches the grass and pebbles he thinks that he is back on earth, and he lets go. He falls with a thump that does not kill him but dazes him, and before he can recover his senses the hunters have stoned him to death.

And they get the coconuts as well.

However, it was the cattle hunts that interested me most, both because they were exciting, as being perilous, and because they suggested a method of escape.

CHAPTER 32

Straight through the Throat

"WHAT DO YOU *do* out there, that it takes you so long?" Eve asked me when I returned from my first beef hunt.

The confinement was telling on her temper. I had looked forward to the time when the sun and wind would bring color back to her face. There had been a hint of this on the beach, and it was exhilarating; but the trudge through the muddy jungle, and the rains, had resulted in a return to her original pallor, and with this went a sharpness of voice and manner. I could not blame her. I had been away for three days and two nights on this particular occasion, and it had rained all the time, so she must have been confoundedly bored in that smelly little hut.

"Well, in the first place we have to go a long ways to where the cattle are. They're wild, of course. Often we have to trail them for hours. That's because of the bulls, which are likely to charge if they think there's something queer going on. And these are big animals! They're nothing like our cud-chewing cows back home. I don't know whether they give any milk—except to their calves, of course—but there's a heap of meat in one. They've got a big hump in the middle of their back, and that's the best part."

I went on to explain how we would stalk a herd up and down hills, through wooded spots, cutting out a straggler now and then, though we had to be almighty careful.

"Then the butchering has to be done very fast, just saving the best meat. That's why they don't save the hide. No time. They have to keep after the herd."

"I thought you said they didn't have knives?"

"I didn't think they did, until this trip. Knives made of bones. They don't use 'em for anything else. And guess where they keep them? In their hair."

"In their *hair?*"

"Yes. It's stiff enough. Stiff with dirt, if nothing else."

The joy of this hunt for cows had been that it was conducted in country to the east of the village, the country in the direction of the mountains. I asked myself why they did not move their village to the east, nearer to their principal meat supply, and I could only fall back for an answer on my previous assumption that at other times of the year they used the swamp for fishing, so that they wished to be near *it*.

Thus, I had a chance to familiarize myself with this country, and even, conceivably, given the right set of circumstances, to hide a supply of food.

Food was our biggest problem. We were given enough, each afternoon, so that we never ached for more, but there could be no thought of putting some aside as a sort of emergency ration. There simply was no place to hide it.

By this time we were sure that there never was a guard on our hut; but by this time too we knew that our captors were among the fastest people on earth. They could cover incredible distances at an untiring trot. In the season of the southwest monsoon, the rainy season, we would leave a track that they could easily follow; and if I had to forage for food .on our way in order to keep up our strength, then we would surely be overtaken. What they might do in that event we did not care to guess.

In other words, when we did break loose we wanted it to be for good and all. Our lives depended upon it.

I went out, doggedly, on every beef hunt. I stayed wet for days and nights on end. I wore out my shoes. And I watched and waited for my chance.

When it came, it came so suddenly that I could scarcely believe it was true.

I had supposed that the rainy time would somehow end as it had begun, abruptly, violently, as is the way with so many natural things in the tropics—sunsets, sunrises—but this was late September (early October, by Eve's calculation) and we were enjoying fine dry weather. We had had, moreover, a lucky day. We had raised a large herd of cattle without half trying. We had cut out several stragglers and were following the herd closely. I had fallen back to answer a call of nature. The others had gotten used to this idiosyncracy of mine: They could never understand it, I am sure, but they tolerated it; themselves, they would do a thing like that right where they stood, without turning around, even if there were women present.

Anyway, the others had swept on ahead, over the brow of a hill and out of sight, though I could still hear the lowing of the cows, the thud of hooves.

I had finished and was about to rejoin the chase when from around a grove of trees only forty or fifty feet from where I stood there came, on the run, one of those very cows.

How she had got there was a mystery. We used to fan out when we were trailing a herd, so as to be ready for any misstep on the part of the hurrying cattle. This particular cow, I suppose, could have slipped between two of the men, who had perhaps seen her and were hot in pursuit of her right now. Meanwhile, she was frightened; and when she saw me she charged.

She was big, with long oxlike horns. As I had told Eve, these wild cattle are the largest animals in Madagascar, where there are no lions or leopards or gorillas or elephants.

She came right at me. However, she did not lower her

head, as a bull would have done. If she had lowered her head I would have been gored. As it was, I had just time to hurl my javelin into her exposed throat. She fell with a crash, at my very feet.

This had been a near thing. I stood a while, panting with excitement, and watching the grove of trees in the expectation of seeing some hunters emerge from it. Nobody came.

Then I realized that this was my own, this kill. This was the chance that I had been waiting for, praying for. The cow was still alive. Hastily I cut her throat.

I did not even skin the corpse, or dress it in any way. That would have taken too much time. I simply cut it enough to tear out a couple of large thick wet flank steaks. The rest I left to the hyenas—or the buzzards.

And now—what to do with my meat? There was not time to bury it: Already the receding sound of the herd, on the far side of the hill, was hard to hear. I took the steaks to the grove.

I did not know what kind of trees these were. I did not care. I picked the one that looked easiest to climb, and I climbed it, provender and all. I crammed the meat into a crotch so that only a high wind could have dislodged it.

Wiping the blood off my javelin as I did so, I ran with all my speed toward the band of hunters, which I succeeded in rejoining just before nightfall.

We did not get back until late the next afternoon.

It must have proved an especially onerous day for Eve Shackleton, who kissed me somewhat offhandedly and not at all with her usual ardor. Her tone, like her manner, was querulous, accusative, as though she was reproaching me for having stayed out late playing cards at a tavern.

"When are we ever going to leave this place, anyway?" she cried.

I looked at her.

"As soon as it gets dark tonight," I answered.

CHAPTER 33

A Path Marked by Skeletons

MY AUNT Harriet Hobbs, who did the best she could for me as long as she lived, used to warn me not to get involved in any conversation about religion or politics. It was bad for friendship, she said.

I could add another topic to that. Never get involved in an argument over the respective merits of cats and dogs. If you bring this up, nine out of ten persons will cry, passionately, either "I *love* dogs but I can't *stand* cats!" or the other way 'round. Why this should be, why the subject should generate such heat, I do not know. Personally, I love both animals, though for different reasons.

All the same, I would like to point out one distinction. A cat that has been cast out into the world, left to fight for its food, will still hold up its head. It may snarl and spit, but it will not cringe. A dog in those circumstances is one of the most pitiful sights imaginable. It might as well be dead: It might *better* be dead. But a cat, no. You never saw a cat put its tail between its legs.

There were no cats in our rickle-of-sticks, but there were about a dozen dogs, sad curs every one, snappish, flea-bitten. Ordinarily we would have avoided these creatures, if only because we felt so sorry for them. However, with an eventual escape in mind, Eve and I had gone out of our way to make friends with them. We would not pat them, for they were indescribably filthy; but a kind word now and then can do wonders; and we reckoned that when the time came for us to depart we would meet with no resistance from this source.

Nor did we. We stepped out of our hut and walked away from the village as quietly as though we were going to church on Sunday. The place was silent.

This lovely lady and I, I told myself, seem to be destined to *sneak out of* places; but whereas our previous stealing-away from the ship had been made memorable by the appearance of William Kidd, nothing whatever interrupted us when we walked out of the village of the blacks. The exit could not have been more banal.

We were barefooted. Eve had had no shoes when she was carried aboard the *Adventure,* and I had literally worn mine out during the various hunts. This was harder on her than on me. My feet, like my leg muscles, had been toughened; and in spite of the fact that I had been walking all day, starting indeed before dawn, I believed that I could keep moving, and moving fast, all night and all the next day. Whether Eve could maintain such a pace was to be seen.

The night was dark, and with no moon or stars to guide me I was not certain of our direction, but we pressed on, and when dawn spread at last we learned that we had been lucky: We were facing in that direction, east, as we had hoped.

So far, so good. It now remained to pick up the track left by the herd of cattle and the hunters two days before. Once we had done this, I believed, finding the steaks in the tree would be an easy matter.

We had killed six cows that memorable day, of which mine was the fifth. None of these had been thoroughly skinned-out, because of the need to hurry after the herd while daylight lasted, and the hyenas and carrion crows, or buzzards, would have a field day following us. I calculated that at least the first ones, and perhaps all of them, would have been picked clean by this time, but if we could find even one skeleton we would have found the track of the herd, which thereafter would be easy to follow.

Again we were lucky, stumbling over the skeleton of the first cow. It had been eaten so clean that it might have been lying there for a long while, except for two things—the bones had not been bleached by the sun, and the droppings of the crows themselves, an excrementive crowd, still were fresh.

Gladly we pressed forward. This was not on our direct easterly course, being somewhat to the south, but the route had been vague at best, and the meat was more important than the actual miles. We were both weak, our legs aching with weariness.

By the middle of the morning we had passed three more skeletons, each almost as clean as the first had been, and we had sighted the birds themselves just a few miles ahead of us. That marked what was left of my kill.

Nothing would sate those buzzards, which drove their beaks into the corpse, refusing to flap away until we were fairly on top of them. It was not a pleasing sight that they had quit, but Eve was so tired that she could not care, and she wrapped herself in our faithful old sail and collapsed on the ground. I dragged her to a spot where she would not be annoyed by the buzzards, which I was sure would resume their meal the moment my back was turned, and I made for the grove of trees.

The previous day had been a notably warm and sunny one, but the meat, which I found right where I had left it, did not smell in the least putrid. Both nights had been chilly, with a heavy dew toward sunup, and that might have helped.

Before I took the steaks out of the crotch, I climbed to the top of the tree and surveyed the land to the west. That land was spottily wooded, and it rolled, and there were clumps of soft rock covered with vines. It was terrain that would have provided plenty of cover for the blacks, who could have dodged from place to place, spread out. But—why should they? If they were coming after us, would they not come directly, without any attempt at concealment?

As I climbed down the tree again I decided to cook the meat right there on the spot. I had first planned to pause only long enough to pick it up raw.

The birds were back, as I had expected. They were gorging themselves untidily. They would dig their beaks deep into the mess that remained, and then stare sullenly at me, blinking their little red beady eyes. They made a horrid splashy sound when they dug their beaks in, a gurgling sound when they withdrew them.

I had brought dry tinder in my pistol box, knowing about the heavy dews, and with a wood nearby it did not take me long to get a fire. I cut the meat with my knife and roasted it on the end of my cutlass. I might have used my javelin as a spit, but it was treen and I feared to burn it.

I did not waken Eve Shackleton until the beef was ready to eat.

At just that time—and somehow it did not startle me in the least—there came across the plain toward us that old Madagascan hand Jan Calkoen.

There was a friskiness about him. He was as sassy as a squirrel in September, and as he approached he almost bounced, as though the earth was pneumatic beneath his feet.

He twinkled at me.

"I'll give you *five* eight-pieces for those pistols," he cried.

CHAPTER 34

Two Gods and a Doormat

EVE WAS unabashedly glad, and he bowed before her with some grace, murmuring "Geachte Mejuffrow," which is a very nice thing to say in Dutch.

Me, I was not amused; and it could be that there was some ice in my voice as I asked what had happened to him when we were captured. He smiled a broad bland smile.

"I was up at dawn that morning—you two were still sleeping—and I went some distance away, behind a big tree, to relieve myself"—he glanced at Eve, but of course she did not understand his language—"and when I started back they were flitting all around me, right and left. Like shadows they were. Why they didn't see me I'll never know."

"You might have at least shouted, to warn us."

"I thought of that, and I almost did. But then it occurred to me that I couldn't help you to get away, though perhaps I could help you in captivity. I know these people, I've had dealings with them. They're a branch of the Betsileos and exceptionally stupid even as natives go out here."

"Yes," I said.

"What's he saying?" asked Eve.

"Later," I said.

"Also," Calkoen went on, "I couldn't see how you two

could possibly expect to make your way to St. Mary's at that season of the year, even if you had me along to guide you. But that wasn't the most important reason."

"And what," I asked, "was the most important reason."

"Well, they know me. They know I'm not a god."

"We know that much, ourselves."

"But they might very likely take you two for gods. But not if I spoke to you, not if I knew you. Then they would know that you're mortal."

"And what would they have done with us?"

He shrugged.

"Kill us?" I pursued.

"Oh, I don't think so. More likely they'd make slaves of you."

"*Slaves?* White slaves of Negroes? How could that be?"

Again he shrugged. He had a slick shrug.

"Anything can happen on Madagascar," he said. "You'd be prestige for them as a tribe. They'd heard of white people before but they had never seen them, excepting me. They would be proud of having a couple of captives of their own. They could use you for trading purposes—I mean, as goods. You'd be worth many a basket of carravances."

"What's that?"

"Those gray peas you've probably been eating all the time, the ones that taste like a blacksmith's bib."

"Yes, I know."

"That's why I went to the village right afterward. I wanted to see if you were being treated like gods or like slaves. If you had been slaves I might have been able to buy you off. They've been after me for years, those Betsileos, to get them a musket. They've never even seen a musket, only heard of them. But I found right away that you were being treated as gods, and that's why I looked right past you when you started toward me there. If I had seemed to recognize you or even so much as *see* you they'd know that you were not gods after all."

"What would they have done then?"

"Why, they might even have killed you in their rage. They don't like to be fooled. The very least that would have happened is that your food allowance would be cut in half and they'd keep a much sharper watch over you. Fortunately you sensed that, Mijnheer, and you walked on past without seeming to see me, which was the right thing to do."

"I'm glad I'm doing *something* right."

Eve Shackleton all this while was bursting with impatience, but I decided, and Calkoen agreed, that the place we were in was not a safe one, the blacks not being so stupid that they could not put two and two together and figure out where to look for us.

"But just a few miles east of here—and that's the way you're going anyway—they wouldn't venture into that territory for anything in the world."

"Why not?"

"It's Hovas territory."

"Whatever that means. What makes you think, then, that *we'd* be safe there?"

"I know the Hovas very well," replied Jan Calkoen.

We ate hastily, standing up, and started east, me first, Eve just behind me, and Calkoen, who seemed to be tireless, following up in the rear. As we went I translated what the Dutcher had told me for the benefit of my darling, who was impressed.

"And now we can't seem to get rid of him," I finished, being confident that he could not understand me.

"Oh, I don't think that we should. I'm glad he's coming along with us, in case we meet some natives."

"He wasn't much good the last time we did."

"I'm thirsty," Calkoen called. "Let's stop for a drink."

"I don't see any water," I said.

He pointed to a tall, oddly shaped palm that spread its fronds, which somewhat resembled banana leaves, in a flat triangle with the point down, like a huge green fan. We had seen several of these, and had wondered about them, for it is a very striking tree.

159

"See that? You can get water out of it, any place, any time, even if you're in the middle of a desert. Look—"

He borrowed my cutlass and hacked this tree through about three feet above the ground, and, sure enough, there was a well of cool, clean, sweet-tasting water.

"It never fails," he said. "I understand that the English call this the travelers' palm for that very reason. The native name for it is zumboo."

Eve, amused, had been watching him, and now, in a low voice, she asked me what it was that I had said his beard looked like the first time we saw him.

"A doormat," I answered.

"And how do you say that in Dutch?"

"Deurmatje."

She pointed to the growth in question, and cried "Deurmatje," and broke into gales of laughter.

Calkoen bowed gravely.

"Geachte Mejuffrow," he murmured.

That night he reverted to his custom of leaving us alone on our sail while he slept behind a nearby tree. Still, it wasn't the same.

Now and then I would glance over toward where he sat. All I could see, really, was one of his shoulders and both of his ankles and feet, and the man never seemed to stir, so that I marveled that he could sleep in such a position. I told myself that he might be very helpful to a couple of babes-in-the-wood like us, such as he had been about pointing out that travelers' palm, for example. All the same, I did not like him. I did not like the way he looked at Eve.

CHAPTER 35

Monkeys and a Crocodile

THE COUNTRYSIDE in this amazing island now was much more in accord with our ideas of what the tropics should be like. We had avoided the mountains by cutting around to the north of them, and though the land under our feet did seem to be rising, if gradually, the weather was milder, the foliage more colorful. There was very little rain now, and those drenching dews were a thing of the past.

Though there were few coconut trees, which seemed to favor the seaside, there were many other kinds of palms and palmettos, also a plant much like Spanish bayonet, and also what Eve and I promptly recognized as bamboo, an identification confirmed by our Dutch guest, who failed to understand our excitement over a plant that for years he had taken for granted. The bamboo was not much to look at up close, being so light and yet strong; but a batch of it on a hillside in the sunshine, from a little distance, its light green tassels waving in the breeze, was a sight to behold. No field of Injun back home was ever half so pretty.

We were seeing a lot more animal life now. Like the birds, for example.

The birds helped to patch my shattered image of the

tropics. Oh, those colors! Giddy reds, greens, yellows! Flamboyant blues! And now and then a dash of the purest white! The trees were generally tall in this part of the island, and the birds, a noisy lot, preferred their upper reaches; but now and then you would catch sight of one swooping across a clearing, and that always was a breath-snatcher.

I never got near enough to one of the birds to think of killing it. I don't believe that I could have killed one anyway, no matter how hungry we might be. They were so beautiful. It is like with deer. I never could understand how any man could shoot a deer.

More than once, in New York, I had seen monkeys. Sailors whose ships had touched at Panama or some other Central American or South American province not infrequently bought these beasts as pets. They were amusing to watch, if dirty, with their peaked faces and their sharp intelligent eyes. I had more than once dreamed of owning one.

The third day out of the village we began to hear and to see monkeys in the branches above us. I never caught one, and never even got very near one, though I tried often enough, not because I wished to kill them but because I hoped to make friends. But they were very shy.

They were of different colors, the commonest being a sort of yellowish brown. The only difference that I could see between them and the monkeys I had met from South America was, however, an important one. It was the face. Instead of the characteristic little-old-man face, these monkeys in Madagascar had a face more like that of a fox—sharp snout, twitchy whiskers, all the rest.

About noon of the third day we came to the banks of a lazy, meandering stream about twenty feet across, and there we surprised a wild pig that I guess had been sleeping. It scrambled to its absurd little feet and started to run right for the water. I had never seen a hog that could swim. Maybe this one could and maybe not. I did not give it a chance to try. It was an easy shot, but not easy to get the thing in the right place, the back of the neck. But I did it, with my javelin. It brought him down on his chin, only a few feet from the edge of the water, and I rolled him over and cut his throat.

Eve made a big fuss over my throwing skill, which pleased me, and so did Calkoen, which didn't.

"One of the Betsileos themselves couldn't have done it better," was Calkoen's comment.

That animal was the ugliest I ever had seen. If I'd come upon it face to face, from the front, I do not suppose that I would have been fast with the lance, so great would have been the shock. It was all covered with rubbery gray little things like warts, and it had tufty whiskers, and very unfriendly lower teeth that jutted up above the upper lip, which itself was curled in a sort of sneer. I certainly would not want to meet one of those creatures in the dark.

"A satra-fotsy," the Dutchman told us. "They're excellent eating."

He was right, as usual. It was like the best roast pork you have ever eaten. We filled ourselves and cooked the rest for future use. Then I took the carcass and scaled it into the stream, where it floated, turning lazily, out of sight.

We had decided to enter that stream ourselves, unless it proved to be too deep, so that we would have a chance to get our clothes dry before nightfall: The nights were not as chilly as they had been, but they were chilly enough. Accordingly I cut a bamboo pole and started wading and probing.

I was up to my knees in the water and nearing the middle of the stream, which was deepening, when I saw floating toward me, from the direction lately taken by the pig's corpse, what at first I took to be a cake of cow dung. It did not occur to me at the time that this was an unlikely object to see in the middle of a stream. It *did* occur to me, fleetingly, that it might mean a herd of wild cattle somewhere not far upstream, a matter that I would do well to investigate.

And then suddenly I saw what the thing really was, and I screamed and lashed out at it with my bamboo.

There was a tremendous thrashing of the water, a great splatter of spume. There was a steely snap, like the sound of a sword, a saber say, being slammed broadside upon a piece

163

of stone. I was struck in the left hip by something scaly. Then the monster was gone, swimming swiftly downstream again.

Those teeth had come not more than a few inches from my left arm.

Calkoen, who had wandered off, now came on the run to give me a hand getting out of the stream. He was a man not easily shaken, but he was shaken now.

"You shouldn't have waded in until I could come and look at the water first," he cried. "Do you know what that was?"

I shook my head, not being interested in another native name, for, unlike Eve, I was cool toward those little lessons in the local language that our Dutcher was forever giving us in an effort to make himself useful. Thus, an owley was a religious charm (for it seems that they had some sort of religion after all), and the priesthood or medicine men were called the omasy; a fonto was any tree or shrub; the kilts that we had seen, short wraparounds, were lambas; a ravina was a palm frond; and all white folks, all strangers of any sort, were called, collectively, zazaha.

These words simply made me impatient, and I shook them off the way a dog shakes off water, but it was not so with Eve, who loved them. She and Calkoen would jabber away at each other by the hour, though what they thought they were saying Heaven only knew. She had picked up some scraps of Dutch, for she used to listen closely when Calkoen and I talked, and he had picked up a little English—from her, not from me—and I guess that the rest they spoke was heathen. They used a lot of gestures, for they always faced one another as they talked, and they laughed a great deal. This, as I say, I did not like. It was not that I was jealous—I was too sure of Eve's affections for that—but I did not think that it *looked* right, her and that tattered old scoundrel, even though there was nobody to see.

So I glared at Calkoen, for I too had been shaken.

This time, however, he came up with a name that was known, if not exactly familiar.

164

"That was a crocodile," he pronounced.

"Most of it must have been under water. All I saw, at first, was a little blob of mud. It looked like a floating cow turd."

"It always does. That's the tip of their snout. When you see one of those—stay away!"

He did not need to tell me that. When I had recovered my breath to make the crossing you may be sure that I flailed the water vigorously with my bamboo to frighten away any marauding saurian.

That night Eve fell asleep early, for she was muscle-weary from a long day's travel, and Jan Calkoen stayed a little, chatting in a low voice. He was meditative, ruminative. He puffed his pipe (what he smoked in that enormous bowl I never was to learn, but from the smell of it it bore only a faint resemblance to tobacco) and he gazed down on the ground between his feet.

He had been around the world a good bit, he said, but he had never known any place like Madagascar. The plants were strange enough, but the people were stranger still, he said.

"There's such a wide range of them. Those Betsileos that at least helped you and the young lady here over the rainy season: They've got no imagination. When they want to execute a criminal all they do is they club him to death."

"Yes, I know."

"But you take down along the coast, and especially in the northern part, the chiefs there have a heap of Moorish blood in them. I knew one—he called himself a sultan—and *he* had the trickiest method of killing criminals that I ever did see. I'll never forget it."

Puff, puff.

"It was a big occasion. Gala. There must have been a hundred spectators, each of them a swell in his own right. The sultan sat on a sort of throne, watching everything with sleepy eyes. He never said a word. There was a charcoal fire in front of him, and they kept it white-hot with a bellows, and over this they had placed a thin steel plate maybe a foot square until *it* was white-hot too. Next to the sultan stood the executioner, a fat man with a big broad curved sword of the sort that down there they call a scimitar. He held this over his shoulder."

Puff, puff.

"When they brought in the prisoner I was surprised to see that he was on his feet. I had supposed that they were going to cut off his head, and for that they would ordinarily make him kneel. But he was upright. His ankles were hob-bled, so that he could just barely walk, but I noticed that the rope had only a slip-knot in it. His wrists were tied behind him, and once again there was only a slip-knot, with a man holding the loose end of it, as a man held the loose end of the line that hobbled the feet. Two other men pushed him forward.

"He was hoodwinked, of course, so that he couldn't see the fire and the heated plate, but he must have smelled it, for he tried to back away, squealing. But they pushed him on. And then, as the executioner stepped forward, the four guards all ducked—and mighty low, I can tell you.

That executioner knew his job. He hardly seemed to move, and the scimitar gave only a whisper as it streaked through the air. And then the prisoner's head just seemed to jump right up, clear off. It plopped to the ground like a squashed melon, and rolled away, the bandage still tied over the eyes."

Puff, puff . . . Puff.

"Then came the funny part. The two men on either side of the brazier lifted that steel plate with tongs, and they slapped it right down over the stump, the neck. It made a hissing sound, and there was a lot of smoke, and it stank. But it stopped the blood. It fair cauterized the wound, as you might say. At the same instant the guards who held the ropes stepped away, yanking them, so that the body, still upright, was free."

Puff.

166

"You've seen a chicken with its head off, how it can run all over the farmyard? That's because its neck is so narrow that the blood can't really gush forth like it would with a man. And that's just what happened to this beggar. The blood was stopped. It was sealed off. And he jumped into the air, flapping his arms. And he started to run.

"I don't suppose it lasted more than half a minute, but he covered a lot of territory in that time. This was in a sort of open grove down near the beach, and at one time this corpse collided with a tree and actually seemed to try to climb it, scrabbling at the bark, before it finally slumped down dead. It was the funniest thing you ever saw."

He laughed. I didn't.

"That's what I mean when I say that they've got more imagination down that way than these hill people up here."

He rose, knocking out his pipe. With a bare foot he ground the ashes into the earth.

"Well, I'd better get some sleep. Big day tomorrow."

A little later, in the pale blink of the moon, curled up beside Eve, I glanced over at Calkoen. Once again, all I could see was the feet and ankles and part of one shoulder, but there was no doubt that the man was asleep. I shivered, snuggling closer to my darling, and then and there I determined that as soon as I could I would get her—and myself—away from this aged monster.

My chance was to come four days later.

CHAPTER 36

Encounter in a Clearing

BOTH EVE and I had remarked, and often, on what a *spikey* island Madagascar was. There were hooks on everything, barbs. If they ever vote to adopt a national plant there it ought to be the cactus. The most innocent-looking vines, bushes, and even trees, which, without these, would look perfectly at home, have the means to tear your clothing and perhaps also your skin as you pass. It was almost as though they reached out for you while you were not looking. This was so in the swamp, and even more emphatically so up in what I suppose we might call the highlands; for though we had skirted the higher peaks, we were in general at a high altitude, as we knew from various signs, and indeed we were hopeful any day of sighting the sea as we pressed in our generally eastern direction. The land through which we now traveled could hardly be called jungle, yet it was tropical, and its growth was lush. It was marked, however, by many clearings, and whenever we sensed the approach of one of these we favored it, switching toward it, in part in order to escape the spikes, in part also because of our aforementioned hope of spotting the sea.

It was in one of these places that we encountered the young man with the musket.

It was a long clearing, and narrow, and he came into the east end of it just as we were stepping out into the west end, whereupon we all four stood stock-still.

He was holding the musket high, almost at his shoulder. It was not pointed directly at us, but a little above our heads. The distance was not more than forty to fifty yards.

Why I acted as I did then I will never know. It was no excess of courage, for I had not even been given time in which to be afraid. It certainly was not a thought-out thing. It must have been inspiration.

I stabbed a forefinger at the musket.

"Drop that gun," I shouted.

Pop-eyed, like a soldier, like a man who has been trained to obey all orders instantly and without consideration or quibble, he dropped the musket. Then he spun on his heel and ran back into the forest.

"He understands English," I cried; and without stopping to think, any more than he had, I ran after him.

I did not snatch up the musket, only jumped over it in my eagerness of pursuit. Nor did I hear Eve Shackleton's disconsolate wail. I was the hunting man incarnate, blind and deaf to everything else. My prey must not escape!

He very nearly did, all the same. He was smallish, scarcely more than a boy, and fleet of foot. I had difficulty, at first, in just keeping him in sight, and he seemed to be lengthening the distance between us, though I strained with all my might.

It was luck, nothing else, that I got him. He caught his foot in an upkneeing root and went asprawl. It did not knock the breath out of him, and he tried to spring to his feet, but by that time I was on top of him.

He struggled, but it was a feeble struggle. He was sobbing at the same time, which somewhat disconcerted me. I got his right arm behind his back, and we both rose, him still sobbing, I suppose in fright.

169

He was, as I said, no more than a boy, though close to manhood. He was neither a Negro nor a white man, but something in between, what the French would call a *mûlatre,* the Spaniards a *mulato.* Also, he had a certain slantiness about the outer edges of his eyes that suggested an Oriental background. He was, in short, a very queer specimen indeed, and I felt sorry for him.

I asked him, sternly, why he had tried to shoot us.

He understood me all right, and he broke into a vehement if barely intelligible denial.

"No, sir," he cried, only the way he pronounced it it came out more like "Noo, suhr." But I will not try to reproduce his dialect, which was the strangest I had ever heard: Time after time I had to ask him to repeat a thing twice or even three times, though *he* knew what *I* said even while I was saying it.

He swore that he had not meant to shoot us or even to point his musket at us. He had been about to aim at a certain bird called (as nearly as I could make out) a rorka, a bird his master, a doughty trencherman, doted on.

We had got this far—and it had not been easy—when we heard Eve coming; and in a moment, disheveled, wild-eyed, she burst upon us. She threw her arms around my neck, thanking God that I was safe. She had been badly frightened, poor girl, to be left so unceremoniously. It was touching, and it raised a lump in my throat. If my captive had taken advantage of that moment he might well have jerked himself to freedom, so wrought-up was I; but he did not stir.

I soothed Eve, and got her quiet, and we started back for the clearing, having in mind that musket. Eve, in control of herself again, retrieved the thing, which was indeed loaded, and she gingerly uncocked it. Meanwhile I went back to work on our prisoner.

"What's your name?"

"Jim, suhr."

"Jim Soor?"

"No, suhr. Just Jim, suhr."

"No last name?"

"No, suhr."

"But you must have! Well, who's your father, then?"

"My father's my master, Cap'n Jenkins."

"Oh?"

"Cap'n Jenkins of Longmeadow."

"Oh?"

He was astounded that it was necessary to tell this. He was implying, though not wittingly, that if I did not know who Captain Jenkins of Longmeadow was I must be mad, nothing less. Then—I could read this in his face—he began to tell himself that of course I *did* know who Captain Jenkins was, and I was only pretending that I didn't, doubtless with some dark design. His eyes slitted, his mouth became pursed.

It made me, irrationally, angry. I shook the arm I held.

"This Captain Jenkins, the way you speak of him, is he some kind of *god* or something around here?" I demanded.

"Yes, suhr."

Here was irreverence, but I passed it by.

"This Longmeadow, where is it?"

"That way," and he nodded toward the east.

"Far?"

"Not far. I take you there, suhr."

I turned him around, for I still had his right arm twisted behind him.

"Yes, you do that," I said. "You take us there."

Now our nosy Dutchman, whom I had plumb forgotten about, spoke up. He did not even glance at the gun.

"I wouldn't advise that, Mijnheer."

I whirled upon him.

"And why not, I'd like to know?"

He shook a gloomy head.

"This man Jenkins—"

"Oh, you know him, then?"

"I know *of* him, and he's got a reputation as a hard driver. He's not well liked in these parts. A retired pirate. A fiend."

"Well, he wouldn't turn us away, now would he?"

"Oh, no! He'll give you hospitality. He dotes on guests.

171

But he doesn't get many of them. The men at St. Mary's don't trust him, and I think that it would be as well for you and the young lady here if you didn't trust him either. He's a hard man."

"We'll be the judge of that."

He shrugged.

Eve was looking at me with large appealing eyes. She could not make out the words that we were saying, but she could guess. She was fond of the old rogue. But I shook my head.

It was not just pique. I had my reasons. Calkoen was as tough as a jackass, and he could endure almost anything in the wilderness, which had come to be his natural home. It was not so with Eve Shackleton and me. Barefooted, almost naked, we had gone as far as we could. We needed clothes and regular meals. We needed a bath. We needed a bed.

If we ever got to St. Mary's we would face a floating colony of the most savage sea rovers in the world. Why, then, should one such, a retired one at that, balk us? It might even be good practice for us to meet him.

I gave Calkoen the meat that was left, little enough. I saw him eyeing once again my pistol box, and I held this out.

"You can have them for eight," I said.

"Done!"

From somewhere in his rags he produced a linen purse, out of which he shook eight Spanish silver pieces. They were good coins, too. I tested them against a rock.

He made an awkward little bow before Eve. "Geachte Mejuffrow," he mumbled.

"Goodbye, Jan," she answered. "Take care of yourself."

He went off without another word, and without once looking back. His shoulders sagged a bit, but his step was firm.

There was a stifled sob at my side, but I pretended that I had not heard it. I turned to Just Jim, whose arm I had been holding all this while.

"All right," I said. "Let's go."

CHAPTER 37

The Offenders

THAT WORD Longmeadow, apparently the name of an estate or a grand manor house such as Mr. Philipse had built in Tarrytown, had fascinated me from the first. We had met with many varieties of natural scenery on our stroll across Madagascar, some mild, some wild, a few downright savage, but never had there been anything to even remotely suggest a meadow. It argued that this Captain Jenkins was not only an Englishman but a *sentimental* Englishman.

I let go of the lad's arm, but I kept the musket in the crook of my own right arm as I walked behind him. He was subdued, and made no dash.

We were now going up, though the slope was not steep. We were skirting the bottom of a mountain, which loomed above us. The forest generally was open, and two or three times we passed Negroes who glanced curiously at Eve Shackleton and me, though they paid no attention to Just Jim, who clearly was well known to them.

After about three miles, all the while climbing gently, we rounded a sort of shoulder of the mountain and abruptly and dramatically came into sight of the sea.

We were indeed high in altitude, almost halfway up this heavily wooded mountain, and the water, a glorious sight, might have been twelve or fourteen miles away. Between it and us there was a downsloping forest or jungle, but near the shore we could see long sullen lagoons caused by reefs on the far side, reefs against which breakers we could not hear furiously pounded. The breakers would cream across the outer edge of the lagoons, from that distance looking for all the world like a piece of chalk being drawn across a blackboard, and then would almost instantaneously vanish, as though erased. Then another streak would appear and go, and another . . . The sea itself, the far side of that muffled turbulence, was as blue as a summer sky and as flat as a mirror.

It was heartlifting, that view. It stopped us in our tracks; and Just Jim, who had gone on around the shoulder, when he saw that we were no longer behind him reluctantly returned.

"What is that island over there?" I asked, pointing to a bright green spot in the sea many miles away, all but hull-down, near the very horizon.

"St. Mary's, suhr."

"Ah!"

I knew of course that there was no science or mathematics involved, only the sheerest kind of luck, but all the same I could not fail to glow inwardly with satisfaction when I reflected that after weeks of toiling and pondering and calculating, without instruments or previous training of any sort, we had crossed a vast unmapped island, over hills and through jungles, and come out on the other side at approximately the place we had planned. I felt like patting myself on the back; but I said nothing, and did not even give a triumphant smirk.

Jim appeared to be annoyed that we were so engrossed in a mere thing like the Indian Ocean, and he stirred restlessly, jogging his head to the right.

"I thought you wanted to see Longmeadow," he complained.

We turned to the right. Still farther around the shoulder of the mountain, and higher, stood a great yellow palace of a building. It was astounding. It was enormous. Though it seemed to be made of wood—we were yet a mile or so away from it—it had turrets and towers, it had crenelated parapets, curtains, bastions, and other trappings of the Middle Ages, even, as well as I could make out, a drawbridge. It was all yellow, but with a white trim, which decidedly was *not* medieval, and it fairly blazed in the sun.

How could they get enough water up here for a moat? was my immediate, disrespectful thought.

"So *that's* Longmeadow," murmured Eve Shackleton; and I felt the same way.

"You live there?" I asked Jim.

It took time to interpret his answers, but we were glad of a chance to catch our breath.

"We all live there," he said, on a note of impatience.

"Oh, you have brothers and sisters, then," I said, just trying to make conversation.

"Of course."

"How many of them?"

He shrugged.

"Seventy, eighty. I have never counted them."

Eve was tart.

"That must be a bit hard on Mrs. Jenkins," she commented.

Jim was puzzled for a little while. Then he said, somewhat stiffly:

"Cap'n Jenkins has many wifes."

"Oh," I said. "A heathen, eh?"

He drew himself up.

"Cap'n Jenkins, suhr, is an English gentleman."

There seemed to be no purpose in prolonging this discusion, so I signaled that he should continue the climb, which he did, Eve and I trudging after him.

We surveyed the building that we approached, the massive, showy edifice. There were small brass pieces on the tower tops, we saw, and sentries who carried boarding pikes paced the parapets. Smoke rose from several parts of what we deduced was a huge inner court.

Thank God Eve was so rapt with the sight that she did not notice the dead men in a little glade on my left. I did. I stopped, though only for a moment, then quickly caught up with her.

There were two men, Negroes, and they were hanging upside down from the limb of a tree, their bare heads clearing the ground by a good four feet. Those heads had been *chewed*, torn, nothing left but bone and wet shreds of flesh, and they glistered with blood, which dribbled to the ground below. Four or five fierce dogs were there, springing up from time to time for another bite. Their chaps were smeared with gore, as were their snouts, and lust was in their eyes. An eye of one of the suspended men hung free of its socket on a long gleaming membrane, and even as I looked one of the dogs with an extra-high leap and a snap of its teeth gained this tidbit.

Those poor devils assuredly were dead, but had they been dead when they were hung there?

I saw Just Jim looking at me as I walked on, and I knew that he had seen the men and the dogs, perhaps on some previous occasion.

"Who were they?" I whispered to him, Eve being at that moment a little ahead of us.

He shrugged. He did not seem to be much interested.

"Somebody that did something bad to Cap'n Jenkins, I suppose," he replied.

I began to believe that Jan Calkoen had had a point.

The ground directly in front of the yellow fortress was level and had been cleared of every bush and tree, a military precaution that did little to enhance the beauty of the building. There was indeed a drawbridge, an affair made of palm trunks, though when we came it was down. There was even a moat, but a dry one filled with crisscrossed bamboo sticks sharpened at the ends instead of water. Just inside of the great open doorway there was a black iron cannon mounted on wooden wheels. The pieces in the tower tops were no more than murderers or falconets, but this guardian of the main gateway was immense, a giant, its muzzle glaring at us like an evil eye.

"I take you to Cap'n Jenkins," pronounced Just Jim as we stepped onto the drawbridge.

"Something tells me," I mutttered to Eve, "that I am not going to like this man Jenkins."

CHAPTER 38

Cutthroat in Satin

THE GREAT gun in the gateway, I saw as we passed it, was not there merely for use *ad terrorum*. It was a serviceable weapon, with not a speck of rust on it, and nearby were the closed but unlocked field magazine, a sponge, a linstock, a rammer, a powder ladle, and a tub with its lighted match. No doubt nearby as well, back among the shadows, were gunners who knew their business, for we could hear a murmur of voices as we passed.

Indeed, the whole establishment was murmurous. It seemed to be heavily inhabited; and people constantly came and went, paying very little attention to us, while muted voices were everywhere to be heard: There was a *singsong* quality to the air, which seemed to *hum*.

We crossed a courtyard open to the sky, and came upon what would appear to be the owner's living quarters, the fancier, more comfortable part of the building, which in truth was not a single building at all but a congeries. Here at a gate of brightly painted bars we were confronted by guards who wore little else besides the bright polished *salades* on their heads but who carried upright *fauchards* that were also brightly polished and that looked to be much more than merely decorative, for they showed as sharp as razors. These personages, by means of gestures, demanded that I turn over to them my musket and cutlass. They did not seem to notice my knife.

I hesitated.

"Better do it, suhr," Just Jim said quietly; and so I did it; and the gates were thrown open.

When we stepped through those gates we stepped out of that curious atmosphere of murmurs, of whispered corner conferences, and into a region of spongy silence, a place where nothing stirred.

We were in the *harem*, or *seraglio*, as some of the heathens call it. I looked around.

The floor was tessellated and very dirty. Monkey droppings and orange peels were strewn about, also women. There might have been fourteen or fifteen of the latter, and they were divided into two classes, the Negroes and the Moors. I do not mean that they were separated according to complexions, for they mixed readily, huddled in small groups, and chatted aimlessly, like women the world over, about this and that. The Negroes stared at us impassively, not as if they found us interesting but like people who do not have many new things in their lives, which could have been the case. These Negroes did not move. The Moors, however, at the sight of us instantly fastened silken biblike veils across the lower parts of their faces from ear to ear. This was not natural modesty, but a part of their training. They were not much to look at anyway, their eyes, which still showed, being their best feature, dark, slanty, mysterious eyes, of which they were well aware. Some of these Moorish women were so scantily covered that you could see their tits through what little they did wear; but they had to have that face veil in place all the time, it being a part of their religion somehow. There is no accounting for heathens.

The females paid scant mind to me, but they studied Eve Shackleton with care, and it showed in their faces that they were contemptuous of what they saw. This inflamed me, but only for a moment. There was not a one of the raddled sluts who could hold a candle to my companion—at least in looks, and I am sure in other respects as well—and at first it infuriated me that they dared to look down upon her. But I quickly divined the reason. They lived for their clothes, these harridans having, I assume, nothing else to live for. And to be sure, they were giddily if skimpily garbed; for they wore the gauziest and gayest of silks and satins, while the hair of many was stuck with bright-colored feathers, making a somewhat savage but undeniably flamboyant effect; whereas my darling Eve stood almost naked, her sleazy brown dress in shreds, her underclothes showing through, her head and feet as well as her legs bare, scratched. She, for her part, leaned slightly forward, her lips spread, eyes agog, while she drank in the glories of the *harem*. She probably had never before seen so much rich clothing. I know *I* hadn't.

Meanwhile, ignoring the splendors of the houris, which no doubt were an old story to him, Just Jim left our side to cross the big room to where a squat swag-bellied man with thick black whiskers sat in a chair that was meant to resemble a throne.

That we had not immediately noticed this potentate, whom we took to be Captain Jenkins himself, is attributable to the fact that he sat in a rather dim corner far away from the door. He was himself not of a retiring appearance. He had piggy eyes that twinkled, and jewels too twinkled in his ears and on his beringed fingers. He had nails like chipped isinglass, unnecessarily smudged, and his short rounded mouth was very red, conceivably painted, while he showed his glittering teeth from time to time as he simpered and tittered. His head was done up in a flame-colored silk scarf wrapped around it like a towel. He was naked to the waist, pale and pudgy but hairy too. Around his middle there was a bright blue satin sash, and his fat legs were crammed into white satin breeches with a great deal of gold braid on them. On his feet, unexpectedly, he wore hobnailed boots.

Now this creature, beaming, summoned us into his pres-

ence. When he crooked a finger at us the motion sent spilli-
kins of light across the ceiling, so many and so varied were
his rings.

As we stood before him he did not look any longer at
Eve than at me, a fact I was quick to notice and remark.

I did not bow, for I am not used to bowing before anybody; but I did incline my head, and he smiled encouragingly.

"Captain Jenkins, I presume?" I said.

"Yes, yes. Our son Jim here has told us he met you when
he was hunting, and said that you thought of going to Libertatia?"

"That's right."

He smiled a smile made of suet.

"Why don't you rest here a little while with us first?
You look tired, both of you. Perhaps we could find some place
for you in our household?"

Besides the way he used "we" and "us" and "our" as if
he was a king, this ruffian had a peculiarity to his speech that
I can only call Londonish, and which I shall not attempt to
reproduce here. I have noticed it in seamen who hale from
that city. It is a distinct dialect, different from anything else
I have ever heard, and it is not always easy to understand. It
is spoken with a sort of whine—despite the circumstance that
in this instance the speaker was smiling all the while—and,
as you might say, through the nose; at least it sounded like
that. Just Jim, behind me, had that same accent. Doubtless
he had learned English from his father.

Men like that, they say "orf" for "off," and "moe" for
"more," and "cheld" for "child," and "wittels" for "victuals,"
and "chines" for "chains." They call a mop a map and a map
a mop, and if they were to try to say "virtuous" it would come
out something like "fartuous."

All the same, and though I did not like him and could
not helping remembering those two upside-down slaves, the
man was being at least conventionally kind. That he had
ample means was clear in everything we saw around us, and
who were we, tattered and torn, limping, bleeding, hungry,

to refuse hospitality so graciously offered? My impulse was to get out of that weird place, to speak a curt refusal and make straight for the sea; but I thought of Eve, who had taken just about all that she could take, and so I inclined my head a second time and mumbled some thanks.

Captain Jenkins tittered gleefully, as though I had said something witty, and he waved us away, in the process setting the ceiling aswarm once again with flecks of red, green, violet, orange, and yellow light.

"See that your acquaintances are taken care of, Jim," he directed. "We will receive them again after they have rested."

To all of this talk Eve Shackleton had paid little attention, so absorbed was she in the details of the women's dresses. Even as we went out of the gate she was looking back over her shoulder, fascinated.

Just Jim was given his musket back, and I was handed my cutlass. The cutlass had been sharpened.

"This way," said Just Jim.

CHAPTER 39

Wicked Lies

WE WERE given a bed, the first we had ever enjoyed, with pillows, with linen sheets. We were given baths, long ones, with hot water and perfume and soap, with sponges, with fleecy towels for drying. We were given pomatum and rice powder and spikenard and all sorts of other ointments that until this time had been only names to us.

There was a dainty damsel of uncertain skin to tend to Eve's wants, and though just at first they had to talk in sign language, they very soon were chattering away like a couple of parrots, my beloved, unlike me, having a knack for picking up the rudiments of a foreign tongue.

As for me, to my amazement, I was waited upon by Just Jim. I should have supposed that the son of a king—for I thought of Jenkins that way, as obviously he thought of himself—would be esteemed superior to all manual labor; but Jim appeared to take the chore in stride, and to give him credit he was both skilled and considerate.

Afterward Eve and I would have admired to try out that bed, which looked enticing, but there were still too many attendants scurrying about—seemingly the servants in this palace had their *own* servants to wait on *them*—and so instead I sallied forth to look around.

I have called the place a fortress, and such it certainly was meant to be. A fortress made of wood might seem contradictory, but I could only conclude that there was precious little stone in those parts, perhaps none at all. How they ever got all that wood and all that yellow paint and all the furniture up there, not to mention the cannons and the powder and the ball, I will never know. The labor supply, for one reason or another, must have been just about unlimited.

The timbers used, especially the lower ones, were stout, and it was unlikely, I suppose, that any attacking force could haul up the hill cannons big enough to batter them down, though there was always that giant in the main gateway to testify that *somebody* had hauled up such a gun. Jenkins' real weakness, as he himself realized, was fire. An elaborate alarm system had been set up, whereby if any sentry discovered a blaze—and all the buildings on the outside were crowded with sentries or watchmen of some sort—he could by means of pulling one cord summon virtually everybody in the place to his side. Additionally, the tower tops and the main walls were lined with barrels of sand and barrels of what I at first took to be water, though I soon learned from the smell that it was urine. It is well known that urine is more effective against a fire than is plain water. I deduced that there was a standing order at Longmeadow that all urine should be saved in barrels; and I later learned that this was so, applying to men and women alike.

Assuming that Jenkins was or had been a pirate—and how could a man be so rich in such a place *without* piracy?—would not tales about Longmeadow be common among the brethren of the coast and the *hostis humani generis* at Libertatia, pirates being notoriously a gullible lot? Was it this that Jenkins feared: That they would plot against him, down there, and, their greed prodded beyond endurance by an imagining of his fortune, at last *proceed* against him—in force? I thought not. Captain Jenkins and his high stronghold would be a hard nut to crack, and pirates, from all I had ever known of them, were not overfond of trying to crack hard nuts, much preferring those that fall into their hands without a struggle. Jenkins knew his former associates of St. Mary's, and he was tolerably sure that they would never hold together long enough to undertake such an arduous and perilous expedition.

It was patent that he was not afraid of the natives of the land, the Negroes who drifted in and out of Longmeadow, who guarded the gates and the walls, who were to be seen everywhere, most of them being armed. He must have made some agreement with the local king or chief, the potentate whose post he had usurped.

The answer, then, lay in the navies of Europe. These, or any two of them, would never co-operate, true; but one alone would suffice. Any time that Spain or Portugal, France or Holland or England, decided in itself to stamp out this gadfly it could do so. It had the ships, the guns, the money, the men —and men, be it noted, who unlike the brethren of the coast did not have individual votes and the privilege of backing out at the last moment, for their only right as members of a national navy was the right to do as they were told. This, beyond all peradventure, was what Captain Jenkins feared. This was the reason for the fortifications.

The very fact that he did dread such an attack, and had prepared against it, argued that Captain Jenkins knew himself to be important enough in piratical circles to justify the cost of an undertaking of that sort. He must be, in his own eyes, a person of such exalted professional standing that his noisy elimination would strike fear to the hearts of lesser freebooters in the Indian Ocean and the Red Sea—somebody comparable, say, to John Avery.

It was a sobering thought; and I had just arrived at it when Jim reappeared to inform me that his father wished to see me again.

The Moors in the *harem* went through their accustomed routine of hastily covering the lower part of their faces whenever they saw me; otherwise things were much the same as they had been a few hours earlier. *I*, however, must have appeared quite different, for now I was dressed in drugget and holland, and I was clean, really clean, for the first time in many months, and my hair was trimmed and carefully combed, though not, of course, powdered. The women, brown or yellow, stared stonily—I suspect that they were obliged to do this as a proof to their master that they could not possibly become interested in any other man—but Captain Jenkins himself beamed his approval, his red mouth open, his little, brilliantly white teeth gleaming. I would not have trusted him any farther than I would trust a copperhead, but he did make a picture of kindly, fatherly interest.

He asked me about myself, how I happened to be there, and I told him, having nothing to conceal. Not at all to my astonishment I learned that he had heard of Mr. Philipse.

"He's the master of Adam Baldridge, the trader, isn't he?"

"Aye."

In the matter of my leaving the *Adventure Galley* I had to be circumspect, for it would never do to tell a man like this that one of my reasons for deserting was the conviction that William Kidd, considering the company he was in, almost certainly would soon go on the account. So instead I emphasized the danger I saw to Miss Shackleton, and enlarged upon my urge to protect her from the filthy paws of the mariners.

"Though of course, that was my *only* interest in her," I added.

"Oh, of course," he said, still smiling, so that I knew he did not believe me anyway, even while I was reminding myself to be sure to ask forgiveness for the lie when I came to say my prayers that night.

It remained a task to understand his lingo, though for fear of offending him I strove to appear as though it was perfectly easy. Just Jim, who surely never had met one, described his pa as "an English gentleman." Now, I do not pre-

186

tend to know much about gentlemen—we did not have many in New York, where most folks had to work—but I was willing to wager that a real one never said "awkurd" for awkward or referred to washing his hands in a "bison." All the same, I stayed polite and even deferential. I had Eve to think of.

The old villain cocked his head, studying me. He seemed pleased with what he saw.

"This might prove a happy meeting"—he pronounced it "appy"—"for both of us," he said at last. "It so happens that our previous secretary left things in a frightful mess."

"What happened to him?"

"But badly though he kept his accounts, we feel sure that any clerk who has worked for Mr. Philipse would be able to straighten them out."

"Did he resign?"

"It has been our wish for some time to have such an accounting, so that we can know just where we stand."

What could I do? I had no desire to grub among this scoundrel's affairs, thus perhaps implicating myself in them, but right then I had to admit that he had the whip hand, as the saying goes. Eve and I needed at least a few days to recover our strength, to reconnoiter the ground, to make plans. Jenkins, it was clear, wanted the satisfaction of having a secretary, and if I turned him down Heaven alone knew what he might do. So once again against my better judgment I inclined my head.

"I should be honored," I said, which was another lie.

After all, I told myself, we could soon sneak away. We were becoming adept at sneaking away from places we did not like.

CHAPTER 40

The Man Who Was Lonesome

THERE WERE many interesting things about Longmeadow, but the most interesting was the master. It might be fairer to say that he *was* the place, which had been built by, for, and about him, a reflection of his own twisted personality. I never did trust that man, but neither did I ever tire of him.

In the first place, why that estate name? Seemingly it was after some large house or country place in England, but how would a man from the middle of London know about it? Again, could it be a figment of Jenkins' imagination? Had he determined, even in boyhood, that if he ever *did* have a large estate he would call it by that grandiose name of Longmeadow? I was not able to get an answer to any of these questions. From time to time the king would toss off something about his "ancestral acres," but I do not believe that even he thought he was fooling me by this, and he never did permit himself to expand the theme.

He was a lonesome man: I very soon saw this. Kings, of course, classically *are* lonesome. Jenkins missed the bustle and din of waterfront ordinaries, the rum, the bumbo, the fights.

He had attained a certain tawdry grandeur, but even grandeur can wax dull. He was bored, up there in that yellow airie.

Also, he was homesick. He longed for the noise and stench and friendly banter of his native city. He yearned to stretch his legs under a tavern table somewhere near St. Mary-le-Bow, and wipe from his mouth the foam of a pint, and laugh and chaff with some of what he himself would call "the right 'uns." But of course he could never go back. He knew this.

Pirates are not pardoned.

There was not at any time a doubt of his past profession, though the word "pirate" itself he never permitted to be uttered in his presence. He would refer to having been "on the account" or "collecting some merchandise consigned to me," and he made no secret of his past association with Bob Culliford, Jack Plaintain, Giles Shelly, Tom Tew, and the great Avery himself. You might call these men "rovers" or perhaps "maritime adventurers," but never—at least while Captain Jenkins was present—"pirates." Somehow, by not mouthing the very word you made the crime less noisome.

How rich was he? He told me that he wished to know and that this is why he had "hired" me—though nothing ever was said about an honorarium—but his ledgers were unintelligible, and such of his storage rooms as I was permitted to see contained no coins. His "finances," in the usual sense of the word, seemed to be nonexistent. He had a staggering supply of dress materials, which, as I was to learn, pass for "treasure" among the Red Sea Men, being the commonest and most convenient form of specie. He had bulging bales of silk, satin, sagathie, drugget, brocade, deerskin, doeskin, chine, camlet, holland, muslin, perpetuana, colebatten, and drap du Barre. With these he was exceedingly generous, which might have been just as well considering that most of the scores of persons working in and around Longmeadow must have started with little or nothing on. Eve and I were served on silver, even at breakfast, and the king himself and all of his sundry "wives" even on the most ordinary occasions clanked with jewels, but if there was a real treasure chest, a chest filled with doubloons or eight-pieces, *I* certainly never saw it.

He was illiterate. That is, he could not read or write. I did not learn this by accident, for on several occasions, complaining of a lack of system on the part of my predecessor, I waved papers before his face, and carefully noted how he brushed these aside, tut-tutting and pooh-poohing. That meant that he was almost blind or that he had never learned to read, and in either case he did not wish to reveal the weakness. Well, he was not nearly blind. Those sharp little pig's eyes of his could pick up a trifle—like, say, a shoe buckle that was askew—clear across the broad dim *harem*. So, he was illiterate. It stood to reason.

I had met persons like that in the past. They let you read them something while pretending to read it with you, but their lips do not move, and when you have finished and they agree to what is written on the paper it is *you* they trust, *your* honesty and integrity, not their own knowledge. Personally I see nothing shameful about not knowing your letters. Some men are lucky and others are not, in this sense. Women do not mind so much; but man after man will go to extraordinary lengths to keep his ignorance hidden. William Jenkins was one of these.

Ordinarily I feel sorry for such men, but there was no feeling sorry for Jenkins, nor was I ever inclined to laugh at him and his absurd, smudged "court." The man was the epitome of evil.

I soon learned why he wore hobnailed boots. He spent most of his time in the *harem*, and though I had never seen him do it there was ample evidence that when he lost his temper he would viciously kick about him, right and left, sparing nobody, not even those who might chance to be pregnant. The women were adroit about hiding their bruises, but they could not hide them all.

Outside, too, when he would make one of his irregular and always unscheduled inspection trips, he was quick to use those same heavy boots against the shins of any guard who seemed to be nodding or who did not show enough visible respect for the king.

A nasty habit, but he had worse ones. I was not likely soon to forget those two upside-down Negroes who were being chewed alive for the sin of having displeased their master, and on the third day of our stay at Longmeadow I witnessed another example of his beastliness.

Along with twenty-odd others I was trailing Captain Jenkins around the outside of the buildings. I never did see just what happened, for I was thirty or thirty-five feet behind the king and not looking in that direction at the time; but there was a tremendous, and earthshaking roar, so utterly unlike his usually high, all but girlish voice that it was hard to believe that it came through the same throat, and I looked around to see Jenkins confronting in wrath a poor quavering slave who had somehow offended him. Jenkins wore the same bright headdress and the same blue sash and white, gold-braided breeches that he customarily wore among his women, but today, assumedly as a symbol of his authority, he had strapped around his waist a long Spanish rapier. He whipped out this blade now and struck the slave with the flat across his bare arms several times, causing him to squeal in pain. But this was not enough to assuage Jenkins' rage. He pointed the sword at his victim, who clearly expected to be run through then and there.

"Take that man to Cell Ten!"

What Cell Ten was I did not know, but patently the slave knew. He started to scream for mercy, trying to throw himself on his face before Captain Jenkins, and he continued to scream piteously while two burly guardsmen dragged him away. I could still hear those screams, from deep in the recesses of the main building, several minutes later when Jenkins, who apparently had dismissed the matter from his mind, approached me to ask, with many a titter, some silly question about the draper's stores. I was to hear them for a long while afterward, in my memory's ear.

This man Jenkins, this monster, then, was my master. I had signed no sort of articles or indenture papers, but as long as I stayed under his roof he had the power of life and death over me—*and* over my beloved. You should never temporize with the Devil. I had not seen Jenkins cast a lecherous eye upon Eve Shackleton, and you may be sure that I was sharply on the watch for any such sign; but all the same, it was common sense to escape.

Still, I procrastinated. The soft life, the easy life, had sunk in. I was supple at making excuses. I used Eve shamelessly. *She* was the one to be considered, I told myself. She was eating well, dressing well, and clearly enjoying herself. Was it right, because of a slight personal peril, to yank her back into the Madagascan wilderness, to all the hardships of life in the tropical jungle, to all the discomforts and dangers, to the semifabulous Libertatia, that resort of the world's most wanted robbers?

Yet—it was Eve Shackleton who at last caused me to take action.

CHAPTER 41

Words in Anger

As ABOARD the *Adventure Galley,* my duties were not onerous. Even if he could have read them I do not think that Captain Jenkins was interested in my reports. We were playing a little game, he and I, but it was a game of which he knew the rules while I did not. Sometimes I had a queer, catchy feeling that he was just keeping me employed until the time came for him to use me in some presently secret, horrible manner—or to use Eve. This chilled; but I used to shake it off, busying myself with my preposterous routine, framing fresh reports.

It was a dull life, despite the fantastic surroundings. The only part of it I truly enjoyed was the view, which at all hours was heart-lifting. The others, passing, sometimes would look strangely at me, wondering why I was so rapt, for it was an old story to them, and often I used to tear myself away before I had had my fill of gazing, being fearful that a report would circulate that I was pondering an escape.

The ocean usually was empty, but not always. Several times I saw small craft plying between the mainland and St. Mary's, from behind which, on clear days, smoke could be descried. There must be *some* manner of settlement down by the shore not many miles away, I reasoned, and if Eve and I could get there well ahead of pursuit it should not be difficult for us to buy passage to Libertatia, using a part of the eight pieces-of-eight I had received for Mr. Philipse's pistols.

The fact that Libertatia was so tantalizingly out of sight, just the far side of the island, somehow made it the more desirable to me as a goal. It might be pointed out, I suppose, that in Libertatia we would find ourselves in the power of not one but a whole colony of pirates, each a minor Captain Jenkins; but what of that? It is said that there is safety in numbers. And in such a city there would be plenty of work for an educated man, a trained clerk, an expert evaluator of dry goods. It would be real work, too, not "made" work.

Still, I drifted. I felt, at Longmeadow, a lassitude that was altogether new to me. Perhaps the air, the great height, had something to do with it.

It was Eve, as I've said, who jolted me out of this.

All of the guards and attendants at Longmeadow, even the lowest ones, could speak at least a little English—they could, that is, grasp simple commands—but most of them could not speak or understand enough to carry on a conversation, as I had learned by trying. Jenkins' children formed a special class of their own in the Longmeadow hierarchy, with Just Jim (unless there were some older girls whom I never met) as their senior, and all of them spoke a good deal of English, albeit in a stilted, rather flowery way. For the most part I, who lacked the gift of tongues, confined myself to them and to their father.

It was not so with Eve, a gregarious girl always, who was quick to pick up new words. She went gadding about, friendly, helpful—or trying to be helpful—and making acquaintances right and left as she jabbered. This was well enough as long as she confined herself to the king's children and to the servants and soldiers. But she went too far.

It was on the eleventh day that I made yet another meaningless report to the king, after first, as the custom was, surrendering my cutlass at the doorway to the *harem*. I was always more than willing to give up the cutlass, temporarily. It was a long, wide, clumsy thing, and I had no scabbard for it, simply tucking it beneath my sash. Walking with it across that low-ceiled, badly lighted *harem*, with groups of squatting "wives" strewn about, would have been difficult; and an accident there, a swiping of one of the females, for instance, might have infuriated the king. So it was just as well.

On this particular day such an incident would have been especially embarrassing, for Eve Shackleton was there.

I saw her as soon as I came in. She was moving from group to group, squatting with them, chatting and laughing with them. I froze.

Do not think that for an instant I supposed that my beloved had left me for the shabby charms of that *harem!* Nothing of the sort crossed my mind. But I was shocked and disgusted, and it was half a minute before I could collect myself and cross to the king, who had been signaling for me to approach him. I have no question that Eve saw me then, no question either that she had the delicacy to blush.

The *seraglio*, like everything else around there, was guarded night and day, but it was not *assiduously* guarded. The checking for weapons was more or less a formality: Nobody took it seriously. Eve, bored, in search of company, had probably just wandered in, nobody stopping her. But she should not have lowered herself.

It was her manners I was concerned about, not her morals.

Captain Jenkins, I suspect, sensed my rage. He asked many questions, all pointless, about my report, delighting to see me squirm with impatience. Now and then he would run the tip of his tongue along a too-red upper lip, as though to savor some exotic sweet. At last he let me go.

I marched right to Eve, who, hunkered down, watched me with round green eyes, the eyes I loved so well. I leaned, and took her upper arm, and raised her to her feet.

"Come along," I said.

She thought fleetingly of resistance, but decided against

it—not because she was physically afraid of me but because she dreaded a scene. So she shrugged, and started for the door.

"You don't need to squeeze my arm like that," she muttered savagely. "I'm not going to run away."

I let go of her arm, and we made straight for the room we shared, where I shooed out a couple of servants and slammed the door.

"Well?" she said.

I was so furious it was some time before I could talk at all. Then I began to fume. What a way for her to debase herself! What a shameful way!

She broke in.

"Toby Franklin, you know perfectly well that I was not doing anything shameful. I was just looking for a little company, somebody to talk with."

"And so you stooped to consort with those—those whores!"

"That's a harsh word, Toby. They're slaves. They do as they're told."

"They're whores," I corrected her. "See here, you are not going to try to tell me that you believe any one of them is actually *married* to Captain Jenkins?"

She sagged suddenly. She flipped her hands, the palms toward me, a gesture that touched my heart. All of a sudden her eyes swam with tears, which was most extraordinary.

"Who am I to reproach them?" she whispered. "After all, Toby, *I'm* not married either."

Bumbling apologies, I took her into my arms. With us, I told her, it was different. We had not been in command of our fate. We had never been given a chance to get married. But she had my promise, and I would promise again, and I did, that as soon as we got to where there was a preacher we would become man and wife.

"And when will that be?" she sniffled.

"Just as soon as I can make it."

Right away I started to make plans for an escape. But I did forbid her to go back to the *harem*.

196

CHAPTER 42

Hell Ahead of Time

THE NIGHT we had named for our break was a curiously quiet one. It was also dark, but the darkness was no surprise, for during the long months aboard the *Adventure Galley* I had picked up a habit of memorizing the moon's movements, and though we were not even in agreement as to which month this was we did know what the moon's risings had lately been, and we knew too that it would not rise this night until very late, almost dawn.

The quiet, however, was unsettling. The main building, the residence, what I thought of as the "palace," which was occupied as living quarters by Captain Jenkins and his concubines and children, together with their most intimate servants, most nights was tolerably quiet, passersby being fearful that they might taste of that terrible boot if they annoyed the master with noise; but the rest of the sprawling, barrackslike structures clattered and thumped all day as all night, ringing with shouts and the clack of arms.

It was not so as we planned to leave. The whole place was swathed in silence, a tomb.

This troubled us. Our plan of escape, an eminently simple one, was based on a business-as-usual atmosphere. As soon as full darkness came we were going to drift outside, nodding to the gatekeepers, friends of ours. There would be nothing suspicious about us. I would wear my cutlass; but then, I usually did. A day's supply of food, our flint-and-steel, my Book, and a few other odds and ends, were the whole of our baggage, and we could readily conceal these about our persons, leaving no telltale bulge. We were leaving behind the sail from the Captain's gig: It was pretty well rotted anyway.

I went to the door and opened it, and peered out. To my right in the direction of the main gate, which most nights would be the noisiest part of the whole estate, the hall was empty and utterly silent. To my left the hall led to a door which in turn led to the large courtyard, on the other side of which was the palace. This hallway too, lighted by a cressetted pineknot by the side of the doorway, was silent, still.

Yet to turn back, to delay our departure, could be a serious strain, and might make us twitchy. I took my cutlass.

"Come on," I said.

There was a slight sound to my right, and I jumped. I closed the door all but an inch, and instinctively I crouched.

Perhaps that crouching position made the oncoming figures seem even more gigantic than they were, but they must have been very big anyway. They loomed as shadows out of the darkness, one by one, in single file, like Indians back home treading a narrow forest path. The flaming pineknot, spluttering and spitting, caused their shadows to jiggle and swoop on the far wall.

Every one of them—and there might have been thirty— had a weapon of some sort, a sword or lance or club.

They made never a sound as they walked swiftly past, their heads jutting forward like those of men with a mission, and we knew that they had planned this for a long time and had rehearsed it often. We could not even hear their bare feet slish against the floor.

Then they were gone. The last one passed into the courtyard.

We waited for maybe ten minutes, but there was no sound, no sign. We crept out into the hall.

The bare space just outside of the main gate at Long-meadow most nights was the scene of some jollity, a gathering place, a place of gossip. Tonight, as we approached it from the inside, it was deserted. Not even our friends, the doughty halberdiers whom we had dubbed Noodle and Doodle, were in sight. This was very odd, for despite the general carelessness at Longmeadow these guards Noodle and Doodle, good natured fellows, were customarily conscientious about keeping their post.

We paused, uncertain of ourselves.

Then out of the shadows that skirted the clearing, in great high bounds like a frightened ape, came the guardsman Doodle. He did not carry his halberd, and there was a look of the starkest terror on his face. He came straight toward us, though I do not believe that he saw us: Probably he was making for the gateway, hoping to get protection inside the fort.

Behind him, also running fast, but with no show of panic, was his erstwhile friend Noodle, who had retained *his* halberd.

For a wild instant, and despite the frenzied fear in the fugitive's face, I thought that this might be some foolish game, some horseplay these two clowns had concocted.

Doodle tripped and went asprawl on his face, his outstretched arms only a few feet from us. Noodle never hesitated, but with a horrid grunt plunged the halberd, which he held in both hands, into the other's back.

I might have shouted something, or Eve might have screamed. The killer was aware of us for the first time, standing right in front of him, me with a naked cutlass in my fist. Once again, he did not hesitate. He yanked the blade out of Doodle's back. It was covered with blood. He got a lower grip on the wooden shaft and swung it against me, a wide, full swing.

As you know, a halberd is both a lance, pointed at the end, and an ax. This one was about seven feet long. Noodle was swinging it high, aiming at my head.

What I did then I did without thinking. I slid my right foot forward, bending my knees, and thrust straight for the man's belly as he came in. It hardly jarred my arm, but it made a loud, hollow, "plonck" sort of sound, as though you had smashed a pumpkin. Noodle dropped the ax and fell forward so hard that I barely got my blade out in time to save it from being snapped.

Whether or not Eve had screamed a moment before, some woman screamed now, loud and long. It was a woman inside of the walls, probably in the courtyard. It went through us as if we had been hit by lightning, so that we could not move.

Then there was another scream, and another, and shouts, and three or four shots that sounded like doors being slammed. It was pandemonium. It was Hell ahead of time.

How long we stood there listening I do not know. The din was deafening—wails, screams, hideous laughs, the clang of metal, the thud of clubs.

A man appeared on the parapet high above the gateway. I could not see him well. He raised something in both his hands and hurled it down toward us. For a fearful moment I thought that it might be a grenado, and I started to pull Eve to the ground. But it landed with only a slight squonch, like a bundle of wash. It was not a grenado. It was a baby.

Eve gave a sob. I knelt by the thing—it had landed only a few feet away—and took a look, just one look but it almost made me vomit. I got up and turned Eve Shackleton around, so that she would not see what I had seen.

"There's nothing you can do for it," I told her.

"Is it—Is it—"

"Oh, it's dead all right, don't worry about that. Its whole head is smashed in. Come on."

Confusing though it was, and cacophonous, we knew by this time what was happening. The oppressed blacks had risen, not in a spontaneous show of wrath but on signal and in the pattern of a carefully planned attack designed to eradicate Longmeadow and all that it stood for. The single-file party we had seen in the hall probably was only one of many, getting into place, preparing to converge. The guardsman Noodle had refused to participate and had been cut down.

That poor squashed babe was one of Captain Jenkin's whelps. *Him* they were no doubt hacking to pieces at this very moment. Then the rest of the offspring, who were hated because of their privileged position, would be disposed of; and the wives; and then—us?

"We've got to get out of here," I muttered.

The going was sharply downhill, as we had known it would be, and it was hard to keep from pitching forward. Once we got among the trees and out of the wan starshine of the clearing we could not see a thing, and yet we did not hold hands because we needed our hands to protect our faces. Faces and hands alike, not to mention the clothes we wore, were ripped and torn repeatedly.

For a long time we could hear the tumult of the massacre behind us, but even after it ceased we kept going, though we did go much slower then, feeling our way.

After a while we noticed a faint, filmy, crimson light on the foliage, plainer the higher up we looked, and when we found that we had stumbled into a clearing we turned around to look back.

Longmeadow was afire. It was like the wrath of God, for it was high in the heavens, and nothing could be seen of the stars beyond or the trees before, or of the buildings themselves, for that matter. There was only the eager licking of the long thick red-yellow flames.

Even as we watched, there was a tremendous explosion that must have made a mighty sound, though we could hear nothing from where we stood. For a little while the world seemed to be filled with sparks, and gradually the flames died down. The fire had reached Captain Jenkins' powder magazine.

We sank to the ground by the side of a tree, and permitted ourselves a little sitting-up sleep.

Soon after we had started to walk again we found the ground leveling off under our feet, and at the same time the trees became fewer, so that we knew we had reached the coastal plain.

Not long after that we all but bumped into a native

village. It was a tiny place, a mere hovel in the dreary dawn, not unlike the one over on the other side of the island where we had spent so much time. The dogs, as startled as we were, barked furiously at us, as though to make up for lost time. Women and children stared, without speech, as we walked right down the main street; but we saw no men at all. We kept walking. We went right through the place and out the other side, the dogs chasing us for a short distance. We walked toward the sea.

Were all the men out hunting? or away at war? or had they been summoned from this far away to take part in the ravishment of Longmeadow? We did not stop to ask.

After a while, when it was fully daylight, we turned again. There was no longer any flame or sparks, but the place where the fortress had stood was marked by a blobby mass of upflowing smoke—grayish, greasy, thick smoke. It looked as though it had been pouring forth like that for a long while, and would continue to do so for a long while yet.

That was all that was left of the Jenkins' pirate treasure —smoke.

"Sic semper tyrannis," I said.

"Amen," said Eve Shackleton.

CHAPTER 43

A Man in the Land of Uz

THOUGH WE might have supposed that we were walking away from our worst enemy—if we gave the matter any thought—this was wrong. We were walking right *into* the worst enemy of all, an enemy with which the air along the coastal plain was infested.

This was a large gnat that hums, especially at night, and stings savagely. I had seen something like it a few times in the summer in New York, and in particular along the waterfront, and sailors had told me that they were common in tropical places, most notably in tropical places where there were swampy low spots and much stagnant water. But I had never dreamed that they could be like this.

Eve had never seen them at all, or even heard of them.

They appeared the very first night, humming and buzzing in upon us as though they had been waiting a long while for our welcome appearance. It was easy enough to kill them—and by the dozen, by the score. All you had to do was slap on the place where you felt one biting; though by that time, of course, it was already too late, and a flattened insect did nothing to assuage the welt that appeared where it had been.

Still, we were lucky. We did not need to make a night

of it, incessantly swatting. We had spotted a light ahead and a little to the left even before full darkness came, and we made for this. It was less than a mile away, by the edge of the nearest lagoon, and as we approached it we could hear the boom of breakers out on the reef.

We did not know whether that light shone upon friend or foe, but it looked at least like shelter, and shelter from those pesky midges was all we asked just then.

The light came through a small square glass window, the first glass we had seen in more than half a year. It was set in a rather ramshackle hut down near the edge of the water, and after I had knocked at the door beside it I peered through.

There was a wan rat-faced man of indeterminate age. He had just risen from a stool, and he seemed not alarmed at my knock but wary. He whipped a kerchief off a couple of large pistols on a low shelf on the wall, and he examined these, cocking them, and making sure that there was a little priming powder in the flashpan of each, after which he put them back on the shelf and covered them with the kerchief again.

It did not startle me that a man should have two pistols, but it was amazing that he kept them loaded. Pistols are highly uncertain machines, as everybody knows, and it had always been the policy of caution to carry at least two, in case the first one fails to go off. If they *both* fail to go off they can be reversed and used as clubs, which is why the lead is put into their butts. But for a man to have two of them *loaded,* on his shelf, suggests that he is expecting trouble.

This man came to the door. He seemed easy-mannered enough, though it was evident that he was somewhat astonished at the sight of Eve Shackleton, as he had every right to be.

"Ah," he said, "the first refugees from the big bonfire, no doubt? Come in. My name is Harrison."

"You know about it?"

"Who could help that? It burned for a long while up there. It must be still smoldering, all that cloth of gold. But

204

—come in, come in! Don't keep the door open. The light attracts mosquitoes."

"What are mosquitoes?" I asked, as we stepped into the little place.

"You're slapping them right now," I was told.

"Oh. Is that what they call them?"

"That's what the Spaniards call them anyway, and I never heard any other name. Means little flies, I believe."

Harrison was an oddly self-contained little man, and he did not at any time show to be suspicious of us, but I did notice that he never got far from the shelf on which the covered pistols lay. He seated us on a plain wooden bench.

"Tell me about it," he begged. "Rum?"

We both accepted, for there was a decided difference in the air down there at sea level and the air up at Longmeadow, and the evening was chilly and wet. The stuff was very strong. It made us cough.

"You don't seem surprised?" Eve offered.

"I'm not. Jenkins had it coming, and the wonder was he lasted as long as he did. If they wipe out a group like that Frenchman Mission and his Libertatia party why shouldn't they wipe out a human swine like Jenkins?"

"Libertatia—"

"Hadn't you heard? Burned to the ground, two years ago."

"The—the whole thing—over there—"

I nodded in the direction of St. Mary's. Our host shook his head.

"Libertatia isn't over there. Never was. It was a hundred and eighty, two hundred miles down the coast toward Capetown. But I expect it's all overgrown by jungle now anyway."

"The same story?"

"The same story. Only, Jenkins was asking for it. Mission and Caraccioli, that Italian priest he had with him, and one of your American rovers, Tom Tew, they had rapturous ideas about the brotherhood of man and all that."

"Share and share alike?"

"Yes, but even more than that. More than just the splitting-up that the Brethren of the Coast used to practice in the West Indies before the Spanish navy made it too hot for them there. These Libertatia men, they *really* made everything equal. No rank. No laws except what they made for themselves, everybody having one vote. No land boundaries, no fences or hedges."

"What about slaves?" Eve asked.

"That's the strangest part of the whole business. They weren't like Jenkins at all. They *liked* the blacks, actually, and didn't believe in slavery. I think they were crazy there. I hope I'm as open-minded as the next man, but it stands to reason that the good Lord put those darkies here on earth specifically to *be* slaves. That's their fate. It's their position in the plan of things. But Caraccioli and Mission and those men, they really thought that the niggers were as good as anybody else, and they treated 'em that way. So you might've thought that they'd be spared. But no. The blacks came creeping out of the jungle one night, and they cut every throat they could find, and they burned all the buildings, and that was the end of Libertatia."

He had been getting us a meal all this while, and I guess he had confidence in our good intentions, for he often turned his back now on those pistols. What he prepared tasted much like chicken, and maybe it was, and also there was some more rum, only this time it was laced with water.

Immediately after the meal Eve began to nod. She'd had a hard day of it, poor girl. We stretched her out on the bench, and our host covered her with burlap sacking.

This news about the obliteration of the city I had been seeking came as a shock to me, you may be sure. But there could be no turning back now. I nodded again in the direction of St. Mary's.

"Then what's over there?" I asked.

"Oh, there's houses. *And* warehouses. And you can imagine what the warehouses are full of. There's a tavern.

And there's a wharf—Shelley's Wharf they call it, after the rover."

Harrison too, I noted, avoided the use of the word "pirate."

I knew Giles Shelley, at least by sight. He was a big, rough, foul-mouthed man who used to swagger around New York chucking away Arabian coins right and left, unless he happened to be sober. Governor Fletcher fairly fawned on him, so I guess he was generous there too. The Governor used to have him in for dinner, and they'd sit drinking together, and the Governor would ride around town with him in the official carriage-and-six, which made a lot of citizens sore because that carriage was paid for out of taxes. It was all very well for Shelley to call himself a privateer, but folks in New York knew better. They were willing to buy his loot, but they disapproved of him riding around at the public expense. And now here, on the other side of the world, he had a wharf named after him.

"Could you sail us over there?" I asked.

"I reckoned that's why you came to me. All right. First thing in the morning. Meanwhile—"

He was eyeing me in a most intense way, and I began to feel uneasy. But it proved that his thoughts were anything but violent.

"That happen to be a Good Book you got under your shirt there?" he asked.

I took it out, in its oiled silk wrapper. It had been through a great deal since my aunt Harriet Hobbs gave it to me.

"It is indeed," I said.

He settled himself on his stool, half closing his eyes.

"I'd admire if you was to read me something from it," he said. "Especially Job. That's my favorite part, Job."

"It's my favorite too," I said. "But maybe if—"

"I'd sure appreciate it if you did that. I'd read it myself only my eyes are tired from the sun."

I sensed from this that he was illiterate. And after all,

he was going to ferry us across to St. Mary's, and he had fed us and was sheltering us. So I sighed, and opened the Book to Job, which was not hard for it all but *fell* open there, and I began to read.

"There was a man in the land of Uz, whose name was Job; and that man was perfect and upright, and one that feared God, and eschewed evil.

"And there were born unto him seven sons and three daughters."

It must have made a strange scene: The darkness outside, the muffled roar of the breakers out on the reef, Eve Shackleton sound asleep, this mysterious man Harrison with a thin wistful smile at his mouth while his eyes were closed, and me doggedly fighting to stay awake. Yes, it must have been strange; but I was too tired to care.

"After this lived Job, a hundred and forty years, and saw his sons and his sons' sons, even four generations.

"So Job died, being old and full of days."

Everything was quiet when I had finished, and for a moment I feared that Harrison too had fallen asleep. But he stirred, and smiled even wider, and opened his eyes, and stood up.

"I sure appreciated that," he said. "Now let me show you your place on the floor."

CHAPTER 44

Like Toys on a Table

St. Mary's as we first saw it was a charming place, polychromatic and perky, smeared with sunshine. St. Mary's the *village*, that is, not St. Mary's the island, which we had been looking down upon for weeks from Longmeadow, though the island too, a small one, was pretty.

It was a bright glittery morning, and we swung around a point of land, plunged through a pass in the reef so close to the lathered seas on either side that our faces were stung with spray, and entered quiet, serenely blue St. Mary's Bay. The village came into sight as we made this turn, the bright little green-and-white houses, the yellow-brown warehouse, the blue-gray fort high on a hill, and stippled all through it the gawky nodding coconut palms that fleered back sunlight. These things did not look real, at first. They looked like toys on a table.

This impression of piled playthings was only slightly marred when we were sighted and people began to appear. Nobody hurried, of course; nobody ever does hurry in that part of the world; but they came from everywhere, the fort, the warehouse, the various huts, even, seemingly, from out of the jungle, and they all drifted down to the beach, where I now perceived that a wooden wharf had been built.

There was a "boom!" high on the hill, and a cloud of smoke blobbed out of one of the cannons. It gave me a start.

"Are they firing on us?"

Harrison grinned.

"No, saluting. They always salute me that way. Just high spirits."

For Harrison's skill in handling the sloop I had only praise, but I had been somewhat taken back when he demanded six eight-pieces for taking us over to the island, especially since I only had eight. The distance was not more than ten to twelve miles, and the weather was fair, and after all I had stayed up half the night reading the book of Job to him. But he said ten pieces-of-eight. I finally got him down to six, but it took a sight of haggling.

There might have been a hundred and fifty persons lined up alongside of Shelley's Wharf when we swung around sideways, losing motion, and Harrison threw a line. About a fifth of them were women, but there were no white women, though some of them were close.

It is the habit of most men in the west to call all colored persons Moors, whether they come from Morocco or Ethiopia or the Malabar Coast, but when you get out there you learn to discriminate in the matter of complexions, and I saw that we had a great variety here, though none, as I said, was a true white, as all of the men were. There were no black women, though there were a few fairly dark browns. Generally the skin tints were lighter and had a yellowish sheen. There were some sharply slanted eyes, and more than a few Semitic noses, suggesting that the Jews or somebody like that had once traded at St. Mary's—and done more than just trade, too. Most of the women were strikingly handsome and young. There were no hags, and very few children.

As for the men, if they had frowned they truly would have made up a villainous crew, and even in the holiday atmosphere that prevailed along Shelley's Wharf they were not men you would have carelessly crossed. They were young, for the most part, and looked rugged. Since they were sea-faring men there was nothing remarkable about the fact that all of them carried knives, but some had two or three knives, which is more than any mariner needs, and there was a siz-able sprinkling of cutlasses as well. I saw no pistols.

Men had made the boat fast both fore and aft by the time Harrison, the first one out, sprang to the wharf. He was in high spirits, probably thinking of how much rum he could buy for those six pieces-of-eight. He spread his arms.

"Ladies and gentlemen of the coast, you are being joined today by a couple of likeminded adventurers. Let me present to you Mr. and Mrs. Tobiah Franklin."

It gave me a jolt to hear it, and I think it did to Eve Shackleton too, though she just smiled. Now, when Eve smiled something happened to men in front of her, and I could see right away that these freebooters were no excep-tions. I almost looked for them to topple over right and left like the pins on a bowling green.

They gave us a cheer, which was gratifying.

"These are folks that ain't going to be asking a lot of questions," Harrison added.

"That's fine," one man cried. "This is a place where we say: 'Ask no questions and you'll be told no lies.' "

There was a great deal of laughing at this, though per-sonally I could not see anything so very funny about it. Eve laughed hard, squinching her eyes shut, opening them with a dazzling pop when she had finished. I began to watch her sidewise.

They were curious about us, understandably, but most of all they were eager to get the story of the Longmeadow fire, which had been seen from a high point in the middle of the island.

"I saw it too, sure, but I wasn't there," Harrison said. "But these people were," pointing to us. "They got out just as it was starting."

Then, and in spite of their assertion that they did not

like questions, they plied us with these, all talking at once. We were swept along, almost literally *carried* along, to one of the two wooden buildings in town, the tavern, which I gathered also sometimes served as a place for public discussions, a meetinghouse.

"Isn't there a church?" I asked Harrison in an undertone.

"Why should there be a church?"

"Well then, how did all these people get married?"

"They didn't."

"Oh."

"They *call* these women their wives. It sounds nicer. But it doesn't fool anybody."

"I see. But don't they have a minister of the Gospel or a priest or anything?"

"Now, what would a man like that be doing in a place like this?"

"You shouldn't have introduced us as Mr. and Mrs. Franklin. But we *want* to be."

"Everybody'll call you that here. You'd better get used to it."

Then we were swept apart.

The women went into the tavern too, and sat right down with the men. I disapproved of this, but I did not say so. Besides, I had so many questions to answer about Captain Jenkins and the attack on Longmeadow that I was given hardly any time to think about the women.

Like Harrison, they all seemed to have expected that attack, and no tears were shed. The wonder was, man after man said, that it had not happened sooner than it did.

Even while I was talking, and though I am sure that they were interested in what I had to tell, I could not help noticing how many men were studying Eve Shackleton through slitted eyes. I could only infer that nobody like her had ever come this way before, which it was easy to believe.

There was a long-legged dark-haired pirate down at the far end of the table—the tables were long community affairs, not much more, really, than planks stretched across sawhorses—whom I particularly disliked. He leaned far over, paying no attention to what I was saying and all but undressing Eve Shackleton with his eyes. He was a handsome fellow, I am bound to admit, and he carried a long cutlass.

One reason why they were so anxious to learn any available details about the attack on Longmeadow, I soon deduced—aside from their dislike of Jenkins—was because ever since the fire had been sighted they had started to form a band to cross to Madagascar and make the climb to what was left of the fortress, which they would comb. I could assure them that all of Jenkins' dry goods must have been burned, but they clung to a belief that he had had more than those, that he had cached away somewhere in that rambling pile of buildings an iron chest full of coins, such as would not have been destroyed or even damaged by smoke and flames. It was this chest they proposed to seek; and they would go in numbers, and armed, on the chance that some of the despoilers were still prowling around the ruins.

It would seem to be mighty small pickings for the famed pirates of St. Mary's, but I reminded myself that there was no vessel in the bay other than that of Harrison, and that these men in fact were not of the main body of Red Sea rovers but only the bits and strays, the lost, the misfits, the left behinds. The *real* ones, who might have scorned such a petty raid, were at sea where they belonged.

When I had finished my narration and had answered still more questions, and when the men had had enough to drink, and Harrison had put away a full meal, we all went outside and marched back to Shelley's Wharf, where those who were going to Longmeadow piled aboard Harrison's sloop, seriously overcrowding it.

I noticed that the long-legged one who had so devoured Eve Shackleton with his eyes was not in the sloop.

"What about you, Franklin?" several called out. "Want to come along? You've been there, you could help us with the route and the grounds. We'll give you a full share."

I shook my head.

"No thanks," I said. "I'll stay here."

CHAPTER 45

So Strange a Town

I WONDER if there ever was so strange a town anywhere in the world. The place we first saw—as we soon learned—was comparatively quiet, tame, routine. The real St. Mary's, when it had filled, as it was likely to do at any time, was much bigger and more tumultuous. The number of its inhabitants might switch, overnight, from fifty to five hundred or back again.

The center of virtually all social activity, and of much business activity as well, was the great sprawling stablelike tavern called Quinn's (apparently there had once been a proprietor by that name, perhaps the founder of the establishment: It was, when we were there, run by a Dutchman called Graaf, with whom I used to chat in his native tongue). There were times when you would rattle around in Quinn's, but other times you had to wait in line to get in.

There were two main reasons for these quick changes. The vessels that visited the island were small, most of them, as the bay itself, the wharf and the anchorage were small; but they were likely to come in two or three or more at the same time, having taken up with one another at sea. If a given expedition had been successful, the members of the various crews would storm ashore after a share-out, and leave their loot in the warehouse, or else sell it for the first price offered. In either event, they would then get roaring drunk at Quinn's, and stay that way as long as their money held out, after which they would go to sea again, sometimes taking townsfolk with them, sometimes leaving a few sick mariners behind. If a cruise had not been successful the seamen would get roaring drunk anyway, on tick; and then, when they had taken on water and firewood, they would depart once more, praying for better luck. Sometimes too they would linger long enough to have a careening job done on the beach, but this never took long, the vessels being so small, the labor so expert. Every man on St. Mary's, including the natives, could help at a careening.

The other reason for the sudden shifts of population was the pirates' habit of hiring themselves out as mercenaries in the various tribal wars that were constantly going on over on the mainland, as they used to call Madagascar, which in truth could be classified either as a very large island or a very small continent. These wars, which were for the purpose of stealing cattle and taking slaves, were a continuous thing, it seemed. The chiefs or kings were always pleading for white men with muskets, and these they paid, ordinarily, with slaves. The blacks on St. Mary's itself managed to keep out of war, and they were never enslaved. They belonged to a tribe called Melagach, and they were in fact a favored lot, never called upon to do hard labor because of the presence of so many slaves from the mainland, and therefore always willing to bring vegetables and chickens and pigs to town. Slavery itself seemed to be taken for granted by everybody.

There were war parties like this putting forth or returning more or less all of the time, just as on our first day there was that party that crossed to Madagascar to search for Captain Jenkins' chest of coins (which, by the way, they never did find). They might number anywhere from twenty to a hundred and fifty, and they might be gone only a couple of days or as long as a month. When they came back they

215

always brought at least a few slaves with them, and these served anybody on the island who happened to need their services. This might have been confusing for the slaves, but it did not seem to bother the residents of St. Mary's.

The people who call themselves anarchists and say that any government is a bad thing, and that man himself, in his natural state, would have no *need* for government, might have found much to interest them on St. Mary's, where there were no rules or regulations of any sort whatsoever at all. Were the citizens of this paradise, then, happy? I wouldn't say so. They were a touchy, quarrelsome lot, among whom fights, flare-ups, were frequent. There was nobody to prevent or to stop these fights. Spectators, indeed, often encouraged them, and if one occurred, as so many did, at Quinn's, the tables and benches would be pushed back against the walls, so that if one of the squabbling parties did not almost immediately give in to the other the floor would soon be wet with blood. I have witnessed any number of these impromptu duels, fought usually with cutlasses, sometimes with knives, rarely with simple fists. Eve Shackleton even witnessed a few, much to my distress.

I had not the slightest trouble finding employment, though this was as irregular and uncertain as everything else on the island. I toiled in the warehouse, appraising hauls, writing letters for the pirates, framing let-passes, and, when they were held ashore, as they sometimes were, presiding at the share-outs. Everybody trusted me. I belonged to no crew and no clique.

Money came easily. I could not accumulate it as quickly as could Harrison, the demon ferryman, who made a modest fortune every time a war party set forth (I was to learn that he had taken us across for a mere six eight-pieces only because he was sure that there would be organized a party to prowl among the ruins of Longmeadow), but I did well enough.

The Spanish eight-real piece was the most usual coin. We got pistareens sometimes, and moidores, and ducats, occasionally a few Peru pieces or some Turkish sequins or

Mexican pillars. There were also Moorish coins with queer figures on them that meant nothing to any of us: We just guessed at their value. But the eight-real piece, or piece-of-eight, as it was called, was the common denominator, the standard by which all of the others were judged, as indeed they always had been in New York, where if *officially* we dealt in pounds, shillings, and pence, we *thought* in terms of eight-pieces.

My conscience never bothered me about handling these coins. After all, I did my own work, and doesn't the Book say (in Luke, I think it is) that the laborer is worthy of his hire? Besides, none of this came from East India Company ships, whether English, Dutch, or French, for our dirty little Davids would never dream of taking on Goliaths like that. No, the victims, in every case, were either Mohammed Aurangzeb, the Great Mogul, who rated as the Emperor of Hindustani, or else some lesser Indian prince, all of them, of course, heathen, which meant that robbing them was no sin.

If any of the money or goods ever came from any other place I was not told about it; and I did not ask.

In one sense, many of the prizes could be said to be meritoriously taken, since the deed itself interrupted or at least delayed a heathen practice. Some of the victims were stripped off the Malabar Coast, which is a part of India, but more were encountered near Bab-el-Mandeb—"the Babs" the men of St. Mary's called it—which is a point of land that marks the entrance to the Red Sea. These latter vessels, nine times out of ten, were carrying pilgrims to Mecca, which is the so-called "holy city" of the heathens. They were the best hauls, too.

The life was not bad, and certainly not dull, but I worried increasingly about Eve Shackleton. She was human, and so she enjoyed having men look at her with lascivious eyes, but she might have been less obvious about that enjoyment, more maidenly, more reticent. There was nothing flirtatious, nothing circuitous, about these ruffians. They did not go in for ogling, for meaningful smirks, or dropped handkerchiefs.

They knew what they wanted and did not mind saying so.

Because of my position, unofficial though it was, I was often able to get pieces of silk and other goods for little or nothing. Almost any pirate, preparing for a share-out, would gladly slice the end off of a bolt of rich material as a sort of tip or gratuity for the man who would preside, who would have the last say; and these snippets I always turned over to Eve, who would work wonders on them with her needle. One day I got her a lace sunshade that the Moorish people call a parasol; but maybe I would not have brought it to her if I had forseen the way she would twirl it—enough to drive a man mad.

We had slept the first few nights in a room in the back of Quinn's, but this proved much too noisy, so we soon rented a hut made of pandanus fronds a couple of hundred yards down the beach. Every morning a little before noon she would sally forth from that hut dressed like a fine lady, like Solomon in all his glory, rouged, her hair powdered, and that parasol over her left shoulder, and walk, oh so slowly, to the warehouse. The ostensible purpose of this stroll was to fetch me my midday meal from the tavern, but she surely was not unaware of the ohs and ahs it provoked, the smacking of lips, the outspoken invitations. She did not even pretend not to hear them.

That tall dark young man I had noticed the first day, and disliked on sight, was not as flagrant as most of the others, but he kept his eye on my beloved all the same. He was French, and his name was Quatremoulins, and he was reputed to be one of the best blades in the business. I had forbidden Eve to talk to him, but I could not control her eyes, and I did not always know what she might be doing when my back was turned. A heap of allowance should be made for her, I told myself, considering the hardships she had been through; but all the same, I was worried.

I bought a scabbard for my cutlass, and now that there were plenty of hones handy I kept it razor-keen.

Eve ignored me when I forbade her to mix with the

females, the so-called "wives." It had been different at Long-meadow, where she was absolutely dependent upon me. Here on St. Mary's she could have had her pick of any man in the place, and she took advantage of this. Even though I ex-plained to her that they were not married, she was soon on friendly terms with virtually every woman on the island. She picked up their lingo in no time at all, and exchanged notes with them about dresses and such. It hurt my feelings, but there was nothing that I could do about it.

Maybe, I told myself, when we get married she'll settle down. Maybe wedlock will have a soothing effect upon her.

It did not.

CHAPTER 46

These Lonesome Men

THE JUDGE wore a chamber pot instead of a wig on his head, and he was invariably addressed as "your dishonor." The witnesses, with their right hands on a roll of privy paper, swore to tell the lies, the whole lies, and nothing but the lies. The prisoner was accused of obeying the law, for which the penalty was being tossed in a blanket—and tossed he was, after much hilarity.

They were fond of tossing men in blankets and otherwise roughing them, these pirates of St. Mary's, though I noted that they never picked on those who were quick with their cutlasses. There was a great deal of heavyhanded clowning, like the mock trial they held in Quinn's our fourth night on the island. Eve, who insisted upon attending that trial, seemed to enjoy it, despite the profanity, which got out of hand as the actors waxed more and more drunk. She laughed heartily, and gasped that I was a vinegarish old prude for not doing likewise. Me, I thought the whole affair vulgar and not a bit funny.

Nor was this an exceptional entertainment. I was told by old-timers that these mock courts, these burlesque trials, were quite common among the Brethren of the Coast not only in the Indian Ocean but also among buccaneers that were left in the Caribbean. When they were not busy defying the law they amused themselves by deriding it. That made them feel better, these lonesome men. They knew that they could never go back, and so they told themselves, with a lot of horseplay, that the real world, the world that they had quit, was not *worth* going back to anyway. It was the story of the fox and the grapes all over again.

There was always a strong element of cruelty in their jokes. They liked to laugh at men in misery.

They laughed often at me. Every time a new vessel would drop hook in the bay I would confront the first batch of crew to come ashore with what was considered my very droll question about a chaplain: Was there one aboard? Often enough the shore party thought that I was trying to be funny.

"Still looking for that pastor, Toby?" the men used to ask me when I hurried down to the wharf.

"It isn't impossible," I would call back.

Nor was it. These were desperate men. They were forlorn. They were lost souls, and they knew it. You would not look for a man of the cloth among them, true; but it *could* happen. Priests and pastors are human, like anybody else. They could stray. They could fall. It was true that if the church, any church, learned that one of its ordained servants was on the account in the Indian Ocean it would presumably defrock the fellow. But—what if it never learned? Captain Mission's second in command at Libertatia, I had been told, was a Franciscan monk. Anything might happen at St. Mary's. What if another one like that were to show up some day? His personal habits did not matter. He could have hate and corruption in his heart, but as long as he was still an accepted servant of the church he was authorized to perform marriages and those marriages were valid. So I kept asking, and hoping, while the others guffawed.

"What's your hurry?" they used to say to me. "You can ride the filly without buying it, can't you?"

Then one afternoon while I was working in the warehouse they came to me, a group of six or seven, and announced that they had found a minister of the Gospel. I snarled at them, thinking just at first that this was their idea of a joke, but they persisted earnestly. He was a member of the crew of the *Rose of Sharon*, a brig that had just anchored. I told them that, as usual, I had asked several members of that crew if there was a preacher among them, and they had all answered no. But, my visitors retorted, I had not canvassed every member of the crew, had I? No, I had not. Come with them, they said. They had learned only by chance, a little while ago, that this fellow was in holy orders.

Fascinated, I followed them into the tavern, and there I met a bewhiskered, portly man who said that his name was William Harkins, Reverend William Harkins. He had been-drinking, and his complexion already was rufous, tending toward purple, but there was a certain dignity about him that moved me.

"Tell me, Mr. Harkins," I said, "you are a member of the clergy?"

He wiped his mouth with the back of his hand and nodded vigorously.

"I am an ordained priest of the Church of England," he replied.

This was better than I could have hoped. I had been resigned to accepting a Catholic.

"How is it that the others did not know this?"

He smiled a little.

"I saw no reason to tell them," he said. "I can assure you that I am not proud of my present position and anything but avid to talk about my past. But when I heard that somebody here was inquiring for one of my calling I thought that I had better speak up. It might be an emergency. What is it you want, my son?"

I told him about Eve Shackleton and myself. I did not like to tell that tale in a public place, with an audience that must have numbered close to twenty by this time; but it meant so much to me that I let it out, and I was perfectly frank.

222

He inclined his head thoughtfully. He stared at me through bushy gray eyebrows.

"Your eagerness to enter into a state of matrimony in the circumstances is admirable, my son," he said at last. "Many men in your position wouldn't be so willing. Do you, uh, know of any reason why you should not be married to this young woman?"

"No, sir."

He looked around the room.

"Do any of *you* know any such reason?"

Nobody so much as stirred. The bearded Harkins nodded, somewhat pompously I thought.

"All right. Bring her here in half an hour, and I shall make you one in the eyes of God," he said.

He took another drink.

"It will cost you five pounds," he added.

Somebody snickered. I was taken aback, and my first instinctive feeling was to beat down the price, I having been brought up that way. But then I reasoned, why shouldn't he get paid for his services like any other professional man? I had the money, and what better way to spend it? So I agreed; and I hurried off to break the news to Eve.

You might have thought that she would fall into my arms for joy, and as a matter of fact that is what I had expected. Instead, she started to go over all of her dresses, fretting about what she should wear—and with what.

When we stood up before that man of God, half an hour later, however, she was perfectly composed, serious of mien, and her beautiful green eyes were radiant with happiness. *He* was somewhat slovenly in his clothing, but his face and hands were clean and his whiskers had been neatly combed, and though once I thought that I heard him stifle a hiccup his manner was stately. He read the service out of a small paper book, and it was the first time I had ever heard this, for the only weddings I had attended in New York were performed in Dutch.

"Will you, Tobiah, take this woman Eve to be your

223

lawfully wedded wife, to have and to hold, in illness and in health, for better or for worse, until death do you part?"

"I will."

"Will you, Eve, take this man Tobiah—"

He finished with the Book put away and both hands raised.

"And so, by the authority invested in me by the Bishop of Chichester and the holy Church of England, I pronounce you man and wife."

He refrained from kissing the bride, while I made it amply clear that I did not want anybody else to even try. However, we could not keep them from cheering, and drinks were called for right and left. We stayed only a little while, mumbling our thanks, a decent period. Once I glimpsed Quartremoulins over against a wall, taking no part in the celebration. He gave me a small, twisted smile.

When we went back to our hut, a whole wedding procession followed us, and for some time afterward they stayed outside, serenading us with ribald songs, so that we did not dare even to undress, for fear that they would come barging in. But at last they went back to Quinn's to get really drunk.

"You were wonderful," I told Eve as we tumbled at last onto the bed.

She twinkled at me.

"You weren't so bad yourself."

CHAPTER 47

No Virgin

"SHED BLOOD, and men believe; shed tears, and they doubt." This is the way an old saying goes, and I am inclined to believe it. I would add that it is particularly true of the men who made their headquarters at St. Mary's. They had lived by the sword and no doubt were resigned to dying by the sword, for it was in the sword, in weapons generally, that they put their firmest faith. Their respect went not to the man with morals, not even to the one with brains, but to the man who could strike the hardest and fastest blow. This I had pondered, and I took it into consideration when I deliberately resorted to violence. I did not lose my head; or at least, not in the beginning.

If I have given the impression that Eve alone was not set in the strait and narrow path of serenity by our entrance into matrimony, then I have erred. I myself continued to be uneasy, and more so than before, after we had been united in holy wedlock. It was curious. I had always supposed that marriage would settle a man, make him sure of himself, that it was a state beyond the uncertainties of courtship, a confirmation of victory, a public decision, irrevocable, immut-

225

able. Yet never in my life had I known such troubled thoughts, such worries, a wavering resolution, as I did in the days after Eve consented to become mine. It was not so much that I doubted *her*—though I did doubt her sometimes, which made me feel guilty and ashamed, as though I had been caught peeping through a woman's window—as that I doubted *myself*. I think I had never been cocksure; but now I positively twitched, and it was as though I was always looking over my shoulder to try to discern somebody who was spying on me. I suffered from the conviction, whenever I had passed a group of men, that they were talking about me afterward.

I had never been a gregarious animal. I could mix with others if the circumstances suggested mixing, but I was not one to seek out companions just for the sake of companionship; and for hours and even days on end I found my own company, if not exhilarating, at least sufficient. Not being accustomed to personal popularity, I did not feel at all dashed to find myself something less than a center of attention at St. Mary's. Yet I believe that most of the men more or less liked me, and I think that many even respected me, if only because of my education, which, if it was not much as educations go in New York, was a thing of splendor and awe among the pirates.

Now I had a feeling that they were holding something back from me, that they were sorry for me. I did not want to be felt sorry for.

Fretting, I wondered if perhaps Eve and I, or one of us, had not made a good appearance at the ceremony of marriage, or maybe had not answered the questions properly, and I started to seek out the Reverend William Harkins to ask him about this. But he was gone. The *Rose of Sharon* had not had a successful cruise, and she was off, with a complete crew, the next morning. Somehow, I hesitated to ask advice in such a matter of any layman.

My wife, clothed in purple and fine linen, her face painted even as was Jezebel's, and that tarnation parasol whirling away over her head, walked every day now along the beach, whenever she wished or the weather permitted, not just at noon. For there was no longer any pretense of bringing me my midday meal. She was out there to show off, and nothing more.

I cannot properly say that she flirted, but she did make a spectacle of herself, which reflected upon me. I should have whipped her, of course, but I was too fond of her, we had been through too much together.

I kept regarding that man Quatremoulins, and I itched to close with him. I do not know why. He did flaunt a somewhat disagreeable sneer, but he did not single me out with it. I had never said a word to him, nor he to me. If he eyed my wife lewdly, why, so did a good many other men at St. Mary's. The Book says that you should love thy neighbor as thyself; but sometimes it is just too hard to.

When I returned to the hut late one afternoon and found Quatremoulins talking to Eve, just outside of the doorway—at least I thought that it was Quatremoulins: He was that height, that build—my blood boiled. I do not fly into a rage easily, but having once flown I do not come down soon.

The scoundrel did not wait for me, but when he saw me coming slipped away into the shadows. Scowling, I summoned Eve inside.

"Was that Quatremoulins?" I asked her.

"And what if it was?" she countered.

"I don't want you to see that man," I said.

She did not reply to this, only sat on the edge of the bed.

I walked back and forth, trying to recover my equanimity, annoyed that she had selected the bed, by which, conceivably, she thought that she could control me.

She seemed to pay me no mind.

"Eve, darling," I cried at last, "we can't go on like this!"

"Can't we?"

"I'm asking all the time for a vessel that's bound for Calicut, but there don't seem to be any. I thought it would be easy, once we got here, but it isn't."

"Calicut?"

"Sure. Your uncle, that you were on your way to visit."

"Oh," she said slowly, and smiled a little, though not at me. "Toby, I never had an uncle, as far as I know, in Calicut or anywhere else. When you found me I just said the first thing that popped into my mind."

"But—your Aunt Stevens?"

"There wasn't any Aunt Stevens. I made that up too. After all, I had to think fast."

"Well then, what were you doing on that ship?"

"I was the first mate's doxy. He'd bought me from a tavern keeper in London. But when the Captain learned about this, off the Cape of Good Hope, he wanted to share me. *I* would have obliged, if only to keep the peace, but the mate would not agree. So I ducked out of there the first way that presented itself. You see?"

"I—I see," I muttered, as I drifted toward the door.

"You didn't think I was any *virgin* when you met me, did you?"

"No," I whispered, going out. "No, I didn't think that."

It was fully dark then, and I walked for a long while. I must have been stunned, in a daze, like a man who has been hit on the head, for I kept bumping into trees and houses.

"No," I kept saying to myself. "No, I didn't think that."

When I got back, Eve was already in bed. I undressed quietly and got in beside her, being careful not to wake her up—if she was really asleep, which I doubted.

She was asleep in the morning, for sure. I rose silently, at sunup, which is usual in the tropics. I got dressed, and went some distance in back of the hut, so that Eve would not hear my honing. I honed the cutlass for some time, and then honed my knife, though they both had been brilliantly sharp to begin with. Then, without returning to the hut, I went straight to Quinn's. Though it was early, I was sure that I would find the place crowded; and I did.

Quatremoulins was there, sitting over in a corner by

himself. Several men haled me, inviting me to eat with them, but I swept past. I went right to Quatremoulins.

"You," I yelled. "You sheephearted bastard son of a pocked whore. *Lug it out!*"

And I drew.

CHAPTER 48

The Crowd Went Wild

HE ROSE, a side-tilted smile at his mouth, and bowed, and said something that sounded like "mercy," though he hardly looked like a man who was asking for mercy. Maybe he spoke in French?

He deliberately turned away from me, took off his coat and hat, and tucked the Valenciennes lace into the cuffs of his shirt. Then he turned back, and drew.

"Monsieur?"

They say that an experienced duelist puts great dependence upon a cool manner, insouciance, slow movements, a scornful smile, which he esteems to be half of the battle. If so, then this man was a master.

The breakfasters, delighted, began to push benches and tables back against the walls, giving us plenty of room, which I at least needed, and they cried "Fair fight! Fair fight!" as they did so. In this they were inaccurate. It would not be a fair fight. I am of average height and build, I suppose you might say, but Quatremoulins towered above me by a good five inches, and his legs and arms were proportionately longer, a great advantage in swordplay. He was only a few years older than I, but he had spent those years, we may assume, among the pirates, and he must have been a veteran of many such affairs of honor, whereas my own experience with a cutlass was made up of those sweaty lessons with Quartermaster Adams on the deck of the *Adventure Galley*.

I wondered how Adams was. I wondered how they all were, aboard the *Adventure Galley*, that ill-omened craft that had been my home for so long. But this was no case of all the events of his life going through the mind of a man who knows that he is about to die! I did not mean to die, if I could help it, though I recognized that the odds were against me, and that I would need every bit of speed, strength, *and* luck that I could muster.

Why, then, had I provoked this contest? Because I wished to keep my wife, and to do this I must talk in the only language these outcasts understood, that of force. "Shed blood, and men believe . . ." Also, I told myself that I was not, yet, dead. I was in perfect health, with an excellent wind, and I believed that I could keep out of Quatremoulins' reach indefinitely.

I had stepped back to give him room, a nicety of behavior that did not go unappreciated by the spectators. We stood a moment facing one another, our blades raised. We did everything but salute.

Then he began to come toward me with small, tight cat-steps. I retreated.

He held his guard higher than I had expected him to, seemingly meaning to parry with it rather than with the body of the blade itself. The point he kept sideways, high. He was a slasher. He probably had a very strong wrist.

Each of us had his knife in his left hand, the point out. This was only an extra precaution. The tale would be told by the cutlasses themselves.

I kept my blade straight out in front of me, the point, high, aimed inexorably at his face. He did not appear to like this. He was muttering something in French. I retreated a little farther. He came after me, slowly.

Then he leapt, his blade high. I jumped back, but he

had allowed for this and he took *two* forward leaps instead of just one, so that I was well within his reach when his sword started down. I raised my own guard high, tipping the blade to the left. I caught the blow low, near my hilt, the strongest part of the weapon. It gave my arm a violent jolt, but it held.

Quatremoulins had danced back out of reach before I could take advantage of his position to deliver what I believe the French call a *riposte,* a counter slash. He was in perfect position, knees bent, guard high, though he did seem a mite astonished to realize that his down-stroke had been parried.

It was a sensational meeting—it probably struck sparks —and the crowd cheered, a sound that was like a distant rat-tat-tat in my ears, like when as a boy I used to run a stick along the pickets of a fence.

I wondered if Eve would hear the cheering, and would come. I hoped not. But there was no time to think of that now. Quatremoulins was edging in again.

I began to sidestep. I had figured from the beginning that he would try to force me into a corner, where with his long arms and long legs he would have me at his mercy; and I meant to avoid this.

I kept my point right toward his face, and he scowled at this, shaking his head, as though to reprove me for not obeying all the rules. But I knew better. There weren't any rules in this fight. We were not a couple of students at a fencing academy. The only rule was—defend yourself.

I sidestepped some more.

The next time he came at me I was ready for him and jumped back two jumps very fast, staying still just beyond his reach.

It flummoxed him. He teetered for an instant, almost off balance, and if I had been a trained swordsman I could have skewered him then and there. But, carelessly, I gave him a chance to step back.

The crowd went wild.

Quatremoulins may have been startled at finding me so elusive, but he kept his wits about him, and he continued to force the fight, coming in . . . and in . . .

I kept circling, but warily, never getting out of guard position.

He stopped, leaning a little backward from the waist, and lowering his guard a trifle, his face a question mark, as though he simply could not understand why he had not yet laid me open.

It was a temptation too great for me to resist. I leaned forward a little, jiggling my point almost under his nose. I hoped that this display of sassyness would infuriate him and cause him to do something rash.

I was a fool. That was exactly what he had wanted me to do. His blade was swished high, and he rose on his toes, bending forward, murder in his eyes.

I swept into a lunge, my right arm straight, my head ducked very low. I felt my sword clug into his belly. I felt it distinctly. But the top of my head was exposed. I yanked the sword out, and started to raise my guard to protect my head.

I felt no pain, though I knew when I was hit. There was a whirlpool of bright red specks, and then I was on my hands and knees, and then a huge cold black wind engulfed me.

CHAPTER 49

A Dead Man Did It

I MADE MY recovery in Dutch. Before I could see again—and for three days it was thought that I never would—I recognized the voice of the person who changed the bandage on my head, who propped me up for feeding, and who handled the bedpan. You might have thought that this would be my wife, but it was not. It was Jan Graaf, the proprietor of Quinn's. No doubt, I reasoned, I had been kept at his establishment because it was feared to move me. But you would think that Eve would be there, now wouldn't you? I asked for her, time and again, but the answers were vague and evasive. I was urged not to worry, for I must save my strength. I was told that I had lost a great deal of blood.

Graaf was not a physician, not even properly a surgeon, but he was the nearest thing to a surgeon that St. Mary's could afford at that time. He could set a bone, cup for blood, restrain a dilirious fever victim, keep a wound clean. He was a large, gentle-spoken Dutchman, warmhearted, easily moved to tears, an anomaly in that abode of wickedness.

If Graaf was reluctant to talk about Eve, he was willing enough to talk about the fight, which he of course had witnessed.

"A dead man did it," he would babble. "You had got him right through the pluck, and he brought that sword all the way down only because he had started and couldn't stop himself. But he was dead by that time. Extraordinary."

It did not prick my conscience, this killing. If I had only wounded Quatremoulins he would challenge me as soon as we had both recovered, and then we would have the whole sorry business over again. It was better this way.

"But—what about Eve?" I would ask.

"Now, you mustn't excite yourself."

From the nature of the sounds that reached me, even before I could see anything, I knew where I was. I was in one of the sleeping stall bunks around the side of the main hall at Quinn's. These were little more than curtained-off niches in the wall, much like the niche I had used for so long on the *Adventure Galley*. Sometimes Graaf rented them to seamen who just felt like sleeping ashore for a change, but mostly they were used to give drunken customers a chance to sleep it off.

My sight came back not all at once but blurred, a little at a time. For most of one day everything I could see was grayish and fuzzy at the edges, and it was hard for me to judge distances. But by the middle of the following day I was normal again, at least as far as my eyes were concerned. It was not until then that Jan Graaf answered the question I had been persistently asking.

"She's gone," he blurted. "She left the island. She's not here any more."

"Who took her? I'll kill the—"

"Now, now! You must be quiet. Nobody took her, mijnheer. She went all of her own accord."

It was the first time that he had called me mijnheer, which is formal in Dutch, like our "sir." Up until that time I had been just "Toby." It makes a difference when you have killed a man.

"Alone?"

"No, mijnheer. She was with Captain Copland."

I could not remember such a person, and said so.

"You never met him. He didn't drop the hook here until the day after your fight, and he left the day after that. The two of them took up right away. She had come here to see how you were doing, and that's when he first saw her. It seems they both came from the same part of London, and it was like meeting an old friend. In a matter of minutes they were giggling and flirting. At that time we thought that you were going to die."

"But she didn't wait to find out?"

"No, mijnheer. She never came here again." There was an acid edge to Graaf's voice, and it was patent that he did not like Eve, for which he could hardly be censured. "Make no mistake about it, she wasn't dragged away by her hair. She had an arm around Copland's waist when the vessel sailed, and she was beaming like a bride."

I swallowed; and it was like gulping a pincushion with all the pins still in place. I turned my head to the wall. Graaf closed the curtains and went quietly away. It was two days later before he allowed anyone to visit me, and by that time I had got myself pretty well under control, and my eyes, I hope, were back to their usual color.

It had been a hellish interval.

I was hailed as a hero when at last visitors were admitted, and many of the men gave me the courtesy title of "captain," as they do sometimes to a man they admire very much, even though he may never have skippered a ship, the same as Jan Graaf had mijnheered me. I smiled—wanly, I fancy—and thanked them. It would have made a difference a little while ago; but it no longer did. Nothing did.

Quatremoulins, I take it, had never been popular.

Nobody so much as mentioned Eve.

I was sick of the whole business. I wanted to get back to New York, to civilization, where people were decent, where there were laws and courts, and murder was never glorified. So long as I had had Eve to protect I could endure the fierce heat, the drenching rains, the almost continuous peril, and the beastly manners and morals of the men around me; but now that she was gone I yearned for home. I began to ask about ships.

I had been in bed ten days, and though I was sitting up from time to time I was still pitifully weak, when I spotted an old friend.

I had finger-Ved the curtains apart, and I saw him right away—William Kidd.

He had a plume in his hat, lace at his chin, gold rings in his ears. He wore a cinnamon-colored drugget coat with white smallclothes, a blue silk sash around his waist, while from a polished leather baldric hung a sword with a silver hilt. He was indeed very grand, quite the smart, no longer a mere privateer.

He was drinking bumbo with Captain Culliford, and both facts were significant.

Bob Culliford was one of the most active and violent pirates in the Indian Ocean—which is to say, in the world. It was not surprising to see such a man at Quinn's, but it *was* surprising to see him in the company of William Kidd, whose commission authorized and specifically commanded him to seek out and hunt down just such persons as Culliford, *not* to hobnob with them.

Graaf, for all his kind heart, charged for his wares whatever he thought that he could get, and his price for rum, though it varied, always was high, the stuff being in short supply most of the time, especially so right then. Bumbo is a concoction of rum, water, sugar, and nutmeg, and what Culliford and Kidd were paying for their mugs Heaven only knew—Heaven, that is, and Jan Graaf. They were the only persons in all of that big place who were so supplied. All of the rest had to be satisfied with the native drink, which is called *taoka* and which they make by distilling the pulped and watered meat of a nut something like the coconut only smaller.

For a fleeting moment I thought of calling the Captain over and asking him if he would take me back to New York, provided I paid my fare. He had been out for more than two years and I assumed that he was fixing to go back, since he was wearing such finery and drinking bumboo. But I quickly changed my mind. In the first place, he might want to know why I had deserted the *Adventure Galley* and what I had done with his gig. In the second place—and this was far more important—I had always had a conviction that the Kidd enterprise was doomed, destined to disaster. That Kidd had gone on the account I did not doubt, and it might be that his powerful political backers would not be powerful enough to get him out of it. I decided to stay where I was until a safer prospect presented itself.

My eyes misted a mite, rather to my own amazement, as I peered out through the opening in the curtain. I found myself feeling sorry for those men out there, just because I did understand them so well. If they were the scum of the earth they were the hunted of all the earth as well. As the lawyers would put it, they were *hostis humani generis*. They were everybody's enemies; and I do not think that they ever meant to be that, most of them. They weren't so much wicked as confused; but they were damned all the same. A highwayman might sometimes be pardoned, even a murderer, provided he will go furtively to another land; but a pirate is legitimate quarry wherever he goes, as well as on the high seas. Every man's hand is against the pirate.

These ruffians I looked upon at Quinn's, they were the irrevocably strayed, the legion of lost souls. They were the men who could never go home.

I never saw Captain Kidd again. He was at St. Mary's for several weeks, but spent most of his time on his own vessel, not the *Adventure Galley*, which he had burned as no longer seaworthy, but a massive prize called the *Quedah Merchant*. If he ever heard my name while there he did not remember it nor did he connect it with the timorous supercargo whom he had once referred to as "Philipse's prowling penman."

It was four months later that a ship put in at St. Mary's

that was to be pointed for New York, but this was a ship untainted by piracy, as I was at pains to determine.

I did not even have to pay the £100 sterling which was the going rate for the New York run at that time. The super-cargo had just died of a fever, and I got his job.

So in more ways than one it had paid me to wait.

CHAPTER 50

Report to the Boss

You could almost *hear* the snowflakes nudging one another as they fell, fat, wet, unhurried. I stood looking through immaculate panes, and I reflected that I was lucky to be looking at snow again: There had been a time when it seemed as though I never would.

"Care for a glass of French brandy?"

It was the first time that Mr. Philipse had ever offered me a drink, and I inclined my head in grave acceptance as I turned away from the window. I was dressed in the "freedom suit" he had given me to mark the termination of my indenture, a handsome piece of sagathie in bottle green with a silver brocade waistcoat, and I felt very grown-up indeed, looking quite as grand as my employer.

"An excellent report," Mr. Philipse was saying. "A most competent report. I knew that I could depend upon you to see things out there as they really are, but I'll admit I had not expected anything as fine as this. Rum and gunpowder, you say?"

"Aye. And wine. A pipe of Madeira that could be picked up on the way out for maybe £19 or £20 would fetch three hundred at St. Mary's. And I told you about the rum. They haven't anything else to spend their money on out there, and they don't dare to come home and start spending it. This man Bellomont"—referring to the new provincial governor—"must really mean business?"

"I'm afraid he does," sighed Mr. Philipse.

"What you pay three shillings a gallon for here they'd be willing to pay three *pounds* for at St. Mary's. And they'll take all you can send."

"And I'll send God's plenty, be sure of that."

"As for gunpowder, they never get too much of that. What they dread is a visit by some navy and a prolonged siege, and they want to be ready for it. I'd recommend, though, that you have your agent paid in gold or silver, as much as possible."

"I always do, as much as possible."

"And if there are Moorish coins, don't take them, or if you have to take them get them melted down. Coins with a heathen figure on it make any seafaring man look like a pirate, these days."

"I see."

"Jewels I'd vote against too. They might be all right for London, which is a big place, but in a small town like this they'd be sure to attract attention."

"You have a point there."

"Your best payment, after metal, is silks. Doesn't take up much room, doesn't spoil, doesn't weigh much. That is, if you think there's a market for it here."

"I'll make a market for it."

"Still another thing," I said. "Your agent, whoever he might be—"

"You wouldn't like to go back there yourself in that capacity, would you, Toby?"

"No." That sounded rather short, so I expanded it: "No, thank you, sir. I've had my fill of the place."

"But your agent," I went on, "he ought to be careful to stay on board his vessel as much as he can, even when he's actually engaged in bartering. He ought to avoid the worst of the pirates. You have no idea what a shock it gave me to

241

see Captain Kidd and Bob Culliford drinking together like a couple of chums. And I wasn't the only one who saw them. I'm sure that that counted against Kidd, though they must have been fixing to hang him anyway."

"They were," Mr. Philipse confirmed. "His political friends are out of office now, and he hasn't a chance. A pity. He was a capable man, in many ways, though he did have a high temper."

"And he drank too much," I added.

It was creepy to talk about a person in the past tense, as though he was already dead.

"Speaking of drinking," said Mr. Philipse, "here's Moe."

The preternaturally solemn butler had no smile for me as he stood there with two tiny glasses on a silver salver, though I am sure that he remembered my face. My glass was so small and so thin that I was almost afraid to pick it up, for fear that I would inadvertently crush it.

Moe bowed and went out of the room, his salver empty.

The firelight gleamed and danced, red and yellow, across a white ceiling. Outside, the rowdydowdy snow fell. The brandy was delicious.

"Well . . ." said Mr. Philipse; and I knew from that that our business was over and that what we were drinking was a goodnighter, what the Scots would call a stirrup cup.

"You heard about Jan Van der Donck?" my host asked suddenly.

He was probably watching my face, and I am sure that I flushed. Yes, I had heard about Van der Donck, the *zuiplap,* who a year or so ago had got drunk once too often. I had heard about it soon after I engaged a room at the Anchor Inn, where several persons appeared to be eager to tell me, wondering, no doubt, as they did so, if the news would start me on a dash for the widow's house. How much they knew I could not guess. Anneke and I had always thought that we were very careful, very discreet.

It was a sobering thought. Did half of New York wonder, like that, why I was not proposing to the Widow Van der

Donck? Would I have to tell them, more or less publicly, that I was already married, that I had taken up with a trull, who left me for the first flashy pirate she had an eye for but to whom I was still linked by the bonds of holy matrimony? Would I have to tell *Anneke* that, as well?

I gulped my brandy, and almost choked on it.

"This is no affair of mine, Toby," Mr. Philipse said cautiously. "It's personal, with you."

I made no remark upon this. I had finished my brandy.

"All the same, I naturally have your interests at heart, you having been with me so long and served me so well. Also, I always like to see a young man get ahead."

Still I made no comment. He had paid me handsomely for my services on the other side of the world, and already it was understood that I should have some responsible and lucrative post in his mercantile organization, in which, additionally, I should be permitted to invest. But I knew what he was getting at now. He was thinking of different money.

"The widow Van der Donck is uncommonly pretty, Toby, as you well know. And she's not old. Not much older than you, I should think?"

"About a year and a half," I muttered.

"She's rich by New York standards, Toby. She may not have much cash, but she owns that house and a good deal of land. For one thing, she owns most of the southern side of Wall Street. I grant you that's nothing but orchards right now, but the way the town is growing, Toby, you mark my words that land is going to be mighty valuable in a little while. It'd be a pity if she had to sell it off, to live."

"Yes, sir."

He saw that I had some reason to wish to end the talk, so he helped me on with my greatcoat and he walked me to the door, which Moe held open for me.

"Think it over, Toby."

"Yes, sir."

"And—good night."

"Good night, sir."

CHAPTER 51

He Did it for Drinks

IT WAS LATE afternoon, and the snow-flakes did not drift as casually as they had appeared to do when seen through the window. They were even larger now, and showed somewhat blue. They hissed as they hit my face.

The snow had enspirited me when I watched it from inside the Philipse house. It depressed me now, out in it.

It was shameful of me to feel so sorry for myself. There I was, twenty-three years old, in perfect physical condition, a lifetime of adventure behind me, a lifetime of prosperity looming ahead. I had money in my purse, and one of the shrewdest merchants in all America was pledged to help me invest it. True, my blood had been thinned a bit by the tropics, so that I shivered as I walked; but again, I wore a greatcoat and stout boots, and I was making for a comfortable inn where there would be waiting for me a good dinner, a four-poster, a warming pan. Yet I never felt worse.

Should I march straight up to Anneke Van der Donck and tell her everything, explaining why I could not marry her? Did I lack the courage to do that? I would be seeing her, not every day but from time to time, necessarily, in a small town like this. Must I turn away, shamefaced, every time we met?

The Anchor was on Broadway near the Bowling Green, and as I approached it the outside door of the tap room was thrown open, and the tapster emerged, propelling a bewhiskered waif.

"And *stay* out!"

The tapster pushed this wretch forward, so that he collided with me, whom until that moment the tapster had not seen.

"Oh, I'm sorry, sir!"

"That's all right."

The thrown-out man gave me one bleary look and then he lurched off, mumbling under his breath.

The solicitous tapster brushed me off. After all, I was a new customer.

"Shall I order supper for you, sir?"

I was staring after the drunkard. There had been something familiar . . . Could it possibly be—No, it couldn't. Yet I went on staring after him as he stumbled away.

"A roast perhaps, with Yorkshire pudding? Or maybe you would prefer a bird of some sort?"

I broke away, running after the waif.

"You! Wait!"

It was easy to catch him, and I spun him around. Used to being treated that way, he only whimpered.

"Look at me!"

I could not remember his name, if I had ever known it, but his face was one I had seen often at St. Mary's.

There was no reason why this should have startled me. New York at all times was overrun with pirates, as I well knew. I was so fresh off a ship that the pavement still seemed to rock beneath my feet. I would get used to encounters like this. Still, I shook the man. He had come from another world.

"D'ye remember me?"

He leered at me, blinking, badly befuddled by rum. He nodded.

"Say, wasn't you that young clerk that Bill Harkins made out to marry that afternoon at Quinn's? Aye, that was great sport, now wasn't it? Like one of those trials, only funnier."

"Made out to—"

"I hear tell she ran off with a cove named Copland afterward? Say, she must have been a rare grind, that one. Did she—"

"Shut your mouth."

He took a better look at me, and fell silent. He had been giggling, simpering, playing up to me, no doubt hoping that I would buy him a drink of old time's sake; but now he saw something in my face that frightened him.

I shook him.

"You say Harkins only *made out to* marry us? He wasn't a real priest, then?"

"Bill Harkins? Lord love you, no, sir! Him a priest? I doubt he was ever in a church in his life. No, he just did that for fun—and bumbo."

This possibility had never even occurred to me, and it was like a slap in the face. I reeled.

"But— But why did nobody ever tell me, afterward?"

My waif was serious now, if not exactly sober.

"I expect they was afraid to, sir, after the way you handled that man Quatremoulins. They're still talking about that, down there."

He shrank away from me, badly scared. No doubt he thought I was about to knock him down.

Instead, I flipped an eight-piece from my greatcoat pocket.

"Here, buy yourself a bottle."

I ran, not back to the Anchor but to the Widow Van der Donck's.

She must have been sitting at a front window. She saw me coming, and flung the door open for me, and she fell into my arms right there on the sill.

"Toby, oh my Toby! I've waited so long!"

I kissed her tenderly. She was prettier than ever, and she had not put on any weight. She was weeping, but then so was I.

"I'll never go away again," I promised her. "Never."

www.ingramcontent.com/pod-product-compliance
Lightning Source LLC
Chambersburg PA
CBHW032212030726
47494CB00020B/990